R'iyah Family Archives: Volume 2

A MAGE'S GUIDE TO AUSSIE TERRORS

AJ SHERWOOD

This book is a work of fiction, so please treat it like a work of fiction. Seriously. References to real people, dead people, good guys, bad guys, stupid politicians, companies, restaurants, events, products, locations, pop culture references, or wacky historical events are intended to provide a sense of authenticity and are used fictitiously. Or because I wanted it in the story. Characters, names, story, location, dialogue, weird humor, and strange incidents all come from the author's very fertile imagination and are not to be construed as real. No, I don't believe in killing off main characters. Villains are a totally different story.

A MAGE'S GUIDE TO AUSSIE TERRORS

R'iyah Family Archives 2

www.ajsherwood.com

CHAPTER ONE

BEL

Nico's family was more or less like Nico, just at half the speed. To say Bel felt overwhelmed in their house at times was the understatement of the year. He'd been here a total of two days, was slated to be here for five more, and was very sure at this point the only way he'd survive the rest of the visit was by taking naps. Many, many naps.

Mama Luna was cool, though. Nico's mother managed her kids, grandkids, husband, parents, and parents-in-law all crammed into her house like it was nothing at all. She kept track of people in her kitchen doing various tasks like she was a specialist in troop supply and deployment. Bel had been on missions less organized than her kitchen. It was a sizeable room, sure, with enough space to have double ovens and a large island in the middle of it, but it didn't feel that way with six adults all crammed inside sharing the same workspace. Not to mention the grandkids running in and out looking for snacks and/or drinks.

He'd found a corner of the bar to sit at to peel potatoes, as the safest thing to do in this house was to sit with a task in hand. Bel had basically grown up as an only child in some ways because of how his parents had shuffled him over to Matt and Victoria to raise, so this much family at once was not something he was used to.

Heartwarming, though. Mama Luna made sure he felt welcome, drawing him into conversations whenever he was nearby. Despite being here a short time, Bel had rarely felt more accepted than this anywhere else in his life. It made him wonder, were all families like this? Was his own? Bel had spent so little time in his own parents' house that he couldn't say. The question reverberated in his mind, threatening to draw him down into a melancholy mood. It was hard not to compare and contrast, his own family coming up wanting.

Bel gave himself a mental shake and tuned back in to his immediate surroundings. He'd rather enjoy the people with him now than reflect on might-have-beens. A smile grew and lingered on his face as he watched people work together and chat, the conversation lively.

"—don't put those in yet, I want the pies baking before anything else goes in the oven," Mama Luna directed her eldest daughter.

Gia gave a grunt, not looking up from her phone. "Yeah, I know, pies first. Well, looks like my date tomorrow is cancelled."

"Why?" Adele asked, pausing in picking up the pecan pie. Out of all the girls, Adele looked the most like her mother with her dark hair and high brow.

"This dumbass just sent me a dick pic. We barely had enough of a conversation to agree to meet for coffee, and he sends me this?"

"Ouch."

The other sister in the kitchen, Bria, looked over her sister's shoulder to see the phone screen. "I don't get why he's bragging. Send the man a sympathy card."

Gia cackled outright, and that expression on her heart-shaped face made her look entirely too much like Nico right before he got into mischief. "Bria, I love you. That's exactly what I should do."

Nico appeared from thin air, popping his head over her other shoulder for a look. "Maybe he thought you'd take pity and have sex with him?"

Gia snorted. "It's not the size of the dick, it's how much of a dick he is. I'm not interested if he's pulling crap like this."

"Good." Nico kissed her forehead before moving on, coming to stand next to Bel. "How did you end up as one of my mom's minions?"

"Er...luck?" Bel was a bit confused on that point himself. Even now he couldn't sort out the chain of events that had led him to sitting on this barstool. It had started with him coming into the kitchen for a drink, but he didn't remember volunteering to help. That had just sort of happened.

Nico shook his head and leaned in, kissing Bel. It started as a chaste kiss, but Bel could never leave it at one kiss, not with his men. He kissed Nico back, the brush of their lips warm and soft with affection.

There was the smack of flesh on flesh.

"Ow!" Nico pulled back, turning to glare over his shoulder. "Mama!"

"You're supposed to make food in the kitchen, not love," she told him firmly. "If you're not going to help, out."

"But Bel is in here," Nico protested.

"Bel is helping. You are just in the way. Go play with Garen. And why are you wearing a blanket around your shoulders like that? Are you cold?"

"It's my cape!"

"Why," Gia drawled, "does the cape take you up a level from lazy to super lazy?"

Nico beamed at her. "It's like you read minds. You're right, but I'm also on a grand quest."

Mama Luna rolled her eyes, clearly praying for patience. "Your grand quest better not involve pies because they aren't in the ovens yet."

One would think she had just announced the end of the

world would happen at midnight. Nico reeled under a mortal blow, clutching his chest like any fainting heroine straight from a bodice ripper.

"No! But how can I complete my grand quest if the pies aren't done yet?"

"You'll live," his mother assured him ruthlessly. Then smacked him on the ass with a wooden spoon. "Out."

Nico wasn't one to follow orders when he wanted something, so he stole another kiss, dodged his mother's swatting hand, and bounced out of the kitchen while cackling. Bel watched him go, shaking his head. So full of mischief, that one.

Mama Luna sat on a barstool, a bowl of green beans she was cleaning in her hands, but her eyes were on Bel. It was clear as day Nico took after her. The same dark hair that liked to tumble over his forehead, the high cheekbones, the hazel eyes. The same love and concern in those eyes, too.

"Talk to me about your parents. I wanted to say hi, now that you've become part of the family."

He really liked the way she said that. It sent a little spark of happiness bursting in his chest. It was a shame the reminder of his parents buried the feeling almost immediately.

With a grimace, Bel said, "I can give you their phone number, but there's no guarantee they'll respond. They haven't even responded to me yet."

Her hands abruptly stilled, eyes sharp on Bel's face. "What do you mean?"

Bel might as well explain. Part of him didn't want to, as the words were bitter in his mouth, but he needed to. She'd figure it out sooner or later anyway.

"You probably heard from Nico that the demon eyes run in the family, right?"

"I did."

"Well, it's not like everyone in the family is magical. It's more a percentage, somewhere around twenty-five percent in each generation. Even then, it's not that everyone who is magical also has the eyes. Usually, just one or two people a generation get them. We're running a little higher in my generation, as there's three. We're already ahead of the game for the next generation, for that matter, as my cousin just had twins. But most of the family aren't magical in any sense, and they work pretty normal careers. My parents fit into that bracket. I think it's because of that, they didn't know what to do with me."

Her expression was growing more and more concerned, brows drawing down into an unhappy line. "Do with you?"

"I'm not the only child, I've got siblings, but...well, I was the only magical child. And my eyes came in early, in my infancy, as they always do. Grandpa came up as often as he could to help seal my eyes since I was too young to manage it on my own, but...it was a burden my parents didn't want or need. They're very career-oriented, and managing my health took a lot of time. I was seven when they finally threw in the towel and asked for official help." Bel shrugged, not quite able to meet her eyes. "They reached out to the Magic Alliance Division and asked if someone could take me in and train me. MAD, of course, said yes."

Mama Luna's voice was eerily calm, like the eye of the storm. "You're telling me that at seven years old, you were deemed too much trouble to raise and your parents shuffled you off to someone else to be their responsibility."

"Kinda. They had good reasons, I guess, but yeah. I stayed in their house until high school, but they didn't really pay attention to me after Matt and Victoria entered the picture. I'm the youngest and an accidental baby. They weren't planning on having me anyway, so..." He trailed off, not sure why he was defending them. "Anyway. It's how I met Matt and Victoria. They're the ones who trained and raised me. Pretty much my real parents. If you want to meet the parents who love me, I'll give you their phone number. If you're looking for my birth parents, good luck reaching them."

Mama Luna was flabbergasted. Only word for it. She also looked like she was contemplating mayhem. There was a light in her eye hinting at destruction.

"You're telling me that you're bonded to two men and your parents haven't even met them yet?"

"I'm not entirely sure they even know. I assume they do? Victoria would have emailed them, if nothing else. Honestly, at this point, I'm so disconnected from that side of the family that I've stopped really trying to talk to them. I don't have a relationship with them. It's my cousins, the ones with eyes like mine, who I'm really close to."

"Bel, that's just..." She shook her head in disbelief. "You're such a sweet man. I can't imagine having a child like you and not having you in my life."

That was because she was a far better parent than his. Bel knew raising Nico must have been a feat of endurance even on the best of days, but she'd never backed down from the challenge. Bel was absolutely sure that if he'd been born into this family, she'd have marched through Hell to make sure he had been taken care of.

Mama Luna would never have given him over to anyone.

Really, his own family was a loss. Bel had resigned himself to that years ago. Moving out of his parents' house in high school had been the final straw for him. His parents hadn't even noticed when he'd moved out.

It still hurt sometimes, though—the rejection.

But living with Matt and Victoria had been so much better, as they honestly cared for him. Bel wished now, after meeting Nico's family, that he'd been born here instead. It would have been the best of both worlds, in a sense. Well, maybe not, because then he couldn't have had Nico. He absolutely couldn't unwish his relationship with Nico.

Bel had often fantasized about what it might be like once he was bonded to a familiar, how his life would change, but his imagination hadn't really gotten close. Bel hadn't realized how small his dreams had been until he'd come to this household and been welcomed with open arms. His connection with Nico and Garen meant he had a great deal of family now who liked him and wanted him in the family.

An unexpected bonus, and a gift, all wrapped into one.

Mama Luna got up from the stool and wrapped Bel up in a firm hug, one hand rubbing his back in a soothing stroke. "Well, they're idiots, but apparently no real loss. You're mine now. My Nico was smart enough to latch on to you. Now that I've met you, I'm not giving you back."

Bel returned the hug, smiling into her shoulder. She had no idea how much those words meant to him, how much he loved having a mother hug him like this. Tears stood in his eyes, and he had to blink rapidly to fight them back. Her love was unmistakable, and Bel basked in it.

"I understand now where Nico got his heart from. I'd love to belong to this family."

"Hey, mine too!" Garen protested, his hand resting on Bel's shoulder.

Bel startled. Now when had Garen come in? Last Bel had seen, he'd been in the living room.

"I know you haven't met them in person yet, but my parents already like you."

Bel lifted his head to give his familiar a warm smile. "I like them, too."

Mama Luna let go but she quizzed Garen. "Your family is accepting of the situation, then?"

"Yeah, no issues there. It took a minute to explain it all—and you have to admit, it's a strange situation—but once they understood, they were good with it. In fact, my mother's exact words were, 'Well, son, when you get your head out of your ass, you do it with style.' My dad high-fived her for it, so he apparently agreed." Garen smiled at the memory, green eyes crinkling at the corners. "They're also happy I'm no longer working a job that stresses me out. Our hours are just as insane as my old job in some ways, but I at least have breathing room now."

It was a sad state of affairs that working with Bel was easier. No one could say MAD had light work hours, after all.

"We'll meet them properly soon, or so I hope. Our schedules weren't matching because of training, but now we're certified without an emergency on the horizon. Maybe in the next couple weeks we can make it to my parents' house for a few days."

Bel poked him in the ribs. "Knock on wood when you say stuff like that! That's just calling on Murphy to give us some crazy job."

"It can't be worse than a magically booby-trapped cave," Garen muttered, nose wrinkling.

Bel poked him again. "Seriously, stop it. You won't believe how weird some of these jobs are. I don't need you calling down bad luck."

Mama Luna looked between them with an inquiring smile. "You know, I never did get an explanation of what-all you do, Bel."

Oh boy. Did he want to explain? It would mean telling her that Nico had voluntarily fought mummies, dodged arrow traps, and generally gone into danger laughing his fool head off.

Then again, she had raised him, so it probably wouldn't come as too much of a surprise.

Bel shrugged and started telling her the gist of what he did, then gave her stories and examples of some of the crazier shit he'd dealt with over the years. Garen took over peeling potatoes so he could talk. Mama Luna tried to continue with the green beans, but she was so fascinated by what Bel was saying, she listened more than worked. Eventually, Gia came over and took them from her mother. Mama Luna let them go without protest, more interested in asking Bel the next question.

Having a mother's undivided attention was rather nice. Bel liked it, no question, and he found himself smiling as he told her some of the funnier things he'd done. He got her laughing a few times, which tickled him in turn.

Bel's birth family was shitty, but his family of choice apparently rocked. Really, he was happy to take that win.

CHAPTER TWO

BEL

Bel had liked meeting his new family, but at the same time, he was glad to be home again. He liked routine, which was odd considering his career was anything but. When he was home, though, he indulged in the predictable. Putting clothes into the washing machine, buying groceries, checking the mail—it was all a nice way to spend time at home.

Of course, Nico and Garen were in the living room leg wrestling with each other, but that was also part of his daily routine now. His crazy familiars liked messing with each other.

Standing in the doorway—only safe place to be when those two got going—Bel drawled, "Are you bored or trying to decide who wins?"

"Who wins," Garen answered, the answer huffed out as he strained to flip Nico.

"What are you betting on?"

"Date spot." Nico let out a grunt of effort and managed to flip Garen neatly sideways. "Ha!"

"Dammit." Garen sighed. "Fine, fine, your idea first. Mine next time."

"Okay by me." Nico grinned and levered himself up without any noticeable effort before offering a hand up to

Garen.

Garen took it, stealing a quick kiss once he was on his feet.

This whole thing was cute but also made no sense. "What date spot?"

Garen moved to Bel, a gleam of pure anticipation in his eyes. "We are taking you on a proper date."

"You are?" Bel responded with bemusement.

"Something I realized belatedly, after talking with Mama," Nico explained, also coming over to join him. "For all that we spend a lot of time together, we have never gone on an official date. Which is just sad. I'm not even sure how that happened."

Garen shook his head, expression sardonic. "Pretty sure it had to do with weird things in caves distracting us. Anyway, we're not letting this continue. We're lovers, we should be doing romantic things too. Therefore, date."

A date? A grown-up date? Bel's only dates had been with teenagers and had normally involved pizza, a movie, and sex. Nothing more complicated than that. It was sad to realize that he'd never been on a romantic date before. On the other hand, he was kind of glad the experience would come with these two. He seriously had lucked out when it came to his men. Bel had no idea what he'd done to deserve them both, but he felt like jumping them just for being the romantic softies they were.

His grin grew wider by the second, stretching from ear to ear. "Do I get to hear where we're going?"

Garen snagged him by the waist, pulling him in to smack a kiss against his mouth. "No. We're going to surprise you. Go get dressed in something nice. I'll buy tickets."

"So this requires tickets? Where are we going?"

"Into Detroit."

That didn't help narrow it down any. Lots of fun date things could be found in Detroit.

Bel didn't actually mind having a surprise date. He liked surprises—the good kind, at least—and really, he was willing to go just about anywhere with these two. It was easy to give Garen a quick kiss in return and just go along with the flow.

"Are we talking business casual or a suit?" he asked, just to clarify.

"I think business casual would be better," Nico opined.

"Got it. I'll be ready in thirty minutes or so?"

"Take your time. It starts at seven, I think."

It was only five now, which gave them time to drive into Detroit and find parking (the latter part being the real challenge).

When it wasn't mission-oriented, trying to get all three of them ready to go out was akin to herding cats. Bel wasn't so much the issue—it was Nico getting distracted by shiny things. Still, Garen managed to get them all into the truck without losing one in the process, which was an impressive feat. He more or less always drove the truck these days, as Nico wasn't as comfortable with a manual, and Bel's driving scared the shit out of both of them.

Bel had never been in an accident, but trying to tell them that fell on deaf ears.

It did give Bel the freedom to admire the view, though. Garen and Nico cleaned up very nice indeed. Garen had put on a forest green button-down shirt with dark-wash jeans and, damn, did that complement his mahogany skin well. He looked damn fine, the clothes accentuating his broad shoulders and all those lovely muscles. Nico was also in a button-down, a cream color that offset his olive skin, the tan slacks highlighting his trim form. Bel very much looked forward to later, when he could strip all those clothes back off.

Even entering Detroit didn't help him figure out what the date plan was tonight. This section of Detroit was full of restaurants, live shows, art exhibits, and whatnot. It could be anything. Bel found himself keen on the surprise. He didn't know Nico well enough to predict what he would choose, which made the anticipation even more delicious.

It was impossible to hold hands and walk on the sidewalk; too many pedestrians coming from the other direction forced one or the other to fall back a little. It gave Bel the chance to study Nico's expression, and also Garen's—those two were a little too perky. It made him suspicious. Just what had they planned?

Their destination was in the middle of the block, in front of a nondescript brick building that blended in with every other building on this street. The black sign popped out over the doorway and announced in cursive letters: *Pitch Black*.

"Pitch Black?" Bel read with mounting confusion.

"You heard of this?" Nico bounced a little, his inner three-year-old coming to the fore. "Where it's a complete blackout, and you eat without being able to see anything."

"Ohhh," Bel said in understanding. "Yeah, I've heard of it. Never knew anyone who did it. Wait, Nico, this was your idea?"

"Always wanted to try this," Nico admitted, rubbing his hands together.

Garen shrugged in agreement. "It's sure to be a fun disaster. Besides, this way we can even the playing field."

Bel's head cocked a little. "Um, what?"

"If it's that dark inside"—Garen flipped a hand to indicate the interior of the restaurant—"then even you won't be able to see everything."

Bel blinked, running that through his head. Then again. No, still didn't make sense. "So...you think that if I don't have any ambient light, I'm just as blind as you are?"

Garen and Nico both studied him with growing confusion.

"Did we get that wrong?" Nico glanced at Garen and then back at him. "Wait, you're telling me you can see perfectly even in pitch darkness?"

Bel eyed him back. "Rather, I'm curious what it is I said that gave you the impression I needed some kind of light to see by."

Garen visibly deflated. "Ah, hell. Well, there goes half the fun of this."

"No, let's still go in," Nico urged, spirit bouncing back like the rubber ball he was. "This might actually be funnier. Bel can watch all the stupid things we're bound to do. It'll be a comedy act."

Bel still wanted to do it, for that matter. He thought it sounded too fun to pass up. He urged Garen in with a hand at his back. "Come on, I still want to try it."

Since Bel and Nico were still on board, Garen let himself be talked back into it and they went inside. He was the one with the tickets, so he went ahead of them, giving the tickets to the hostess at the podium. The three of them were taken to a center table and seated. The lights were still on at this point, guests coming in and finding their tables. Bel looked around curiously, not seeing anything about the restaurant that was unusual—except the blackout curtains covering the walls and windows.

It took fifteen minutes or so for all the guests to get settled, then the hostess came in and tapped a mic. "Attention everyone, let me explain the rules. As you're aware, you are at Pitch Black, the total blackout dining experience. We will be serving you a four-course meal. During that time, all lights will be off, except for medical emergencies. Our waitstaff have night vision goggles on, so if you do need to get up, raise a hand to signal them and they'll come and lead you out. Please don't try to get up by yourself. This dining experience lasts one and a half hours. We start—now!"

All lights went off, leaving the room in total darkness.

"Enjoy your dining experience."

Bel had to blink, adjusting to the lack of light, but it only took a few seconds before he could see perfectly. Having no light like this made everything a monochromatic grey—still visible, just washed of all color. Bel imagined this was how a truly color-blind person would see the world. Garen, sitting across from him, had his head tilted as if he was now trying to track things by ear. Nico was just grinning into the dark, apparently already enjoying himself.

"So, how is it?" Garen asked Bel.

"Hmm, really kind of fun. There's a couple near us who are mildly freaked out and trying not to let their nerves get the better of them. I could people-watch right here all day." Bel turned his head to take in the people behind him. "I see a few people who might be on first dates; they don't seem to know what to say to each other."

A hand came onto his shoulder and slid upwards, finding the nape of his neck.

"Can I help you?" Bel drawled to Nico.

"I'm channeling my inner bat," Nico explained.

"Oh, really. You have an inner bat?"

"What's he doing?" Garen asked.

Bel apparently needed to narrate this better. "He's got a hand on my neck for some—"

Nico leaned in and smacked a kiss against his cheek with unerring accuracy.

"—Nico, the hell are you kissing me for?"

"Because I can?"

Bel really should have expected that answer. It had been a stupid question.

You know what, two people could play this game. Bel caught his chin and smacked a kiss against his mouth.

Nico chuckled. "This whole blackout thing is fun. We can do this often, right?"

"You two are kissing each other over there, aren't you?" Garen guessed dryly. "I should have expected mischief."

"You really should have," Nico agreed, still chuckling like the demented gnome he was.

A waiter came by and skillfully deposited plates in front of them, along with water glasses, before moving on. Bel watched in amusement as both men cautiously started well away from their plates, moving in by touch until they found utensils. Even then they were using the pads of their fingers to feel the edge of their plates, cautious about stabbing an appendage into their food.

"How's your inner bat doing, Nico?" Bel inquired, all innocence.

"I think the fucker's gone AWOL on me. Bel, what are we even eating?"

"That would be telling."

"He's getting far too much enjoyment out of this," Nico grumbled at Garen. "Whose bright idea was this, again?"

"Yours."

"Dammit, I was afraid of that."

Bel snickered as he cut into an excellent steak and popped a bite into his mouth. He had the feeling this needed to be an anniversary date spot. Bel definitely wanted to drag them here again. This was far too much fun.

Garen fared better than Nico over the course of the meal, mostly because he was willing to take it slow and try everything. Nico was too impatient and willing to wing it, which prompted several misses and at least one moment when it was only Bel's reflexes that saved his water glass from going right off the table.

It didn't feel like an hour and a half had passed by when the lights abruptly came back on. Bel felt like a vampire stepping out into the sun, his night vision destroyed in a second flat. He had to put both hands over his face to mitigate the damage.

Nico snorted. "Wow, we made such a mess. Except perfect Bel over here, of course. You okay?"

Blinking, he cautiously lowered his hands. "Night vision took a second to switch off. Ahh, that's better. Well, this was fun!"

"You got far too much enjoyment out of watching us struggle," Garen accused him, a grin twitching up the corners of his mouth and eyes.

"Guilty." Bel shrugged, not at all apologetic. "Dessert?"

Nico nodded fervently. "Calories. Sugary goodness. Yes."

The best ice cream parlor was in Plymouth. No competition on that. Garen drove them back to town, then stopped at Dairy King, where they ordered sinful creations of sugar and consumed them without care. Well, really, Bel shared his banana split with Nico because there was no way in hell he could eat the thing alone. It would take Andre the Giant to finish a bowl this large. Or someone with Nico's metabolism, as he had no trouble eating whatever Bel couldn't.

Bel found his thoughts wandering as they ate. He wasn't sure if this date was really just his men wanting romance, or if they'd felt Bel's unease. He'd tried not to focus on it, or think of it at all, but the anniversary of the day Spencer had left him was this week.

It shouldn't still smart, after all this time. Surely he should have healed by now?

Unfortunately, it still hurt, like a wound that throbbed whenever something reminded him of it. One that oozed and whispered that it was his fault Spencer had left, and that Nico and Garen would leave, too.

The simple happiness of being with them on this date fought with that haunting sense of rejection. Bel kept having to wrestle his mood back into a positive light. This wasn't new; he'd been in this fight for three weeks now, trying very hard to ignore and bury the feeling, to not let it carry at all along the bond. It wasn't fair to his lovers. Being with Nico's family had been a nice distraction while it lasted.

His men laughed at something, effectively turning his attention back to them, and he felt a burst of love rush through him. Bel took himself firmly in hand. Nico and Garen were the best familiars, boyfriends, and lovers anyone could ask for. Hell, both men had demanded to stay with him, it wasn't like he was a second choice for them. There was no reason for this insecurity, this self-doubt, this insidious fear that he'd lose them too.

This fear was stupid. Bel would just weather this week, and the anniversary would pass without anything happening, and then things would be fine again. He just had to keep it together, was all. Without his men noticing something was off.

Considering how observant both of them were, that was something of a tall order, granted, but Bel was determined. It'd be fine.

He'd be fine.

With his men being so sweet on their date tonight, Bel wanted to give back a little. Part of it was needing a distraction from his own thoughts, but he also wanted to prove to himself that he was loved. Sexy times were definitely in order.

When they got home, he drew them into the bedroom, a lecherous smile on his face. Sex with these two was always fun, and they could take their time tonight. Multiple rounds were in his immediate future.

Garen caught him just inside the bedroom door, lifting him up and in, his mouth finding Bel's. Garen was always a pleasure to kiss, but tonight was different somehow. He was more intense, the kiss never separating, growing deeper and deeper until the only thing keeping Bel upright was his hold on the man's shoulders. Garen pulled back, just an inch, but all Bel could do was breathe, just breathe, the intensity of the kiss dazing him.

Nico caught the nape of his neck and leaned in from the side, kissing him with the same intensity, his tongue dueling with Bel's. He had to gasp for breath, the sound of it obscene even in his own ears.

Bel wrestled with the buttons of Nico's shirt, caught up in

the lust coursing through him. Even with his eyes closed, he knew it was Garen's hands that dealt with Bel's shirt, Nico's hand that struggled with the button at his waist, Garen's shoulder he clung to for balance as the kiss drugged him past all sense. He barely registered his own pants and boxers hitting the floor.

Garen shifted Bel fully into Nico's arms, and his lover lost no time in getting a firm grip under his thighs, lifting him up. Bel went without any complaint, peppering kisses along Nico's jaw, under his ear, along his neck. Skin to skin like this felt wonderful, even if Nico was still wearing pants. Pants needed to go, definitely.

Bel lifted his head enough to complain to Garen, "He's still wearing pants."

"Working on it," Garen assured him, brow quirked in amusement.

Oooh, but Garen wasn't wearing pants. Or anything else, for that matter. A naked Garen was a very impressive sight; no one could claim otherwise.

With two men determined to get him into bed, it happened quickly. Bel's back hit cool sheets, the soft fabric a caress against his bare skin as he welcomed Nico's weight on top of him. His head tilted to the side, giving way for Nico to press hot kisses against his neck, their bare skin brushing up against each other as Nico made his way down Bel's body.

The bed dipped at Bel's side as Garen joined them, and he rolled Bel and Nico on to their sides. Bel grabbed Garen's hand as he moved, bringing him flush to his back, as he wanted the man close. Also preferably fucking him, but he did not doubt they'd get there shortly.

Nico's mouth found a nipple, nipping at it, sending little shocks of pleasure straight to his dick. Bel's hands threaded through that thick, silky hair, enjoying the attention very much. He felt Garen's mouth press a kiss on his shoulder, then trail his way down along his spine, and Bel felt his skin jump and shiver under the caresses. He really, truly liked where this was going. Bel's entire body felt hot to the touch, toes curling under the excitement of two very sexy men giving him one hundred percent of their attention.

Garen's teeth scraped along the top of his buttock, and Bel shuddered with anticipation. Yes, please. Oh please, oh please, Garen was amazing at rimming; he could make Bel melt in less than three seconds. He was so focused on Garen that he almost missed Nico moving further down as well, like they were in perfect sync with each other, until he felt a tongue swipe a wet glide up his happy trail.

A groan escaped Bel's mouth as Nico moved even lower, taking him into the warm cavity of his mouth. Reveling in that hot touch, he writhed and gasped, his hold on Nico's silky hair almost punishing. The gentler Nico touched him, the more it melted him, to the point it almost felt suffocating.

Bel's attention snapped to the back as Garen's hands spread his cheeks apart, and that very talented mouth pressed in close as he swiped a hot, wet tongue over Bel's hole. Bel's hand flung out and grasped the sheets to the point of ripping them, trying to somehow process this pleasure overload. It was in vain. Every time he thought he had some sort of grip on himself, they undid him all over again. Nico bobbed his head, sucking him without mercy, rubbing the flat of his tongue against a too-sensitive tip.

Garen's tongue was fucking Bel in and out in a deliciously sinful mimicry, loosening him up. They were driving Bel's senses right to the edge, sweat dewing at his temples as his blood burned. That telltale tingle was in his groin, tightening and clamoring for release.

He tried to get a warning out, some kind of word that wasn't just sounds, but Bel's coordination was long gone. He gave a groan, pushing at Nico's shoulder, and that was all he could manage.

It didn't matter. Nico drew him in tighter, swallowing

him down as Bel came hard. Bel melted into the bed, breath shaking in his mouth, a pleasant wave of endorphins washing through him.

Nico moved off the bed, not far, before he was back again. Garen lifted his head as well, and Bel tried to track what they were doing, but it was a lost cause. He was too relaxed to get his head off the mattress.

Or at least, he was until he felt the tip of Garen's dick, slick with lube, press slowly into him. Bel spasmed around the intrusion, hands latching on to Nico's arms as he was the closest thing to grab.

Garen leaned in to whisper against his ear, his voice deep and rumbling, "I'm going to fuck you hard, take you until you can't think of anything else but coming."

Bel might have let out a pleading whimper.

"When I'm done, Nico will take over, and he'll tease you, let you taste a climax without actually coming, until he feels like coming himself. And we all know Nico's stamina is something else."

If this was punishment for something Bel had done, what was it? He really needed to know so he could do it again.

He had no chance to ask. Garen bottomed out, and the burn of penetration robbed him of all words and breath.

Garen was barely settled before he pulled out again, a good inch, then thrust back in, his hand on Bel's stomach keeping him in place. Nico shifted to lift Bel's leg up a little higher, giving the man better access and turning the angle into something perfectly amazing. Bel damn near lost his mind, the sensation was that overwhelming. He scrambled for purchase, his free hand reaching up to twine around Garen's neck, keeping him close. The heat of Garen's cock felt divine, and Bel felt a truncated gasp leave his mouth with each thrust.

Nico watched them with dark, intense eyes, a smile playing around the corners of his mouth. "You two are seriously sexy, I hope you know this. Damn, it's better than porn. Garen, we need to fuck him on his side like this more often, I didn't know he could make these sexy little sounds."

Bel moaned. Yes please, fuck him like this more often, it felt amazing. Despite having come not even five minutes ago, Bel started to rise to the occasion again. It was that good.

Garen was shaking a little, a fine tremor that signaled he was reaching the edge. Bel could recognize it easily after making love with this man so many times. He knew that Garen had maybe a minute before he lost all control. Bel reached forward, gathering Nico in closer, then dropped a hand to Nico's dick, giving it a squeeze.

"Mm, like that," Nico encouraged, eyes falling to half-mast.

Garen's arm around him spasmed, snatching Bel impossibly closer, his hips jerking in and out for a second in a rough rhythm before he came, pressed as close to Bel as he could manage. He came down with a satisfied sigh, his hold on Bel loosening.

With gentle hands, Nico took Bel out of Garen's arms, turning him so that he was in a mirrored position with his back to Nico's front. His far-too-energetic lover pressed a kiss to his shoulder even as he pushed in, thrusting easily after Garen had worked Bel's hole loose. Bel sighed into it, letting Nico do as he liked, as he had not a word of complaint.

Bel kept one hand on Garen's chest like an anchor, the other finding a handhold on the back of Nico's thigh, gripping it as the man found a good angle for both of them. Ah, perfection. These two knew precisely how to satisfy him.

Garen pressed in closer, catching Bel's face with a gentle hand, and leaned in to kiss him. Unlike before, this kiss wasn't meant to arouse, but had the taste of affection. Garen's lips were sweet on his, hand gentle as he played with strands of his hair. The dichotomy of it, with Nico thrusting in hard and heavy from behind, brought tears to Bel's eyes. The rhythm of his and Nico's bodies colliding echoed through the room, Nico's pants hot against the bare shoulder of his skin. Bel was mostly hard thanks to Garen, but with Nico grazing his prostate with every thrust in, he was quickly getting to the point where he wanted release.

"Garen—" Bel whined against his mouth.

"What is it, my heart?"

He caught Garen's hand and put it around his erect dick, not so subtly demanding attention.

"Mmm, but it's Nico who's going to drive you crazy first, remember?" Garen's smile was not nice.

"Already crazy," Bel responded, vision going dark around the edges. "Please. I—ahhh—I need—please—!"

"I'm a bit crazy, too," Nico panted. "He's just too giving, I can't—G, I'm too close."

At least they were in accord on this. Bel felt it in the way Nico's thigh jumped and quivered under his hand, the slightly erratic rhythm his thrusts were taking. He was perilously close, and Bel wanted nothing more than to come with him.

Garen did not do what Bel wanted. He pulled him in a little tighter, his hands tender as he cradled Bel's face. It brought so many emotions to the fore, as Bel felt perfectly cherished in that moment. It heightened the pleasure even more, making it impossibly intense. He was twisting under Nico's hands, trying to drive himself harder onto that hot cock, so anxious for climax that he was almost coming out of his skin.

Nico tilted his head back and Bel went with it, not sure what his lover was up to. He felt a nose brush aside hair, hot breath on the tender skin of his ear—

Oh shit, was he?

Teeth caught the tip of his ear and bit, just on this side of painful. Every nerve ending came alive, all in a rush, caged lightning racing along his nerves without warning. Bel screamed, the intensity turning his vision to pure white, body shaking under the hands holding on to him. He came so hard his spine arched with it, and he slammed his hips back onto Nico.

Nico groaned, loud and long, as he thrust in once more before coming just as hard. Heat flooded Bel's interior, leaving him under this lethargy of satisfaction. He had words to describe this. Maybe. Braining was beyond him just then.

Garen left the bed long enough to fetch a damp towel, cleaning them both up. Nico pulled out and turned him, snuggling Bel against his chest. He was still breathing hard, and Bel found himself stroking his back and shoulders, calming him down. Nico hugged him tighter, pressing a kiss against his forehead.

"Love you, Ruby." The husky words were soft with emotion.

"I love you, *carus*." Bel pressed a kiss against his shoulder. Turning, he caught Garen's hand, pulling him back in. "I love you, *amasio*."

Garen leaned in to kiss him, oh so softly. "I love you."

He watched as Garen and Nico exchanged a soft kiss, saying the same I love yous, and felt his heart impossibly expand even more in his chest. The moments like this, when Bel felt perfectly loved and cherished, were few and far between. He'd never thought he'd be loved like this.

He was ever so glad he'd been wrong.

It was the last thought he had before he fell asleep, tucked in against Nico's chest. For a moment, all was right in his world.

CHAPTER THREE

GAREN

Garen lay on his side, propped up on an elbow, eyes roving over his young lover. Bel was curled up against Nico's chest, sleeping peacefully, but even in his sleep he had a firm grip on Nico's waist. One of his feet was hooked over Garen's ankle, too, his way of keeping Garen close and connected. It was cute—or would be, if there wasn't this nagging sense of something being off with him.

With gentle fingertips, he reached out and brushed some of the hair from Bel's face, revealing the tip of a pointed ear in the process. Garen was careful to not touch it, though. As sensitive as he was, Bel would come right out of a sound sleep at even a brush against his ear, and Garen wanted him to rest.

"You sense it too, don't you?" Nico murmured softly, the words barely a whisper.

Garen looked up to meet his eyes. "Yeah. He's off-kilter. I can feel it through the bond. I can't put my finger on why."

"It started a few weeks ago, but I really felt it as we were visiting my family. I kept looking for something that might be bothering him, but I haven't been able to pinpoint anything. He's keeping up too good of a front."

Bel was, unfortunately, a master at masking pain. He'd

had too much practice at it in his short life. Garen wished he could get it through Bel's head that, with them, he didn't have to. Neither Nico nor Garen would ever be impatient with him. Especially not with something that hurt him. It would likely take time and patience to get that through to him. In the meantime, though, how could he convince Bel to open up? To confess what was wrong?

"He's been a touch clingy with us since coming back." This moment being a prime example.

"Not in a cute way, either. More like he needs to keep tabs on us." Nico let out a soft sigh, brows drawn into a troubled line. "Maybe this has something to do with his parents? They still haven't called or responded to his email."

"Maybe." Garen personally didn't understand it. Bel was an amazing man; what parent wouldn't be proud of him? Yet they really didn't seem interested in keeping up with Bel or being involved in his life at all. "Bel didn't seem to think they would respond, though. He was doing it more out of courtesy than anything."

"I know that's what he said, but if my parents acted like that, I'd be hurt."

Garen grunted in agreement. Then again, he and Nico were both close with their parents. Bel hadn't really seen much of his since he was fourteen years old. It had to be different when there wasn't any history between them.

"We need to corner him tomorrow." Nico got a mulish expression on his face. "Just waiting for him to open up isn't going to get us anywhere. It feels like he's unhappy, which is making my bond twitch, and it's becoming this itch I can't scratch."

Garen's nose wrinkled up. "Same. We'll try asking nicely in the morning."

"When nice fails—'cause you know it will—I vote we tickle it out of him."

"Tickling is a perfectly legitimate tactic."

Nico gave him a high five, although they kept the tap gentle to avoid making noise.

"I knew I liked you for a reason." Nico settled in more, his hand finding a spot on Garen's hip to rest. He was clearly ready to sleep now that he and Garen had a plan.

Garen let his eyes fall shut as well, the promise of deep rest drawing him under.

It felt like he had been asleep maybe five minutes when the phone rang. It wasn't the usual ringtone, either, but Bel's *Avengers Assemble* ringtone. That ringtone meant something, somewhere in the world, was on fire and they needed Bel yesterday.

On autopilot, Garen rolled over and put a hand on the phone, trying to get his eyes open as he swiped accept. "Dallarosa."

There was a beat, as if the speaker had just changed their mind about what they were going to say. "*Agent Dallarosa, this is Director Tesfay—*"

Bel's immediate boss, in other words. Uh-oh.

"*I'm calling for Agent Adams.*"

"Can you run it by me first? He's sound asleep."

"*Well...hell, you're his familiar, sure. Try to shake him awake, though. I'm sure he's going to ask questions.*"

"Knowing him. This is an emergency, I take it?"

"*When is it not?*" Tesfay's voice was painfully dry. "*We've got missing people, most presumed dead, near one of our joint operation bases in northern Australia. It looks like something either magical or supernatural is at play. Frankly, the picture is weird enough that I don't know what it is. No one on site has any better idea. You see how Adams will probably ask me questions?*"

"Oh, he'll have a ton of them. Just give me one minute, sir." Garen put the phone down and rolled over, shaking Bel awake with a hand on his shoulder. "Bel. Red, you need to wake up."

Bel grumbled and rolled into him, head flopping on the pillow as he forced one eye open to half-mast. His expression was belligerent in the extreme, like a waking ogre not ready to crawl out of his winter cave yet.

"You spent that much energy wearing me out, and now you want me up again?"

"I want you asleep—"

"Oh good." Bel rolled back over.

Garen pulled him back, regretting saying those words. "But your boss is on the line. Something's wrong in Australia."

Bel stared up at him. Glared, really. "Something's always wrong in Australia."

"People missing, presumed dead," Garen tacked on, hoping to tap into some kind of sympathy. Empathy? Something that would get Bel motivated enough to take the phone. "Either supernatural or magical, they're not sure. Near a joint base."

"Fuck," Bel grumbled, sitting up to take the call. "Adams. Yes, sir, I got the gist. What details do we have?"

Garen went to wake up Nico, only to find his other lover already awake and looking at his own phone.

"Dammit, we only slept for an hour." Nico sighed, pushing himself up into a sitting position. "What's on fire?"

"Australia, apparently."

"I assume since they're calling us at three a.m., they want us on a plane tonight."

"That would be my assumption, yeah," Garen agreed sourly. This was the downside to being a first responder. You got called out of your warm bed at all hours.

They listened intently as Bel spoke. He didn't say much, but the questions were enlightening. Also scary.

"How many people? In what time span? Hmm, that is worrisome. Is this base near water? Oh. I was hoping territory would narrow down possibilities. Has anyone else gone in? Ah. Well, I can't blame them for that, sir, not when they don't even know what they're facing. Yes, sir. Yes, sir, we can get on a flight this morning. Can I have my team? Oh good, thank you. I'll try to keep you updated, sir. Good night."

Bel hung up the phone before dramatically flopping sideways, landing on Garen's lap.

"On a scale of one to ten...?" Nico inquired.

Garen shot him a look. He was far too perky and excited. He was no doubt hoping for more magically booby-trapped caves, or the fun equivalent.

"I honestly have no idea," Bel answered, looking exhausted already. "Probably a six or seven. The problem is, the base is right along the coastline and it's got rivers, swamps, and forest area all around it."

Garen didn't follow. "How is that problematic?"

"Terrain dictates what kind of creatures and magic likely live there," Bel explained, eyes falling shut. "That much water, especially, spells trouble. Lots of things in water. Too many things."

Nico leaned over, his voice venturing into three-year-old-excitement land. "How many scary things are in the big bathtub?"

Their mage opened his eyes to slits so he could glare up into that hopeful face. "Far too many things. You. You are much too hyper and happy about this."

"I get to play with Wicky," Nico explained without any apology whatsoever on the horizon. "And maybe kangaroos."

"No kangaroos. No." Bel shook a finger at him, expression stern. "Knowing my luck, they'll like you and try to take off with you."

Garen could strangely see that happening. He took control of the conversation before it could get even further off track. "If we need to catch a plane tonight, we better shower and pack. Nico, shower first. I'll call Victoria and Matt, make sure they're moving."

Nico was up in a second, pulling Bel along with him. "Come on, Bel Bel, come shower with me."

Bel went with the same energy as a dog heading to the vet, but he did go. Garen couldn't exactly blame him. This didn't sound all that fun, and it was hard to brace for something when you didn't even have a firm grasp on the situation. Garen punched in Victoria's number, letting it ring.

On the second ring, she answered with a brisk, *"We're up. You got the call?"*

"Yeah, just now. We'll try to be out in thirty minutes."

"Okay. We'll take the van so we can all ride together. Do you know if Zia and Wicky are coming too?"

"I believe Bel asked for the full team and got approval."

"Good. I don't want to go in there without those two. Besides, if something happens, Wicky's the only one who has a prayer of keeping up with Nico."

"Sad but true. Alright, see you in a bit." Garen hung up, then put the phone back on the charger. They needed all phones charged as much as possible before they left. And sanity.

Sadly, he didn't know how to charge sanity. Someone somewhere should get on that.

CHAPTER FOUR

NICO

Since Nico was the only one really awake when they hit the airport, he took charge of herding everyone onto the plane in Detroit. Garen had his eyes open and was moving under his own power, but Nico was not fooled. He'd seen that man sleep while standing up once. Garen could impersonate a functioning adult so well that it was rather scary.

The flight from Detroit to LAX was five hours, and Bel spent the entirety of it asleep against Garen's shoulder, all cuddled in and cute. Garen was also dead asleep, his snores thankfully on the quieter end. Matthew and Victoria were in the row ahead of them, also cuddled up together and sleeping.

Nico tried to nap, but...naps. He and naps had never gotten along. His mother had given up trying to introduce him to naps when he was a year old. He'd managed a cat nap once in his adult life. It had been about two years in to him and Garen dating. He'd had a Frappuccino, done the Spartan race, sexed up Garen for a very fun few hours, and eventually he'd dozed off for a cat nap. Then woke up and sexed up Garen some more. Really, if he had the promise of sex afterwards, Nico could pretend to nap. He just wasn't motivated enough most of the time.

When they arrived in California, it was much brighter, to say the least, and people were less inclined to murder someone because of sleep deprivation. It was hitting eight a.m. local time when they landed, and they still had a few hours' drive to go, as they had to reach Edwards Air Force Base to catch a military plane bound for Australia. Really, the logistics of getting to another continent hurt Nico's brain, and he was just glad he wasn't in charge of anything more than keeping zombified people shuffling in the right direction.

As they hit baggage claim, Nico heard the *Avengers* theme song—this one from the awesome cartoon—blare up. Mobius was calling for him, making Nico laugh in delight. He looked over the other people shuffling around and spied a familiar head of fair hair, and Zia, who he could always spot in a crowd. The huge bun of braids sitting on top of her head gave her several extra inches of height, and she was a tall woman to begin with. Oh look, two of his favorite people!

Nico bounded ahead, catching Wicky up in a firm hug. "My favorite partner in crime, how are you?"

"Relieved," Wicky responded with a firm hug in return. "I've been so *bored* without you. Zia keeps saying mean things like 'that will break a limb' and 'I'm not taking you to the hospital if you survive that.' I need to move closer to you guys."

"You totally do," Nico encouraged, already on board with this plan.

Zia made a high-pitched noise in protest. "Michigan won't survive if you two are neighbors. No. Hi, guys, you look exhausted. I vote coffee before we head for the base."

"Coffee," Victoria moaned. "God, yes, I need coffee. I was asleep the whole flight here. Do we have the file yet?"

"Can't tell you, I was also asleep on the way here."

Nico let them talk, figuring he'd better fetch suitcases as no one else was awake or coordinated enough to do it without tripping. He took Wicky with him, as he didn't know what his or Zia's suitcases looked like, and besides, this way they could plot without it being obvious.

"Kangaroos," he told Wicky.

"Absolutely, that's happening. Glad you're on board. Mobius, you rat us out on this, I will forget to plug you in for a week, don't think I won't."

Mobius made the sad two-beep sound like R2-D2.

"And use your words, dammit. I just bought you the Samuel L. Jackson voice package. You said you wanted that one."

"Motherfucker," Mobius chimed in helpfully.

"*Aside* from that one word." Wicky glared at his familiar in his hand suspiciously. "Was it just for that one word you wanted the voice package? You better tell me that wasn't the sole reason."

Mobius was suspiciously quiet.

Wicky growled.

Nico had to ask, curiosity compelled him. "So...how much have you spent on voice packages?"

"Fortunately, they're all reimbursable, so it's not like I'm out of pocket on them, but..." Wicky was still glaring at Mobius as if seriously contemplating the merits of water. "I estimate it's about twenty thousand at this point."

Nico's jaw dropped. "Seriously?! How many voice packages is that?"

"I can't tell you. I honestly can't. Some of them were more expensive than others."

"Damn, man. Good thing it's an expense you can get reimbursed for. You can buy a car for that amount of money."

"Tell me about it. Oh, the bright purple case, that's Zia's."

That was faster than Nico had expected. He went ahead to grab suitcases, getting everyone's off in the next five minutes. People claimed theirs, and they managed to get outside and loaded into a big passenger van without losing anyone in the process. Near thing, though. Victoria's familiar had found a bright, sunny spot in a window and fallen asleep curled up in it. Victoria had literally gotten a foot inside the van before she realized she was missing a cat and frantically doubled back inside for her.

They stopped for food on the way out of Los Angeles. Hamburgers, fries, and coffee for the most part—except Nico, who wasn't allowed a milkshake, soda, or coffee. No one wanted him to have much sugar, the meanies. Or caffeine. Not even a Frappuccino. He took his hamburger and water and frowned at his teammates. He'd remember this later. See if he didn't.

People kind of fell asleep again after eating lunch, dozing off on each other. Nico sat in the front seat with the driver and kept her entertained. Lovely woman, name was Chelsea, mother of two kids, and she had a wicked sense of humor. They had a mutual love for swords, as it turned out.

Two hours later, Nico was once again in charge of jostling people up and out of the vehicle, herding them to the tarmac.

Edwards Air Force Base's location had been chosen specifically because of the fair-weather conditions in California. It was the secondary choice for landings, just in case Houston's weather was insane. That said, it hadn't been chosen for its beauty. There was a lot of sand out here. Sand, Joshua trees, and clear blue skies. That was about it.

He couldn't say that he missed California. Not one bit.

They were met on the tarmac by a young lieutenant in fatigues, a folder in one hand and a smile on his face. "Hello. I'm Lieutenant Abernathy, welcome to Edwards. I've got a plane idling on the tarmac for you, ready to take off. We received a report containing the latest intel, which I printed out for you."

Nico, judging he was the most functional, took point on this. "I'll take that. Thanks, Lieutenant."

"No problem, sir. Hope you have a good flight."

"Thank you."

Like any other military plane, it wasn't built for comfort. There were jumper seats on both sides near the cockpit, basically just places to strap in, and a cargo net nearby to hold the luggage. The rest of the plane was open and empty, meant for large cargo. They dropped into different seats, strapping in, and their pilot came out of the cockpit long enough to verify everyone was there and then went right back.

It would be a long flight, no doubt there. All of the other familiars were curling back up on their people, going right back to sleep, which was the sensible option. Nico cracked open the folder and read through it.

Which wasn't hard, it was basically four pages.

Bel leaned in against his side, head tilted on his shoulder to read. "Hmm. That's really not a lot to go on."

"Tell me about it."

"Please do," Zia said, waving at him from across the aisle. "All I got before leaving was 'people are disappearing near a base,' which doesn't tell me much."

"I don't have much more to offer." Nico paused as he felt the plane roll into motion, the engines louder as they picked up speed. He pitched his voice to carry more to compete with the sound. "Basically, we've got nine people confirmed dead, two people missing who they suspect are tied to the case. They're disappearing at night, no witnesses, and the only sign left behind is blood. A lot of blood. Too much blood loss for anyone to survive, really."

Bel's finger came up to point at a line. "It says the disappearances are all along a riverbank—isolated areas where there aren't any people. Campers or people who live off the main roads. Frequency is also picking up."

"Water." Victoria's nose wrinkled. "Nothing good comes out of the water."

Matt grunted in agreement. "I have PTSD from the last

water case. Damn hard to fight and breathe."

"But it's coming up on land to attack," Garen pointed out. "Which means it's amphibious, right? If we can lure it on ground, we stand a better chance of fighting it."

"I'm banking on that." Matt shared a frown with Bel. "Can you think of something that would be able to take on people like this, that's amphibious?"

"Yes. Does it live in northern Australia? Not to my knowledge." Bel leaned back over Nico's shoulder. "Does it say anything else?"

"Only that most of the investigation files are with the police and will be available to us if we want to take a look at them."

"I definitely want to. More data." Bel flipped to the last page and sighed. "That was an annoyingly short report."

"Like a teaser to a movie." Garen settled back, arms crossed loosely over his lap, head tilting back. "I suppose we'll just have to wait until we get there."

Which would be in far too many hours.

Nico wasn't good at waiting. In fact, he could reliably say he sucked at it.

People pulled out iPads, books, things to read and occupy themselves. Nico had a really good game on his phone he could play, but he wasn't really in the mood to sit still. They were airborne now, the ride smooth with little turbulence, so he wanted to take advantage and get up, move around. He hadn't been able to run this morning so he had too much energy to spare.

He caught Wicky's eye, one of the few who wasn't doing anything to entertain himself, and gestured toward the cargo area. "Wanna leg wrestle?"

Wicky's grin was evil. "You think you can beat me, former Ranger?"

"Oh, it's on now." Nico popped open his seatbelt. Just for that, he'd flip Wicky right over without even trying to take it easy on him.

Bel glanced up at him, eyes crinkled up in amusement. "Don't break each other."

He ducked down enough to kiss him on the forehead. "I'll only bruise him a little. Promise."

"Mobius, be our referee." Wicky stood, already moving for a clear spot.

Mobius gave a little ditty that sounded suspiciously like the opening refrain to *Mortal Kombat*.

Now this would be an excellent way to pass the time. Assuming they didn't shake the plane. Meh, it should be fine, right?

CHAPTER FIVE

BEL

They were all exhausted by the time they got off the plane at Robertson Barracks. Even Bel's familiars were feeling it, and he had thought nothing could drain Nico's battery. Not really. A corporal met them on the tarmac and, bless her, she had coffee in cups, just waiting to be passed out. Bel liked her already. She was in the Australian uniform, still fatigues but with more brown and red.

"Welcome to Australia," she greeted with a smile, holding out a hand. "Corporal Williams. I'm here to get you to the right place this afternoon."

Ye little gods, it really was afternoon. Bel's internal clock insisted it was some other hour altogether, but there was a thirteen-and-a-half-hour time difference between here and home, and his body couldn't figure out what time it was supposed to be. Damn time zones. Bed. That's all he really knew. He wanted a bed.

Because Bel was an adult, he shook her hand and gave her a smile in return. "Bel Adams, nice to meet you."

"Here, figured you'd need a pick-me-up to carry you through the meeting."

"You are absolutely correct." He accepted the nirvana in

a cup and sipped at the magic beans that promoted life and function. It was even hot. She'd managed to get hot coffee to them. Bless her.

She introduced herself to the rest of the group, handing out coffee and getting smiles and thanks in return. He almost stepped in to take the cup she offered Nico, because Nico and caffeine was a definite no in anyone's books, but Wicky intercepted it so smoothly, Bel didn't have a chance.

Nico came in closer and leaned heavily against Bel, head on his. "Beeeeel, he stole my coffee!"

"If he hadn't, I would have," Garen muttered behind Bel.

"But I'm tired too!"

Ladies, gentlemen, and gentlefolk, they finally had the answer. What did it take to tire Nico out to the point he wanted caffeine? Well, you had to take him on an evening date, sex him up, then take him on an international trip that meant sixteen hours on various planes, plus the three hours in a car to get to those planes. In short, you had to keep him up at least thirty-eight hours.

And to think, the Army thought putting this man behind a desk forty hours a week was a good idea.

Nico leaned harder, a solid weight against Bel's side. "Bel Bel, just one sip? One itty bitty sip?"

Bel didn't see how one sip would do anything drastic. Maybe. He let Nico have a sip and watched him like a hawk to make sure it was only a sip.

Nico made a face and handed it back. "How can you drink that? It's so bitter."

"Trust me, I need it to be black right now." Bel took another healthy swallow, praying it would keep him awake and thinking for the rest of the day. Presumably that was another four hours. Going to bed at seven wasn't too early, right? Right?

Corporal Williams got their bags loaded onto a jeep, promising they'd be delivered to the nearby hotel where they'd been set up for their stay, then herded them all into a van. She did so with smiles and efficiency and, frankly, everyone was too tired to do anything but blindly follow.

They drove all of five minutes to a two-story building that had the words Joint Movements Control Office on a sign out front. It looked like every other government building Bel had ever seen—blocky, efficient, and nothing about it ornamental.

They offloaded and went in, getting signed in with visitor badges at the front desk before going down a white hallway with grey tile, then promptly into a rather large conference room where two men and another woman stood by waiting. Bel took them both in carefully. Both men were middle-aged, the steady sort of military-career men who had seen it all and dealt with most of it.

The American commander had a receding hairline and a nose that had been broken and badly set sometime in his youth. He had a neutral expression on his face, but there was something about him that seemed a little...pleased? Bel couldn't figure out why. Unless he was just happy they'd finally arrived.

The Australian commander looked like he hadn't slept well in several nights. There were bags under his eyes, and the lines around his mouth and eyes made him seem ten years older than what Bel suspected him to be. His fatigues were crisp, though, like he'd changed just for this meeting.

"Welcome, everyone." The American commander approached first, a hand outstretched in greeting. "I'm Andrew Martin, commander of the American side here at Robertson Barracks. This is my co-commander, Harris Kelly."

They went the round of shaking hands, getting names, and taking a seat as they finished. The woman seemed to be the secretary to one of the commanders, as she passed Bel two thick files, both of which he took with a smile of thanks.

Victoria and Matt sat on either side of him so they could read over his shoulders. It left everyone else to arrange themselves around the table, with Nico and Garen directly across from him. Bel flipped open the top of one and realized this was some of the data he'd been promised. A quick profile of the missing people, along with the locations and photos from the scene. Excellent. Bel still wanted to go out to the places in person, as a file could only tell him so much.

Commander Kelly sat at the head of the table, to Bel's right. He cleared his throat, expression troubled. "Agent Adams, you'll forgive me if I ask some questions. Martin's had experience with you R'iyah mages before. He swears up and down that you can get to the bottom of this."

Bel's eyes flicked to Commander Martin's. "You have, sir?"

"I worked with an Agent Chantelle last time."

"Ahh, my cousin." Bel gave him a slight nod. "Then yes, you're very aware of what we can do."

"Well, I saw her waltz in and untangle a problem that had plagued us for a solid week, with a smile on her face while she flirted with her familiar, and then she waltzed out again, problem solved. I liked her solution. Not even a grave for what had plagued us."

That did sound like Chantelle's work, alright. "And knowing my cousin, she didn't really stop to explain."

"Not really. I didn't care, either, as long as she got results."

Martin might not care, but Kelly obviously did. Bel tried to explain. "A R'iyah's eyes aren't like your average mage's. We can see everything. I do mean everything. Every layer of this world, every trace element, every whisper of magic or energy. There's nothing we can't see. When we are called in, it's specifically for situations like this one, where no one knows what's going on. To you, this is a baffling mystery. To me, it's a case I need to assemble the pieces of for an overall picture."

Kelly's eyebrows compressed. He was a touch resistant to this, like most people were when first hearing it. "When you say you can see everything…"

Bel arched an eyebrow at him in amusement. "I would suggest laying off the coffee, sir. The ulcer in your gut will thank you for it."

Kelly's eyes blew wide in his face, jaw dropping as he spluttered.

Ahh, those reactions never got old. Bel should probably behave himself but, well, it was too much to resist. He'd blame Nico's influence for his mischief.

At least Martin was amused, as he chuckled. "Yes, you and Chantelle are definitely related. I can see the same sense of humor. Alright, Adams, here's the situation as it stands. You got the general brief about people disappearing. We just put it down to missing people at first, as nothing seemed especially strange about it. It was campers that went missing first, you see. Then the first house was hit, and that's when we knew something was very awry. The first set of pictures in that folder, they should give you an idea of what the scene's like."

Victoria leaned over Bel's shoulder to get a look. "That house is practically demolished. Like a vehicle just rammed right into it."

"That's what it does look like, on first impression. A few things contradicted that theory. One, there was blood spray everywhere, and it wasn't consistent with a car crash. We're talking arterial spray that hit the ceilings." Martin's face scrunched up in memory, and he had to take a second before he could continue. "It was like a horror house, only worse because it was, unfortunately, real. No hint of bodies to be found except the blood. The other odd thing was the claw marks in the ground. They were huge, easily a five-foot span."

Bel flipped to another picture showing the claw prints,

now cast to make them easier to see. There was a tape measure nearby to give the prints' scale. Damn, the paws were nearly wider than he was tall.

"That's unnerving."

"Tell me about it. No one has any clue what this thing could be. Nor are there sightings of it, whatever it is. I would think something this big, that could snatch grown adults without a fight, would be visible in the area."

"Not necessarily," Zia warned. "I've had more than a few cases where the thing would burrow into a hole during the day, or live in the water away from people, and only come out to feed. They've adapted to modern times. They've learned how to hide and hide well. This area we're in is populated, I could see that from the air, but what about further east?"

Kelly fielded this question. "Not as populated. There are several nature reserves, rivers, and whole sections of land where practically no one lives."

Bel had a grim feeling that was precisely where the thing lived. Whatever it was.

"I don't expect you to start the investigation tonight," Kelly continued. "You're all clearly exhausted from the long flight here. Rest up tonight so you can start fresh in the morning. Just tell me what you need from me."

Bel was able to rattle this off without thinking hard about it. "First, I want to go to the nearest sites where people have gone missing. The sooner I can get eyes on them, the better. If this started as a missing persons case, then I assume there's an active police file?"

"There is."

"I want to review those files and talk to the detective in charge."

"Done. What else?"

Bel stopped at that point, thinking. "A guide who's familiar with the area. We don't know where we're going, and I'd rather not rely on GPS as I'm sure we'll go off-road at some point or another."

Martin cleared his throat. "I think more than a guide. Why don't I send some Marines with you? We've got people who've been stationed here a while. They know the area, and I'd feel better if you had backup. I know you mages are formidable, but I don't want to take chances with all of you."

Bel mentally flinched at the mention of Marines. Spencer was a Marine, and any time he thought of one, he thought of the other. The two things were intrinsically linked in his head, like a word association game. He shook it off and tried to focus on the here and now.

"I won't turn them down. The more eyes the better on something like this. They will need to understand they have to take orders from us. If we say duck, they duck. Often, the things we tackle can't be subdued by firepower."

"I'll make sure that's clear. Will you need them by tomorrow?"

"Not if we're just visiting the sites already hit. I doubt the creature will hit the same spot twice, not when it's cleared of prey. And it only attacks at night, correct?"

"Correct. Or at least, we think so. No one's disappeared during the day that we know of."

Bel took that with a grain of salt. There were a lot of things they didn't know at this point. Far too many, in fact.

Victoria tapped the file. "We'll study this and get up to speed as fast as we can."

"Agents." Kelly looked at them all, one by one, concern drawing his face into a frown. "I don't know how you operate. I don't know what you've faced before. Tell me, if this really is some kind of monster, can you defeat it?"

"Oh yes," Wicky answered confidently. "Won't even be the first one. Or the thirtieth. We'll let Nico have first stab at it, though. He'll sulk otherwise."

Nico flashed his friend a brilliant smile and knuckled a tear from his eye. "You're a true friend, bro."

"You know I look out for you." Wicky winked at him in return.

Kelly did not look reassured, so Bel leaned in and murmured, "Nico is a former Army Ranger. Nothing gets past him. He's my familiar for a reason. Wicky specializes in fire magic. Trust me, those two joke a lot, but nothing's gotten the better of them. And yes, sir, I've defeated my share of monsters. The last batch were ones that liked to phase right through solid stone, making it impossible to predict where they would attack from."

Kelly's eyes went to him with a snap. "How did you deal with those?"

"Full-range magic attack that killed everything in a certain radius." Bel shrugged. "It does the job. Alright, sir, anything else you want to tell me?"

"Ah, no. Just leave your phone numbers with my secretary so we can reach you in case anything else goes down tonight."

"Absolutely." Bel turned to the woman in question and handed her one of his business cards from his wallet, which had all the pertinent info. "Here you go."

Martin stood with them, catching Bel's eye. "One more thing, Agent. I know it's impossible to give me any kind of timeline on matters when you don't even have your feet wet, but how long do these kinds of cases normally take?"

"Anywhere between a day to two weeks, depending on how fast we can find it." Bel shared a speaking look with Victoria.

"On things like this, the faster the better," she finished with a grimace. "Trust me, sir, we'll get through this as fast as we can. We don't want any more victims."

CHAPTER SIX

GAREN

Early the next morning, Corporal Williams took them to the most recent sites. Garen dared to eat breakfast before they went, assuming a site this old wouldn't have fresh gore and make him regret eating.

The first site wasn't very far from the base, roughly an hour's drive, which was alarming. He now understood why they'd been called in so quickly. Granted, the sites were going up and down the river, but the river was in national reserve territory and close enough that any training maneuvers would put people in jeopardy. It brought to mind that saying: The map was not the territory, the file was not the man. There was a stark difference in seeing it all himself.

When he thought of Australia, he normally thought of desert and swamps, mostly because of the *Crocodile Dundee* movies. This area seemed to be more forest and swamp, with a lazy river nearby. It was rich with trees, grass, and animals, all of it looking peaceful and undisturbed. Right up until they reached the taped-off site, at least.

Garen looked at the one-story bungalow house and made the uncharitable observation that it looked rather like a giant Kool-Aid Man had busted right through it. The sides of the house were still standing on either side, but the interior was smashed in. Roof, wall, door, windows—all of them obliterated and in shards on the floor. The back wall was intact too, and the room was covered in pieces of furniture, roof, and blood. A great deal of blood. Any horror movie set would be proud of the amount of blood. He could see why the report was firm on the fact that whoever had been attacked couldn't have possibly survived this.

Treasure was flying above the area, doing an aerial scan for them, and Matt's attention was solely on him. Garen looked to his mage, who was standing just ahead of him, scanning the area carefully. It wasn't that there was any physical difference between when Bel was using his eyes to their fullest power and when he was in relaxed mode, but Garen had picked up a few cues. Bel's eyebrows were always a touch furrowed, and it wasn't that he squinted, but he always looked right on the verge of doing so. He'd looked like that for a good five minutes already, walking up and down the length of the house without venturing all the way in, only to back up and try a different angle.

Nico leaned up on Garen's side, hand propped on his shoulder. "He's looking hella confused right now."

"Yeah, caught that. He didn't think he'd know what this is to begin with. He said that, but it's not stopping him from trying to figure it out."

"Our Bel Bel loves a puzzle."

Garen snorted. That he did.

Bel finally gave up and retreated to them, where the full team and their guide awaited him. He looked dissatisfied and irritated, mouth scrunched up.

"I can't figure out what this is. She's amphibious, that much I can tell you."

"It's female?" Victoria asked, intrigued.

"That much I can say for sure. It's female. If you follow the path"—he turned and gestured to the river that wasn't even a full stone's throw behind the house—"she clearly came from there. I think she tracked a person from there and into the front of the house. She followed another's footsteps in, the trail shows that. She took two people and dragged them back into the river."

Williams blinked at Bel as if he'd said something surprising. "We're still waiting on the lab reports to come in. We can only confirm one person lived here. The second person is suspected, not proven."

He looked at her in black amusement, as if she'd said something humorous. "As I said. Two people."

Seeing that she was perplexed about this, Garen leaned in and murmured an explanation. "A R'iyah's eyes can see everything. I do mean everything. He can tell how many people were here. Mark it down as two confirmed missing."

She turned to look up at him, blue eyes wide. "When you say everything..."

"Assume there's nothing he can't see. It's why he was brought in. We're just backup for him on this case."

Bel walked toward them, shaking his head. "For all that I can see what happened, I can't figure out what this is. For now, take me to the next location."

Williams nodded uncertainly. "Okay. It's only a kilometer down from here, in fact."

They loaded back up into the van for the short ride there. Garen glanced at Bel, wondering how he was doing. The bond between them still had this unhappy thrum, nothing obvious, but like a single note off-key in a melody. Garen still had no answer to what'd been eating at him over the past few weeks. It was hard to pinpoint it now as he seemed to have gone entirely into work mode.

The next house looked much like the first. Same style, also backed up against the river, with the same sort of squashed look, although this one was from the back and side, not the front. They unloaded but stayed back so as to not be in Bel's way as he went over the area again with his x-ray vision. His frown was more pronounced this time, and he kept squatting to get a closer look, only to stand and shake his head.

Wicky sidled in next to Nico and Garen, muttering, "I'll bet you five dollars right now that whatever he's seeing doesn't match up to the last house."

"I'm not taking that bet," Nico retorted. "That's obvious from the look on his face."

"Damn, I was hoping for a sucker bet."

"Yeah, wish you luck on that. I know my mage better than you do."

Even to Garen, something looked off. The damage wasn't the same, somehow, the hole not as large. The footprints he could see weren't the same size, either. Smaller, for one, and was he imagining that they seemed to have fewer toes? The ground here was damp, encouraging footprints, but it was still grassy enough that Garen couldn't see every single detail. Garen wasn't trained in this, either, although the crash course they'd had to be Bel's familiars covered the basics of tracking. He could follow the path to the river easily enough.

Bel finally came back to them again, expression even more confused. "Okay, this just got weirder."

"Weirder, how?" Victoria prompted.

"It's not the same creature."

Garen groaned. That wasn't what he wanted to hear. "We've got two different monsters eating people?"

"Apparently." Bel turned and outlined the situation with his hands. "We've got two different body signatures. Even the claw prints in the ground are different, although similar enough to be mistaken for the same creature at first glance. I can see why forensics got a bit confused there. They're both huge, both amphibious, probably the same breed, but they're not the same creature. We've got two running around."

Williams looked downright disturbed. "Can you tell me how many victims were here?"

"Three. I believe that matches the report."

"It does." She passed a hand over her face, and Garen didn't have to guess this would fuel her nightmares for the next few weeks. "We have lab results back on this case, at least, so I know there were three victims here. No idea what this is?"

"I wish. Trust me. You wanted to show me one more site today?"

"Yes."

"I think I need to see it before we return to base. I'm now going to ask some very different questions of whomever we talk to."

Wicky bounced a little on his toes, looking excited. "Do you think there's a third creature?"

Bel shot him a quelling look. "Bite your tongue. It's bad enough we have two."

"But three would make it more interesting."

"You just want more things to stab."

"You're not wrong."

Universe, why did you create a second Nico and then decide to give him magic? Really, one wasn't enough for you? Garen shook the thought off as they once again loaded back into the van.

This house was a bit farther out, closer to three kilometers by the time they arrived, but it looked amazingly similar to the first two. It had more outbuildings—two in fact—both of them intact. The house had been added on to in the back, and it was the add-on that was crushed to splinters, the main part of the house almost intact except for the missing back corner.

There also seemed to have been more of a fight here. Garen picked up on the trees near the riverbank with their broken limbs, a few broken trunks, and the paddock of one of the outbuildings that had been torn right out of the ground.

Bel pointed to the outbuilding, slowly asking Williams,

"They kept horses here?"

"Correct. Two. We believe the creature was going for the horses, the horses fought back and made enough noise their owners came out to defend them."

"They lost a horse and their own lives. The other horse lived."

"Also correct. They had chickens, pigs, and a few cats that all went to a rescue farm. They were the survivors of this attack."

Interesting. So, this thing, whatever it was, didn't just attack humans. It attacked anything living? Although the idea that it would comfortably attack a horse, thinking it was food, was alarming. A human was so much smaller in comparison, after all.

Wicky went around to put his chin on Bel's shoulder. "Bel, different creature?"

"Sorry to disappoint," Bel drawled, not bothered by Wicky's proximity, "but it's the same creature as the first house."

"Boooo."

"If it makes you feel any better, this thing is a good twenty feet tall, so it's not like you're facing an easy thing to defeat."

"So...in gaming terms, is this like the final boss of this area?"

"I sure as hell hope not. We don't have a full raiding party."

They'd definitely have to augment with Marines, although how much they could help, Garen wasn't sure. Bel had said the humans here responded and tried to defend their animals, after all. Garen didn't see how anyone would do that barehanded.

"Bel, can you tell what they fought back with?"

"Hunting rifles, from the look of it. I see a few shells in the grass over there."

"So something that should have been able to take out

large game, or at the very least hurt this thing enough to drive it off."

"Yeah. I would have thought so. I think all it did was piss her off. As callous as this sounds, it would have been safer for them to abandon the horses, get in a vehicle, and run for it. They probably would have lived if they had done that." Bel shook his head sadly. "I don't blame them for going on the defensive, though."

Neither did Garen. He would have fought back in their shoes, too. It wasn't in his nature to let something attack without at least trying to defend.

Bel blew out another breath, both resigned and amused as he glanced at Wicky. "I hate to say this, as it's only going to encourage you, but I think lightsabers and fire are the best weapons against this thing. Water-borne as it is, it'll be weak against fire."

Wicky punched a victorious fist into the air and did a little impromptu dance. Nico offered him a hand and they did a do-si-do with each other, all happy energy. Zia, Victoria, and Matt didn't look as enthused, but then, they were the sane ones.

Bel did a circling motion with his hand before gesturing for the van. "I've seen all I can see here. Let's go."

Garen fell into step with him and asked as they walked, "Do you think the Marines can help us if we arm them properly?"

"Yeah, and it's probably not a bad idea to bring some along. Just so we can do proper bait tactics, if nothing else. We've got a few tricks for how to arm someone short-term against things regular bullets won't work against." Bel rubbed at his chin before inclining his head to Matt. "He's the expert, I'll let him handle that. There are two questions that bother me more than backup, though."

Garen had more than two. "First question, I assume, is what are these two creatures?"

"That's definitely the first question, yup."

"What's the second?"

"Why now?" Bel gestured to the area at large. "This place was unmolested for years, decades. No one in living history can remember any attacks like these. That goes without saying because they're alarmed and have no idea what this can be, otherwise we wouldn't be here. So these creatures, whatever they are, either lay dormant for many, many years or they're not native to the area. They've either been woken up by something and came out to feed, or they were pushed out of their own territory and into this one."

Garen didn't like either theory. They didn't suggest good things. "Usually things that come out of hibernation and eat tend to breed next, right?"

Matt grunted in agreement. "That's a concern, yeah."

Victoria tacked on with love and brightness, "And if they're not native to this area, then that means something bigger and badder pushed them here, which means we have a potentially bigger problem waiting for us in some other location."

"You see why I'm concerned."

Garen stared at his lover in dismay. "Bel. What if I don't like either option?"

"Do I look overjoyed to you?"

"No, but...which one's easier? Finding a nest and killing off eggs before they hatch, or dealing with a bigger enemy?"

Bel paused with a foot inside the van and shrugged. "I don't know, Stoney, which would you prefer to do? Tramp through thousands of acres of swamps looking for a nest or fight something that could probably swallow you whole?"

Garen could honestly say neither appealed, and could he have an Option C please?

Nico and Wicky behind him chorused, "Giant creature, please!"

Garen shot them an irritated look. "If it really is a giant

creature, I'm sending you two in first."

This did not deter Nico. In fact, he looked like a child promised a shiny toy. "You promise?"

Okay, that was Garen's misstep. He should have known Nico would react like that.

Nico closed in for a back hug. "Awww, G, you do love me."

"Absolutely, Nico. I volunteered you as bait because I love you." Garen shook his head, already resigned. On the one hand, he had his mage who tracked down dangerous creatures. On the other, he had his lover who liked to fight dangerous creatures.

If this wasn't a match made in heaven, he wasn't sure what could qualify.

CHAPTER SEVEN

BEL

When Bel went to the police station to speak with the detective, he didn't want to look like one of those Korean CEOs in the dramas where they went everywhere with six lackeys following them. He chose to split off from the team after lunch, letting them go back to the hotel and rest, and only took Garen and Nico with him. Well, and Corporal Williams, who was still driving them around. Bel was rather grateful to have her. She served as an excellent ice breaker.

An Australian police station, as it turned out, didn't look all that different from an American one. It had the same busy air, with phones ringing, people going back and forth with documents or evidence in hand, surly-eyed people in cuffs shuffling along. The atmosphere was no different in the bullpen from any other place Bel had been.

Corporal Williams had clearly been here before, as she went straight for a back corner and the middle-aged man sitting hunched over at the desk. "Mick!"

Head coming up, he spied her and gave a wave. He was a bit heavyset, with something of a beer gut, sleeves rolled up at the elbows revealing tanned skin. "Hows't, Williams. Who've you got there?"

"Experts from the States." Williams planted herself between them and waved a hand as she did introductions. "Detective Mick Sorenson, this is Mage Bel Adams and his familiars, Garen Dallarosa and Nico di Rocci."

Mick did a slow blink, his brain clearly short-circuiting while trying to connect "familiars" with "human beings." Bel got that reaction a lot. He knew precisely how to interrupt that baffled uplift of his eyebrows.

"You heard that correctly, Detective. Hello. I'm here specifically to talk about your missing persons cases in this area over the past, say, six months."

Mick sat back in his chair and regarded Bel in a slow head-to-toe sweep. "That right. Why?"

"I think it might tie in to the cases I'm here to work. You and Corporal Williams have already discussed this, right?"

"More like, she took the case files from me when we realized they weren't missing, but dead. You think more of them are?"

"Quite possibly. May I review your files, perhaps see the sites of their disappearances? I can tell you if they're dead or not."

"Well, I'm all for a lighter caseload, but..." His brows furrowed even more. "You can tell that with a spell?"

"I can tell that in a look." Bel gave him a rueful smile. "I'm a R'iyah mage. My red eyes are not just for show."

"Huh. I've heard of your type. Crikey, they really did pull out the big guns for this case." Shaking his head, Mick waved him to the chair in front of his desk. "I can pull the files. Last six months, you said?"

"Correct."

"I think I have most of those on my desk."

It certainly looked that way. The stacks on all sides weren't in danger of toppling, but a good wind would certainly put Mick's computer and coffee cup in jeopardy.

He started sorting through the stack, handing things

over to Bel one by one. Bel took them but, four files in, was in danger of dropping something soon. Garen came to the rescue, taking files out of his hands and then handing them to Nico.

"Why am I the file holder?" Nico gave his lover a wry lift of his brow.

"Would you rather be the file reader?"

"Uhh...I feel like this is a trick question."

"Just hold files, Nico."

"Roger, roger."

Bel started on the file in his lap and read through it quickly, eyes skimming through the report. Adult female, lived alone, no signs of forced entry but car was found running in the driveway. Assumed snatched before she could get into her house. That was a pretty good candidate, right there.

The second file also had all the right earmarks: a young man returning from college but his parents found his vehicle in the driveway with no sign of him anywhere.

Mick went through the stack on the right side of his desk and then grunted in satisfaction. "The rest of these are older than six months. Right then, whaddya think?"

"I think two of these are quite possibly related. I won't know until I can look over the area itself, though." Bel tapped the files in his hands. "Can we start with these two?"

"Tell you what, let's go for the farthest one out, then work our way back in. Logistically, it'll make more sense than crisscrossing back and forth."

"Fair enough. Corporal Williams will drive us."

Mick snorted. "Trust me, you don't want to get in my car."

Ah. One of those, eh? Bel personally liked having his car clean enough for people to get into, but he knew multiple people whose cars were never cleaned out. Ever.

They filed out and back into the oversized van, Corporal Williams driving with the detective riding shotgun to navigate for her. Nico sat with Bel in the middle, leaving Garen in the back row of the passenger van.

As they drove, Nico leaned into Bel and asked in a low tone, "How many of these cases do you suspect are part of ours?"

"I hope very few. The further back this goes, the more of a problem it becomes. It gives these creatures that much longer to create a nest."

"Ah. Shit, I didn't think of it from that perspective." Nico pulled a face. "Like, all joking aside, tracking something down into a nest that it's protecting is fun, but...I really don't want you that close to danger. My familiar bond goes apeshit just picturing that."

"I second that," Garen piped up.

Bel grimaced. "I both appreciate the sentiment and totally agree."

"But? I see the *but* on your face."

"I just have this nagging sense in my gut that something disastrous is going to go down, and soon. Don't you?"

"Yeah." Nico tried very hard to maintain Serious Face, but it kept getting spoiled by the childlike glee in his eyes. "I promise to protect you, Ruby."

Bel sighed. Deeply. Why, despite the fact that he was thirteen years younger, did he feel like he was the responsible adult?

"Nico, just try not to get eaten. Okay? I kinda like you for some reason."

The grin broke out as Nico leaned in and smacked a kiss against his mouth. "Love you too, Bel Bel."

Garen leaned in over the back of the seat. "Nico, keep in mind that if you get injured on this job, neither of us will let you play alone with a swamp monster ever again."

Nico reeled in his seat, a hand over his heart. "How dare you suggest something can get past my defense!"

"Oh, I dare. I'd like to remind you of a certain training incident while we were in boot camp—"

"You said you'd never bring that up again!"

"I lied."

Bel's curiosity was piqued. Something had gotten past Nico's reflexes? Really? Bel hadn't thought that was possible. "What happened?"

Nico's glare at Garen promised death and no nookie if he breathed even one more word. "Don't you dare."

Grinning, Garen just shrugged. "I won't tell him, but keep in mind that you're not infallible. We like you without holes in you."

"Yeah, yeah."

Turning to Bel, Garen's expression turned more serious. "I do have a thought. I, for one, don't like the idea of tracking these things through a swamp or along a riverbed. That's bound to get us into trouble. You said these things would be weak to fire?"

"Right. I mean, that's basic Magic 101. If you want to counter something, go with its primal opposite. They're water based, so fire is bound to be the most effective thing to combat them with. Why?"

"Any chance we can borrow some hellhounds? They'd be good to track with, good protection, and I know your grandfather wouldn't mind lending us a few."

Now that was a brilliant idea. "Garen, bless your brain. Come here, I need to kiss that brain."

Garen chuckled and obligingly leaned in so Bel could smack a kiss against his forehead.

"I will totally call him later and borrow a few. Not right now, of course, there's no good place to keep them. They'll destroy a hotel room just walking into it." Bel wasn't sure what the precise timing should be, but definitely before they started hunting actively in the swamp.

Nico was all smiles. "We get to play with the doggies again?"

"Nico, Monkey, hellhounds are not pets. They are

ferocious guardians and incite terror in men's souls."

"Yeah, no, don't buy it. They're too cute playing fetch and getting belly rubs."

"You and Wicky are outside the norm, somehow, getting them to play with you." Bel shook his head, still amused at the memory. How the hell they even managed that was still a question for the ages. The hounds had been oversized puppies for them, super happy to have such attention. One session of fetch in, the hounds, Wicky, and Nico had become best buddies.

Corporal Williams pulled off the main road and onto a gravel driveway that wound between the trees. Bel turned back, facing forward, and paid more attention. He couldn't see much from this angle, but...was that a hint of a trail there?

She stopped and parked the van, turning off the engine. Bel followed Nico out of the back, stepping once again into the hot, humid air. He could hear the river clearly even though it wasn't in sight, the slope of the land just obscuring it.

Bel's eyes switched to his other vision, where the world was all lines of energy and imprints. He stepped forward, eyes sweeping the area, starting from the driveway.

There. It was there. He could see the signature of that amphibious monster, the one from the very first site he'd seen this morning. It was fainter, older. Just over four months old was his guess. There was some blood spatter mixed in with the trail, but nothing in great quantities. Likely why no one suspected foul play. There was nothing here to suggest attack by giant monster unless you knew precisely what to look for.

Turning his head, he inquired of Mick, "Which case is this?"

"The missing college student."

Bel's heart swam with pity. So young, likely his own age. He didn't envy the detective the job he'd have to do next. "Are the parents still living here?"

"Yes, why?"

"You better tell them to move. It's not safe here."

Corporal Williams came in sharply, eyes locked on his face. "This one ours?"

"Yeah." Bel used a hand to trace the path, illustrating it. "The monster snuck up behind him, I think. He wasn't even able to fight back. She more or less swallowed him whole on the spot. There's barely any blood splatter. She went directly from the driveway, then back toward the river. The trail's a good four months old. This matches the energy signature from our first site this morning, by the way."

She nodded grimly, not at all happy with this finding.

For that matter, neither was Bel.

Mick blew out a breath, head hanging. "Shit. Mage Adams, what are the odds this poor bloke survived the attack? You sure he was swallowed whole?"

"His energy signature died right there on the driveway. I'm sorry, he's dead. There's no doubt of that."

"Shit," Mick repeated more forcefully. "I better go and talk to the parents, then, assuming they're home. I really hate this part of the job. Mage Adams, can I ask you to back me up on this? Bad enough I have to tell them their son is dead, but I have to tell them to move, too. Or at least stay somewhere else until you can defeat whatever this is."

Bel didn't want to, but then who would? Still, Mick needed the backup, and doing so might be the final push to get these people out of harm's way. It was a miracle they hadn't become victims themselves. If it could save lives, Bel would say whatever he needed to.

"Of course."

"Thanks. Alright, I'm knocking on a door." Looking a little heartsick, Mick turned on a heel and marched for the front of the house.

Bel took one more look at the direction of the river, and wished he could at least tell the parents what had taken their son. It grated that despite having seen so much evidence, he had no idea what this thing was. That would be his next task, after he figured out the area of the attacks—to call the agency's research department and tap in to their hivemind. Surely someone back home would be able to figure this out for him.

For now, though, he could at least promise them that whatever this was, Bel would not rest until it was hunted down and killed. He hoped beyond hope that the rest of the missing person cases weren't related. Either way, it was going to be a long afternoon checking out every site to verify it, one way or another.

CHAPTER EIGHT

NICO

One of the things Nico loved best was Bel's intelligence. He practically radiated it, and it was just so hot watching all that intellect in action. That said, when Bel went into research mode, like now, it didn't really give Nico much to do. He tried to be patient during moments like these, though, because the research was necessary. They had to figure out what their target was before they could hit it.

Research mode started right after breakfast that morning. Bel had his phone out on the conference table on speaker so he, Victoria, Matt, and Zia could all hover around it. On the other end was Jack Yoshikawa, Bel's favorite agent in the Magical Theory and Research Department. Nico had heard Bel describe him as "simply brilliant," and that was high praise coming from his genius mage. If Bel had a choice of who to call, Jack was number one on the list.

Jack's voice was calm and steady over the speakerphone. *"I read your initial email to me three times, and this still doesn't make complete sense. You've got two amphibious creatures over there? You're sure on that, that they're two different creatures?"*

"Completely sure," Bel confirmed. "Same breed, but different ages and different genders. The energy signatures alone are starkly different from each other. But the body signatures are very similar. There's no mistaking the two."

"*Alright. Give me the information you have on the first one.*"

Bel ticked things off on his fingers as he went. "Female, large, probably about twenty feet tall? Sixty feet or so long? That's my estimate. She has six legs, five claws on each foot. The tail reminds me of something on a lizard, it leaves that kind of trail in the mud."

Now, some of that information was news to Nico. Bel hadn't elaborated on the details, just that this thing was massive. At twenty feet tall, with that kind of length, a human being probably looked like an insect to her. The ratio was about right for that.

"*And this thing has been dormant in the area for how long?*"

"Living memory, at least. No one has any idea what this is."

"*So a hundred years at least. Hmm. Alright, what about the second one?*"

"Male, and there was something different about him. He didn't have six legs, he had five, like one was amputated? And some of the toes were missing on one foot."

"*Was he still amphibious, same general size?*"

"Yes, slightly smaller than the female."

"*Hmm, not much to my knowledge fits that description for Australia. Let me plug all of this in our search engine, see what pops up.*"

"We're on standby."

Zia leaned back in her chair, crossing one leg over the other. "If they really are amphibious, then we're tracking these things through a swamp. This does not fill my heart with joy."

Nico piped up. "Garen suggested borrowing hellhounds from Grandpa to help us track them down and attack."

Wicky immediately gave Garen a high five. "You are awesome, my dude. We should totally do that. Bel, will your grandfather let us play with the puppies again?"

The look Bel gave him was wearily amused. "I love how no one at this table is terrified of *the* gatekeepers of Hell."

"Hey, I'm trying to make friends before I get down there," Wicky riposted cheerfully.

Nico snorted a laugh. And that was why he and Wicky were friends, right there.

Jack cleared his throat. "*I second the hellhound option if you can get them. Just make sure to put it in your report to us so we're not surprised later. Anyway, I have a possible hit.*"

Nico was all ears. Target info, please!

"*It's called a Moha-Moha. I...have no faith I pronounced that right. Anyway, it's the wrong area for it—should be in the Great Sandy Island area. It's a giant turtle fish, standing about ten feet high at full extension, full length unknown. It has four legs not six, though.*"

"That does not match what I'm seeing. Anything else?"

"*Not under this search parameter. Let me mix this up. Sometimes, too narrow of a search will skew the results and not give me the right creature. Our database needs a serious overhaul.*"

Every government agency's database needed a serious overhaul. It was a universal truth.

Nico's attention started to wander at that point. He knew how these sorts of meetings went. They'd go back and forth for hours before either calling for a break, wanting food, or suddenly tripping on the answer. He'd been through so many meetings like this, he could smell it.

Wodge and Treasure had apparently also figured out what was up. They'd found a sunny spot on the conference room floor near the window and were curled up together, taking a midmorning nap. Zia's familiar, Maddeus, apparently decided it was a great idea and glided off the table's edge to join them. Wrapping Wodge's fluffy tail around his body, he got comfy and went right to sleep.

Eyeing them, Nico, for the first time in his life, contemplated the benefits of a nap. It wasn't that he was tired. He was just bored. Also, it looked comfortable and fun to get all cozy in a pile like that. It wouldn't be strange if he joined them, right? He was a familiar, too, dammit.

From under the table, Nico felt a light nudge against his shin. He didn't think someone was trying to play footsie with him; it didn't feel like that. More a poke to get his attention. He looked up to find Wicky waggling eyebrows at him.

Waggling eyebrows meant Wicky had a perfectly terrible idea.

Nico was all ears. He perked up, expression asking hopefully, yes?

His phone chimed and Nico took it out to see Wicky had messaged him through Mobius. *Let's go outside. We need to figure out how to defeat a giant lizard.*

Sold. Done. Nico was more than ready to move.

An old hand at getting out of meetings, Nico knew precisely what to say to his lovers. He waved at Garen and mouthed, *Just getting up to stretch my legs.*

Garen, knowing full well that trying to keep Nico still in a meeting for more than thirty minutes led to things like paper airplane fights, just waved him on. Bel was focused on Jack, so he missed this initially, but the minute Nico stood up from his chair, his head snapped up. There was a twinge of immediate unease along the bond, stopping Nico right in his tracks.

Bel did that a lot these days. Track Nico and Garen as if hyper vigilant of where they were at all times. It wasn't an entirely healthy response, more a fear-based one, and Nico had no idea why. It wasn't like he'd given any indication that he was unhappy with Bel. It was probably trauma-related because of that damn first familiar. It smelled like that, at least. Nico decided to be patient and just wait him out, hoping love and time would heal the wound and help Bel overcome it. That seemed to have been working, at least until this past week, when Bel was triggered by something. Nico still had no idea what.

Seeing Bel's concern, he gave him a reassuring smile. "Just stretching my legs. Keep going."

Bel relaxed again and gave him a smile in return. "Okay."

Success! Nico escaped out of the room before anyone could question him more or ask why Wicky was going with him. Freeeedom!

As soon as they were back out in the bland grey-on-white hallway, Wicky offered him an arm, like a lord escorting a grand lady to the ballroom. "My dear sir, would you care to accompany me?"

"I would, good sir." Nico took the arm, linking their elbows together and sharing a naughty smile with his friend.

Mobius, because he had an excellent sense of humor, played the *Mario* adventure song that you always heard as you were jumping levels.

Truly, an excellent choice in music. Nico beamed at him. "I really like your familiar, Wicky. He's got it."

"Oh, he's got something, alright." Wicky just rolled his eyes. "I'm glad you were down for escaping. I felt my brain leaking out of my ears."

"Dude, I was so bored I was contemplating a nap."

"I thought you didn't take naps?"

"Exactly."

"Maybe I should have given this another ten minutes. It would have been funny watching you try."

Nico poked him in the side. Some friend he was. "Anyway, you said something about mock-fighting a giant lizard?"

"Right. I had this idea last night. I'd rather try this out on something that can't actually kill us, get our bait-and-switch tactics down, before we engage with the real thing." Wicky cast him a quick study from head to foot. "You do have your lightsaber on you, right?"

"Of course I have my lightsaber on me."

"Good."

"But where can we even practice something like this?"

"Well, we passed this place on the way into the building that no one's using. Looks like an unused parking lot. It's all fenced off, but I saw an opening. It'll keep the bystanders out of harm's way."

The way that Wicky said this promised something fun was about to happen. "You think we're going to attract bystanders?"

"My man, I guarantee you we will." Wicky was back to waggling eyebrows in pure mischief.

Nico opened the door and stepped out into the Australian heat, which, frankly, felt amazing after being blasted by that overexuberant air conditioner. Nico really preferred being too hot over being too cold.

Once he was free of the building, he turned back to Wicky. "I can see why you think that, I guess. Two men fighting a conjured monster in a parking lot is sure to get some stares."

"Oh, I'm not going to conjure just any monster."

Nico's hope rose steadily. Wicky was planning something awesome. It was written all over his face. "What are you going to conjure?"

"What's the biggest, baddest lizard you can think of?"

"Godzilla," Nico answered promptly.

"Exactly."

"You're...going to conjure Godzilla?"

Wicky's chest puffed out with pride. "I am."

Nico couldn't contain himself. He just had to hug this man. "Wicky, you're awesome and I'm proud to know you. Be my best friend for life."

Laughing, Wicky hugged him back. "Done. Come on, let's

go fight Godzilla."

Nico felt like several of his childhood fantasies were about to come true, all at once. He got to fight Godzilla with a *lightsaber*. What child didn't fantasize about that?

So, so much better than a boring meeting.

CHAPTER NINE.

BEL

Bel felt frustrated that he still didn't have a firm answer of what this could be. He could tell Jack wasn't much happier about it. The agent promised to do some more research, call a few people he knew, and give Bel a short list of possibilities before the week was out. Bel happily took the offer.

He just hoped no one else died while they figured this out.

They broke for lunch, and it was then that his head came out of the problem and informed him of something serious: Nico was still not back.

Worse, Wicky was also absent.

Oh. Oh, no.

Rightfully alarmed, he demanded of Garen, "Where are Nico and Wicky?"

"Outside." Garen shrugged as if this wasn't anything to be worried about.

"I thought they were just going to walk around the building, stretch their legs, and return?"

"You honestly thought Nico would willingly walk back into a meeting he escaped from?"

Okay, put like that, Bel felt stupid. Of course Nico wouldn't return of his own accord. "But why didn't you go look for them?"

"Bel, relax. They're on an Army base. It's not like they can find much trouble here."

Bel had no such faith. Find trouble? No, probably not. Create trouble? Absolutely. He loved those two to pieces, but Bel was also under no illusions.

Unable to sit still, he left the chair quickly and went hunting for his other familiar. He didn't know precisely where to go, but the familiar bond between himself and Nico would give him a direction. He could close his eyes and point with unerring accuracy to where exactly Nico was at all times. He was over...there, somewhere. Not far.

Bel followed both the bond and his own ears, walking out of the building and then behind it, into a fenced off parking lot that seemed out of use. Well, out of use for the inhabitants of the base, at least.

Nico and Wicky had found a use for it.

More than a little bemused, Bel looked up at the conjured form of Godzilla and the illusionary buildings along the edges of the AOE area, looking like something straight out of a bad Japanese monster movie. He wasn't sure if the scale was accurate or not, but that seemed beside the point.

With far too much glee, Nico and Wicky were battling Godzilla with their lightsabers, dancing in and around its feet, hacking at anything they could reach. Godzilla fought back, reaching down with its arms or trying to kick them with its legs. The magic behind the spell was rather impressive, really, as Godzilla could move or lift them if it caught hold. It was set to non-lethal damage, but it would at least leave bruises if it landed a hit.

Of course, with Nico's speed, it didn't stand a prayer of catching Bel's familiar. Wicky was doing a damn impressive job keeping up with Nico, too, although it was clearly more of an effort on his part.

They looked like nothing more than two little boys playing

make-believe, fighting off the monster from under the bed. Bel couldn't begin to take this seriously. If he stopped them and asked, they'd give him some bullshit reason like "training." He had no doubt of that. It was why he didn't bother to stop them.

If they wanted to play, let them play.

Besides, a tired Nico was a well-behaved Nico.

Bel shook his head and decided, for sanity reasons, to let them be. He turned and walked the opposite way, thinking as he went. Lunch did sound good, and he'd join his teammates in a minute, but if they really had to hunt this thing down? Whatever it was? Then he'd better give the commander here a heads-up that he'd need that promised backup soon. Hellhounds were all well and fine, but this called for manpower. Also, if they got them ready now, then Zia and Matt would have a chance to modify their weapons and equip them with magical shields before going hunting. It evened the odds and gave them a better fighting chance.

Decided, he texted Garen, *going to talk to commander about backup. tell me where you'll get lunch, I'll meet you there*

He got back the reply: *Sure. Where's Nico and Wicky?*

fighting Godzilla

Is that a metaphor?

sadly, no. wicky conjured Godzilla. they're still on base

I choose not to ask more questions.

you are wise

Alright, this conversation should hopefully take ten minutes. The commander's office was right across the street. If he wasn't in—it was entirely possible the man was out to lunch himself—then Bel would just leave a message and have him call later. No big deal.

Bel took himself across the street and into the blocky main building for headquarters, transitioning from hot air to arctic. Why did government buildings always crank up the

A/C? It was seriously a universal mystery.

The commander's office for the US was to the right, the one for the Australian CO to the left. The one to the left looked closed—the doors were shut and lights were off—so Bel went to the right. It didn't really matter which country's troops he took. He just needed support.

The secretary sitting at the desk looked up with a professional smile. "Hello, Agent. Can I help you?"

"I just need five minutes with the commander, if he's available."

"I think he is." She popped up from her desk and went through the connecting door to the commander's office, leaning in and asking, "Sir, do you have a moment for Agent Adams? He's here to speak with you."

"Of course, send him in," Martin's voice said firmly.

She leaned back and waved Bel through the door with another smile.

Bel gave her one in return as he walked through, taking in his bearings as he moved.

Bland blue-grey carpet, white walls, the usual art of the American flag and an aerial shot of the base on the walls, yadda yadda. Bel had seen one version or another of this office many a time. Decorators had no sense of creativity on a military base. Any branch, for that matter. Martin was behind his desk, glasses perched on the end of his nose, which he took off as Bel entered. He looked both tired and professionally welcoming as he indicated for Bel to take one of the empty chairs in front of his desk.

"Agent, please. I'm eager for an update."

"I have one for you. It won't take long. I'm sure you want to get to lunch like I do."

"For this, I'll delay a few minutes. What have you found?"

Bel sank into the chair, leaning his forearms lightly on the wood of the arms as he answered. "First, this problem is more widespread and has been going on longer than you reported to me. We have, in fact, eight cases altogether, going as far back as four months ago."

Commander Martin winced. "How do you know?"

"Yesterday I spoke with a detective in charge of missing persons and went through their recent files, visited the sites. It was obvious enough to my eyes what really happened to some of these people. I'm sorry to report this, sir, but you should be aware this problem has been going on far longer than you believed, and it started much further north of here. One of the sites involved four victims."

He rubbed at the bridge of his nose, clearly disturbed. "I'm so glad now that I pulled you in. We'd never have gotten closure for those families who've lost someone otherwise. What else can you tell me?"

Bel shared what he knew, and the commander's wince grew.

"You're sure there's two of them?"

"I'm sure on that part. I'm thankful I haven't found a third yet."

"So am I." He frowned. "If I remember correctly, at one of the sites hit, the people there fought back with hunting rifles."

"Correct, sir. Big game rifles should have made an impact, at the very least scared it off, but they didn't. I don't know if traditional weapons will do much to these things. That said"—Bel met his eyes levelly—"I'd like to take you up on the ground support. I'm making an additional request to modify their weapons. Two of my teammates are good at adapting technology with magic; they'll enhance the weapons so whoever you assign to me will be able to protect themselves."

Martin's brown eyes narrowed in his tanned face. "You're going to hunt these things down in the swamp?"

"I don't know of any other method to stop them. It's not like I can predict where they'll hit next, not really. They seem to be hitting places along the river, but that means they could be anywhere along that stretch of water. There's no way for me to pinpoint them. Their attacks have certainly been random. Likely they just swam about until they caught the scent of prey and then attacked. It depended totally on availability."

"Dammit. Still, to go in like this...you've got balls, Agent. I give you that."

Bel took the compliment. "Thank you, sir. May I have permission to modify their weapons?"

"Hell, I can't deny that request. Do so. I want my people to have a fighting chance. I'll give you a squad of Marines, how's that?"

Bel had to squash his first emotional reaction. He really, truly wished he could have an Australian squad instead.

Calm down, he counselled himself. *Calm down. It isn't like Spencer would be here, of all places, anyway.*

He summoned a smile for the commander. "Absolutely, sir. Marines would be welcome. I promise you, we'll do what we can to safeguard them and prepare them before we go in."

"When do you want to go?"

"I really don't want to leave this any time to escalate. Is tomorrow morning too soon?"

"Of course not. I'll issue the order this afternoon and have them prepare. Are you team lead?"

"I am not, sir. Matthew is."

"Ah. I'll make sure to put the right person on the paperwork then and inform the squad that they're under his command. I realize this is more a joint operation, but in situations like this, you don't want questions when it comes to chain of command."

"A thing I know all too well, sir. Thank you. I appreciate your willingness to support."

"Thank you, Agent, for being willing to go after those things despite not knowing what they actually are." He paused before tacking on, "You seem to know how to fight them, though? You said you'd prepare the Marines to help them be more combative, so that indicates you have a plan of attack in mind?"

It was a sound question. "Yes, sir. Anything water based is weak to fire. It's Magic 101. We'll equip them with fire-based ammunition and protective shields. Even if the ammunition fails, for whatever reason, they can hunker down under the shields and ride it out."

"Good, good. I don't want to send my boys in as cannon fodder. I appreciate your attitude, Agent. Let me know if you need anything else. We're more than ready to support you and get this danger out of the area."

That seemed a good dismissal, and Bel took it. He rose and offered a hand. "Thank you. I'll keep you informed. Oh-eight-hundred? Oh, and I'll need boats. I'd like to scout the river first before diving into the actual hunt, see if I can't pinpoint this thing's den. Or dens." He grimaced at the thought.

"Of course, I'll put in the req order myself." Martin gave his hand a firm shake.

"Thank you so much. Alright, I'm off to lunch. Please call me or Matthew if there are questions."

"I will."

Bel took himself back out the way he'd come, satisfied he'd gotten the right help. He didn't look forward to spending half the day on the water, trying to find monsters that thought people made good snacks, but them's the breaks. It was all part of the job.

Really, what he didn't look forward to was Nico and Wicky, stuck on a boat for hours on end with nothing to entertain them. He'd seen what they did on planes. It wouldn't be much different.

He was going to have to convince them to not leg wrestle on the boat, wasn't he?

Shaking his head in amusement, he checked his phone

and found that Garen had texted him the location for the burger joint on the corner. An easy walk, then. Bel almost went directly there, then decided against it. He felt brave enough to go back to Nico and Wicky. Maybe, if he was very convincing, he could persuade them to put Godzilla back in the toy chest and come eat?

Worth a shot.

CHAPTER TEN

GAREN

Garen absolutely hated misplacing his phone charger. Especially in hotel rooms, because there really was no telling where he'd put it. It forced him to walk around looking at everything like he was suspicious of it. What about you, nightstand? Huh, you sketchy piece of shit, did you eat it?

Nope, didn't look like it.

He'd normally poke Nico and make Nico find it, but the man had already ducked out a half hour ago for his morning run. (He swore he wasn't going to secretly meet up with Wicky to play with Godzilla again. Garen only believed him because there was no way in hell Wicky would choose to be awake this early.) Bel was only semi-conscious and not really awake. He was snuggled in the middle of the bed, hugging a pillow, about three seconds from falling right back asleep.

Garen leaned in and pressed a kiss against his forehead, breathing in warm skin. "Bel?"

"Mmm."

"You understand that unless you say actual words, I don't believe you're awake?"

"Mmm."

"Come on, Red, wakey, wakey, eggs and bakey. Eyes all the way open."

Bel grumbled some more, then tried yanking Garen in closer. Garen knew what that meant—he wanted snuggles, and as soon as he had something warm to cuddle into, he'd be right back asleep. He was predictable that way.

"No can do, you've got to get up."

Whining in the back of his throat, Bel protested and tugged at Garen some more.

"Nope. I'll cuddle you later. I need you up now."

One eye creaked open. "I thought I liked you. I'm no longer sure."

"Words, ladies and gentlemen, we have words!" Garen just chuckled when he got a poke in the ribs for that. "Come on, up. I'll get you coffee."

"Coffee?"

"If I give you coffee, can you manage to ignore the siren song of your blankets?"

Bel made a scrunched-up, adorable face of thought. "Yeah."

"Just one thing first, where did I put my phone charger?"

Bel might be only marginally awake, but that intellect wasn't ever slow. He was quick on the uptake. "Did you wake me up just to find your charger for you?"

Knowing better than to answer directly, Garen misdirected. "I can't go get coffee for you with my phone dying."

Bel made a noise of disbelief, as if he knew on some level this logic was bullshit but wasn't awake enough to connect the dots. He gave up and blinked both eyes, taking a good look around the room. He was damn handy in moments like this, when he could see absolutely everything without needing to move an inch.

"Bathroom counter."

Garen kissed the top of his head. "Perfect, thank you."

As Bel stretched, moving around to sit upright, Garen went to the little coffee station inside the hotel room and got the Keurig going. The first cup done, he handed that over to Bel and let him sip at the brew, making happy noises. He started a second cup for himself.

As it percolated, he mentioned to Bel, "Nico's already on his morning run. He said he'd go a little further today, run longer, so he's not as antsy on the boat."

Bel snorted. "The day Nico isn't fidgety is the day I check for a pulse and call for an ambulance."

"Fair. Maybe we should invest in a fidget spinner for him."

"Now there's an idea. Let's do that this afternoon. It's not like I can be on the river looking for more than three hours, anyway."

"True." Garen fixed his coffee the way he preferred it, then returned to Bel, sitting next to him so he could snuggle Bel in. Garen smoothed back that silky blond hair, looking at the pillow creases on Bel's cheek and wondering just why this man was so adorable. Garen had cute-aggression sometimes with Bel, where he just wanted to squeeze the breath out of him.

Bel leaned up to kiss him on the lips. "Love you, too."

"Is it that obvious, what I'm thinking?"

"Yeah. I can see it in the way you look at me." Bel leaned into his side with a soft sigh. "You have no idea how glad I am that you and Nico wear your hearts on your sleeves. I am never in doubt of how you feel about me."

Something in his tone hinted that this, this was the thing bothering Bel. The issue he was burying and not speaking about. Garen felt a tug at the bond, a soft pang there that spoke of deep trauma and sorrow. Old, now, no longer fresh, but the scar was still there. What was this? Garen didn't like the feel of this at all.

As much as he wanted to get to the bottom of it, Garen put it in matter of priority and reassured him first. "I do love you."

"I know you do. You turned your entire life upside down in order to stay with me."

"I've never once regretted that, either. Having you and Nico has made me far happier than that soul-sucking job I was in. Even if there are times when Nico seems determined to scare me into an early greying—"

Bel snorted on a laugh, in complete agreement.

"—and you do dangerous things that make my familiar bond get the heebie-jeebies, I still don't regret it."

Bel leaned even more firmly into him. It'd been the right thing to say, he could feel that along the bond, as something settled in Bel. "I love you too."

Was he not reassuring Bel enough through words? Was that the problem? Or did this tie back in to being rejected by his first familiar? Garen wasn't sure, and it bothered him that he didn't know how to address the problem. Or even what the problem actually was. He wished Bel would talk to him frankly about what was bothering him, so he would know how to address it.

The door clicked open and Nico strode through. He wore the satisfied smile he always had on his face after a good run, a drink carrier in his hand that held two cups. "Oooh, morning snuggles? Me too!"

Garen pointed a stern finger at him. "Not until you've had a shower. I can smell you from here. How far did you run, anyway?"

"About fifteen miles. It's getting hot out there, by the way. Make sure we have sunscreen for Bel."

Bel made a face at him. "I find it very unfair that I'm the only one who burns."

Nico's eyebrow waggle was both lecherous and ridiculous. "We like all that fair skin, don't worry. Here, I brought you— oh, you have coffee already."

Bel held up his cup. "This cup is to motivate me enough to get me out of bed. Yours is to ensure I am a functioning member of society."

"That's fair." Nico put both down on the nightstand, then skipped off to the bathroom. "I'll be quick."

Garen wasn't sure if Nico had any other speed, so why he'd said that was the question.

Either way, the moment to cuddle and ask questions appeared to be broken. He gave Bel another kiss before getting off the bed. He too needed to take a shower and put on actual clothes.

It took effort, some maneuvering, and all the coffee, but they managed to get out of the room more or less on time. Nico went next door to pounce on Wicky. Probably for the cheap entertainment value. Even in the hallway, Garen could hear Mobius playing maniacal laughter, so the familiar clearly found Wicky's wail of protest about being woken up entertaining.

Zia met them at the elevator, giving them a smile. "I'm really glad Nico likes waking up Wicky. That man's a chore to get out of bed some days."

Garen shrugged. "Nico thinks of it like a fun challenge. That might or might not end up in taking HP damage."

"I used to just lob ice cubes at him from the doorway." Zia shook her head on a laugh. "Bel, I know we only have about four hours before your eyes give out. What do you plan to do this afternoon?"

"Hmm, that's the question. I'm still waiting on Jack to get back to me with an idea of what this is."

Zia suggested, "I think maybe properly prepping the Marines, and maybe doing some drills with them might be the best use of time. If they don't know how to fight with us later, it'll be bad."

That was a really good suggestion. Also a great way to further wear out Nico after spending hours sitting in place.

"I'm all for it," Bel agreed. "We just need to make sure they don't conjure Godzilla again."

Zia flicked a hand in disagreement. "I think Godzilla is fine. It'll make it more fun for the Marines' training, too. If you make it fun, they're more inclined to do it. If we make it a game, too, they're more motivated to win."

"Ah. Well, okay, said like that it makes more sense. I guess we'll leave it up to them." Bel made a face. "And it's not like we actually know what we're going up against, so I can't offer a more realistic suggestion."

"There's that, too."

Nico bounced back to them about the time the elevator dinged open. He wore a shit-eating grin that suggested he'd had far too much fun. "Wicky's awake."

"Good job, alarm clock." Zia gave him a high five.

He smacked his palm against hers lightly, still pleased with himself. "I promised him pancakes and coffee waiting for him downstairs. We are eating here in the hotel?"

"We are."

"Okay, good."

As they rode down, Garen caught Nico up on the plan for the afternoon, which he thought sounded fun. No one was surprised.

They all ate a hearty breakfast in the hotel's dining room, which was rather good. Wicky joined them at some point, and by looking at him, you'd never know he was a zombie on shuffle not a half hour ago. Garen was very curious how much coffee went into that transformation.

Matt herded them all outside and into the waiting van. Corporal Williams was once again chauffeuring, taking them toward the Adelaide River. A great deal of the problems had occurred near the Harrison Dam. There was a whole stretch of river there that led up to the coast and through a swamp conservation area, which led to a lot of possible terrain for their monsters to have come from. It would probably take two or three days to comb through all of it.

Assuming the monster in question didn't find them first.

They drove along the freeway and east, through green country thick with trees. The Marines were meeting them there with boats already waiting. Garen took in the area, especially the heat of the day, and was glad they would be on the water this morning. It would be cooler that way. He wouldn't have to worry about anyone overheating.

The van pulled up and parked in a rather large parking area, and it was only then Garen realized this wasn't just a dam. It was a tourist attraction. There was a large sign in yellow with white text proclaiming *Jumping Crocodile Cruise meet here*! right at the entrance to the blocky green building. The hell?

Bel leaned in from the middle seat and asked Corporal Williams uncertainly, "There's a cruise ship that goes up and down this river?"

"More than one." She gave him a speaking look. "You see why we're all so concerned."

"Fucking hell. I don't like the look of this at all."

"We're actually borrowing a cruise ship this morning for your squizz."

Garen blinked at her in surprise. "Uh...squizz?"

"Not a term you Yanks use? Look about."

Oh. Aussie slang was something else. How did that word even develop...? Garen shook off the question and went back to the matter at hand. "We're taking a cruise ship?"

"Easiest boat to get on short notice. Plus, their boats are shaded and meant to hold a large number of people. You'll want that shade on the water, trust me."

Garen had no doubt of that, but...a cruise ship? Really? Then again, it was an Army base, not a naval one. They probably didn't have many ships at their disposal.

Bel didn't look entirely happy about this but shrugged and got out with everyone else. If it was a problem, he'd find a different boat for the next day, Garen had no doubt about that. His mild-mannered mage could make things move when he was of a mind to.

They trooped up the metal stairs and then back down again to a shaded area near the main building that looked like a waiting area. Small tables and chairs were set up, encouraging people to relax as they waited. Even in the shade it was a bit sweltering. Garen did not look forward to the rest of the morning.

The Marines were already in place, although it looked as if they'd barely beaten them there by five minutes. Most were standing and chatting with each other, a mix of men and women in uniform, weapons slung over their shoulders. They were relaxed now, but Garen had no doubt they'd react quickly if danger showed itself. He didn't see their captain yet, but Corporal Williams was beelining for someone in the crowd. They'd get introduced shortly.

Like a Mack truck, a barrage of feelings slammed through Garen along the bond: pain, regret, horror, denial, all edged in panic. Garen felt bowled over by it all, so much so that he staggered a step, the breath knocked out of his lungs. What the hell?!

Nico, faster than he to react, was at Bel's side in a second, latching on to him. Garen was a beat behind him, alarmed, as he had no idea what had set Bel off. What was wrong? Why did Bel look like someone had just walked over his grave and then cursed it for good measure? He didn't see anything wrong, there wasn't any danger or hint of something off.

Bel stared straight at one of the Marines, who stared back at him with the same sort of shock, neither of them moving.

What the hell was going on?!

CHAPTER ELEVEN

BEL

Spencer. Oh god, Spencer was *here*. Panic slammed into Bel, raw and hot, and all he wanted to do was run. His breathing became scattered the longer he stared, and his entire body trembled, mind on the verge of shutting down completely.

God above, how he wished Spencer was a ghost. Bel would pay good money for this man to be a figment of his imagination right now. He'd never, ever, wanted to see Spencer living and breathing in front of him again.

Some part of his mind wondered if he'd conjured the man, just because the anniversary of breaking their bond was today, and it was some cruel trick his subconscious was playing on him. The emotions rampaging in his chest were all too real, though. The regret of ever summoning Spencer to begin with, the remembered pain of that broken bond, the anger of Spencer hating him for no reason, enough to walk out. All of that flooded back to him as if it had happened yesterday instead of three years ago.

For a moment, Bel felt outside of his own body, this whole situation feeling strange and unreal to him. Spencer looked a little different than Bel remembered. His time in the Marines had filled him out more, bulked him up some. He was tan, red hair more sun-bleached blond, but the anger and disgust in his green eyes were all too familiar. That hadn't changed at all.

"Oh, shit," Victoria breathed.

Bel heard her, but she and Matt seemed as rooted to the spot as he was, disbelief shocking them into stillness. Of course, no one else would recognize Spencer, so they couldn't know shit was about to hit the fan.

Bel barely felt Nico's hands on his shoulders, the weight of Garen's hand on his back as Spencer marched toward him. His entire focus was on this man who should have loved him. Bel had no idea how to feel about him now. He did know, though, that no part of him wanted a confrontation with him.

He was about to get one, anyway.

"You freaky little shit," Spencer snarled, marching for him. "You followed me out here? You seriously tracked me down and followed me way out here?"

"No," Bel managed around a tight throat. His eyes burned, maybe from tears—tears of horror and regret—but they didn't spill. "I didn't. I had no idea you were here. Trust me, I wish I had. I would have put more effort into avoiding you."

"Bel," Nico murmured near his temple, "who is this?"

This was going to open a can of worms and probably sound the starting bell to a fight, but Bel had to tell him. He didn't take his eyes off Spencer—he frankly didn't trust him enough to do that—as he said, "This is Spencer."

Nico and Garen both went still.

"*That* Spencer?" Garen's voice was the epitome of calm.

Bel managed to choke out, "Yeah."

"Why the hell are you here?" Spencer demanded. "You can't be the hotshot agent they called out here."

Bel swallowed hard. He could feel everyone's eyes on him, staring and taking in this drama. It was extremely uncomfortable, and he had to fight to stay still. To not just turn and bury himself in Garen's arms, or Nico's, and wish this whole day away. Being an adult sucked in moments like these. It was one of the hardest things he'd ever done, to stand there and face this ghost from the past. The only thing that kept him there was his determination not to let Spencer have the upper hand ever again.

"I am, in fact. This is my specialty, remember? Or I guess you wouldn't, as you ditched me before we could even start working."

Spencer's eyes roved over him again, this time taking in the windbreaker with his department's letters on it, taking stock of him in a different light. "Shit. Are you fucking serious? I guess your freaky eyes would come in handy for something like this. I don't believe you didn't maneuver your way here, though—"

He tried to stab a finger into Bel's chest, but it never hit. Nico's hand whipped out, quick as a viper, and deflected it, throwing the hand back into Spencer's face. It startled him enough he took a step back, eyes snapping to Nico.

Nico was all rage, red high in his cheeks, as he took a half step in front of Bel. "You don't touch him. Ever."

For the first time, Spencer really examined the two men flanking Bel. Bel could see when it connected, when the realization of who they must be hit. After all, the defensiveness in how Garen and Nico were standing over him was unmistakable. Especially to Spencer, who had been in that position before.

"Holy shit, you're the new familiar. Ha! Of course he had to call someone else; no familiar, no working. That's how the rule goes." Spencer snorted in derision. "Wow. That didn't take him long. And he made such a big deal about breaking our bond to begin with."

"It took me a full fucking year to recover from you." Bel's anger surged as he stared at Spencer. He welcomed the anger, as it was vastly preferable over the panic. He didn't remember this man being such an arrogant asshole. Had he gotten worse over the past three years?

"You still managed just fine, apparently." Spencer's lip lifted in a curl of derision.

"The lion, the witch, and the audacity of this bitch," Nico growled.

Victoria was right there with him. "He's always been a little bundle of bitch."

Garen shifted at his side, distressed because of Bel's emotions. He rubbed a hand up and down Bel's back, coming in close enough that Bel was almost against his chest. The contact helped steady him as nothing else could. Bel wanted to lean in to it desperately, just tuck his head under Garen's chin and re-find his center.

Spencer's eyes flickered over Garen and Nico all over again. "What, it took two of you to replace me? That's funny."

Oh, he did *not* just say that! Bel snapped upright, ready to defend his men and tear Spencer a new one.

Nico beat him to the punch. "Wow, your ass must be jealous of all the shit your mouth is spewing."

Spencer got right in his face, although he had to tilt his head back a smidge, as Nico was taller. "I'm right, aren't I?"

"Naw, you're hella wrong. Bel summoned me. Garen we brought in because we happen to like him very, very much."

"Love you, too," Garen drawled.

Nico shot him a wink before focusing on Spencer. In a rare showing, Nico went full captain mode, his voice clipped and hard, something used against a younger and stupider subordinate.

"Now, let's get this straight, you arrogant jackass. You can't compare yourself to us. Why? *Because you left.* You couldn't even cut it three weeks before you called it quits and hightailed it out of there like the coward you are. You took a look at what Bel can do, what he'd be asked to do in the future, and tough Marine that you are, you decided it was too dangerous."

Spencer's mouth opened on a hot retort. "That's not—"

"You couldn't hack it, Soldier." Nico took a step forward, forcing Spencer back a step in return. "You can't compare yourself to us. We chose to love this man, to help and support him, to be the defense he needed against the world. We stayed. You left. *You are not our equal.*"

Bel was in awe watching Nico because, damn. He'd never seen the man this enraged before. Part of his brain catalogued that look for future reference. This was what Nico looked like when he was utterly pissed off.

Spencer didn't seem to know what to say to that. Nico was entirely right, and everyone listening—well, those who knew the story—knew it. Spencer hadn't even lasted a full month before running for it. He couldn't compare to Nico or Garen. Garen especially, because he'd had no magical tie urging him to stay but had chosen Bel anyway.

"Do not come near him again." Garen's voice was firm, his hold on Bel protective in the extreme. "For the duration of our stay here, you stay as far from him as you can manage. If you try to touch him again, there will be hell to pay. I promise you, you will not get past us."

Spencer sneered and took a half step around Nico, his intention to challenge Nico's words clear. "You're not all that—"

Out of Bel's peripheral vision, he could see when Garen's gargoyle genes activated. In the blink of an eye, his skin changed from soft and supple to rock hard, covered in grey stone like he was donning armor. It went over his arms and hands, up to his jawline, clearly visible to anyone looking. The whole squad, standing behind Spencer, was visibly taken aback.

Spencer stopped dead, eyes flaring comically wide in his face. "Shit! The hell, man?!"

"He's part gargoyle," Matt explained cheerfully. "When Garen says you can't get past him, he's not just blowing hot air."

This show of force and love gave Bel what he needed to face Spencer down properly. And really, he couldn't let his men steal the limelight, now, could he? "Spencer, let's be clear on this. The men who came after you are very much your superiors. In every way."

Nico shot him a smile, warm and full of affection. "Love you too, Bel Bel."

Bel gave him a small smile back. Truly, he felt the love from both of them. It was impossible not to.

A tall woman in a Marine uniform came forward, a sergeant's stripes on her collar. She was easily as tall as any man there, powerful in figure, and the look on her face did not herald anything good. "Davis!"

Spencer clearly hated it, but he turned and came to attention. "Ma'am."

"Stand there." She pointed to the ground, and the look in her eye dared him to move. Only when he was properly cowed did she turn to Nico, and her demeanor noticeably softened. "Di Rocci, isn't it?"

"Yes, ma'am."

"I'd like to talk to your mage. Can I do that?"

Smart of her to realize that both Nico and Garen were on high alert and would be highly defensive toward anyone who came near Bel until the issue with Spencer was somehow settled.

Nico had years of *obey superiors* ground into him, and still he hesitated for a long second before ducking his head in a nod. "Yes, ma'am."

"Thank you." She was still cautious coming around him to face Bel and stopped a good three feet away. It was clear from the way she reacted that she'd had experience with mages and familiars and was smart enough to heed that experience. "Mage Adams. I'm Sergeant Lee. I think I got the gist of the situation just by the yelling. Clarify two things for me. Davis was your familiar, but he chose to leave and break the bond, which means he has no further claim on you. Is that correct?"

Bel swallowed hard and gave her a curt nod, emotions still in enough turmoil that he found it hard to answer her. "Yes. That's correct."

"You had no idea he was here and came only because the higher-ups requested your help. Your sole purpose here is to track down what's eating people and help us root it out. Is that correct?"

"Yes, Sergeant, that's also correct."

"First, thank you for coming. And for trying to talk this hothead down. I can tell how upset you are, but you're being calm and reasonable, and I appreciate it. I will try to keep him as far away from you as possible, okay?"

As first impressions went, hers was good. Bel liked her. A lot.

"I'd appreciate that very much."

She softened into a smile, an expression that made her look like a person you really wanted to be friends with. "Then that's what we'll do. Davis, first of all, let me tell you something. You're a fucking moron if you mess with these three. Crossing a familiar by trying to get at their mage is suicide. I expect the men in my unit to have better sense than that. Is that understood?"

Spencer looked ready to swallow gasoline rather than admit to that.

Her eyes cut to him in the same expression a mother would give a particularly rebellious child. "I asked a question, Davis."

"Yes, ma'am," he gritted out. "Understood."

"Good. You're to keep as much distance between yourself and Mage Adams as you can possibly manage. At all times.

Is that understood?"

"Yes, ma'am," he gritted out again, skin flushing angrily along his neck and cheeks.

"Understand that if you ignore that last order and deliberately antagonize Mage Adams, I will not be the least bit sympathetic when his familiars take you out. I just watched how combat ready they are, and frankly? I don't give your survival good odds if you start a fight with them." She shook her head. "Now, get on the boat. Everyone, board!"

The Marines moved, and there was whispering amongst them as everyone moved. Only Spencer wasn't spoken to, and he was surly in the extreme as he pivoted on a heel and stalked along the metal ramp leading to the boat.

Bel's gaze went to the sergeant. She was quite possibly the tallest Asian woman Bel had ever seen, and pretty, not to mention tough as nails. Bel was incredibly happy she was the sergeant of this squad, as apparently she had no patience with stupidity. Lee was his kind of people.

"Sergeant Lee, thank you."

Her smile turned rueful. "I can't promise I can keep that idiot totally in line. Davis has a history of choosing stupidity first and foremost. He's in danger of a blanket party at the rate he's going, as no one in the squad really likes him. If he starts hassling you guys again, report it to me. I'll handle it. If he does more than hassling, then act with extreme prejudice."

Nico beamed at her. "I really like you."

She snorted a laugh, eyes crinkling up. "I've worked with mages and familiars before. I know the score. I'm just justifying the inevitable. Now, Mage Adams, can we get on board? We've got dangerous creatures to find."

"Yes, Sergeant, we can." Bel liked the idea of working on the same boat as Spencer about as much as he liked the thought of lying on an anthill, but what could he do? People's lives were in danger. He was here for a reason. Someone had to track this thing down, and he had the best bet of doing so.

Still, today was going to suck.

Garen dropped the stone coating over his skin and leaned in, pressing a kiss to Bel's temple before whispering, "We've got you, my heart."

"I know," Bel whispered back. He did know. And it was only because of them that he had the strength and the willpower to get on that boat despite Spencer being on it.

He turned in Garen's arms and hugged him tightly, trying to absorb the other man's strength. He'd need it shortly. He could feel the love both his men sent along the bond, and the very strength of that bond, and it bolstered him as nothing else could. Still. The idea of spending any time with Spencer at all sounded like torture. The memory of that broken bond was a livewire of pain in him, and only his hold on Garen and Nico kept him on his feet and breathing.

The rest of this day was going to suck. Majorly.

CHAPTER TWELVE

NICO

Bel was at the very front of the boat, the better for his eyes to pick up some kind of trail. Treasure was once again up in the air, scouting from a higher vantage point. It might have been early morning, but the heat of the day was already a promise on the air, the sun coming in strong. The boat had a metal top to it, a shield over the rows of seats, but Bel couldn't really take advantage of it. He had to lean on the railing in order to have the best view. Nico didn't like that, for various reasons, but at least it kept him on the opposite side of the boat from Douchebag.

The trip was barely underway when Garen magicked a small tube of sunscreen out of his pocket and started slathering it on Bel's porcelain skin, starting with his face.

"I'm really okay," Bel assured him, although his expression showed he was touched by Garen's actions.

"You won't be in about an hour," Garen retaliated, still smoothing white cream over his nose. "And remember, this might take days of being on the water. You don't want to get burned now only to make it worse for the rest of the mission."

"Urk. That's true."

Nico made a mental note to bring an umbrella tomorrow

to give Bel portable shade. He'd need it. Nico turned sideways, staying at Bel's side but keeping an eye on Spencer at the same time.

The scumbucket was on the far side of the boat, as ordered, but his eyes were pinned on Bel. There was an expression there, a look Nico couldn't quite decipher. Surprise? Awareness? Spencer's gaze kept roving over Bel from head to foot, taking him in again and again, as if he couldn't quite believe his eyes.

After a moment, he must have sensed Nico's stare on him, as his eyes snapped to Nico, and he flushed angrily, then resolutely turned his back to him.

Too late, Nico internally grumbled. Caught you staring, jackass. Nico swore right then and there, if that dickhead even tried to come near Bel, he'd throw hands without thinking twice. Just having him nearby and causing Bel such heartache made Nico agitated. He could feel along the bond how upset Bel was, that remembered agony still throbbing, even though his mage kept his gaze on the river. Bel might look calm, but inside he was an emotional mess. His heart was in turmoil.

Bel would feel better if Nico killed Spencer, right? Right? He felt good about this decision.

Wicky sidled up next to him, leaning a little into Nico's side as he murmured, "Can I have a page or two of this story?"

Of course he would want to know. Nico stepped away from Bel's side—just a few feet—so he could relate it all to Wicky without pouring salt into an open wound. As he did so, Zia joined them, also huddling in so they could speak in whispers.

"I can't actually add much more than you overheard," Nico admitted sourly. "Bel gave Garen and I the gist, but it's painful for him to talk about, so I don't have all the details. What I can tell you is this: Bel called for a familiar at sixteen and got shithead over there. Spencer was twenty at the time.

Bel said it all went to shit pretty quickly. Within three weeks, Spencer had had enough and demanded to be let out of the bond. It took Bel a year to recover afterwards."

Zia made a face. "Damn. To have a familiar reject you... it's so rare that happens. It's like, what, a one in a million chance?"

"I think it's even rarer than that." Wicky, for once, looked dead serious, and the way he looked at Spencer was chilling. Nico had seen kinder eyes on contract killers. Nico wholeheartedly approved of this expression. When he killed Spencer, he knew precisely who to call to help him bury the body.

Victoria joined in, leaning between Wicky and Zia to tack on, "What's worse is I think we all saw this coming the first day Spencer was there. He didn't take the initial summoning well. Not like you, Nico. You were all curiosity, interest—you took it really well. Spencer was demanding, asking question after question, not liking the answers. Once he really got the lay of the land, he started throwing things, yelling at Bel about just yanking him out of training without warning—like he didn't even understand how summoning worked. It took two days to calm him down enough to get a full explanation out. The first real question he asked was about salary and seeing a contract. A fucking work contract."

"Ouch." Zia winced. "That's a terrible sign, alright. Why would Bel's magic choose someone like that?"

Now, that was Nico's question.

"Magic isn't infallible. Spencer did have the right fighting skills, the right talent, to be a good familiar." Victoria shook her head, disappointment tugging her mouth down. "He just let his temper get the best of him. He was too self-centered to really focus on anything but himself. Bel bent over backward those first weeks, trying to overcome Spencer's objections. But I think he knew. He had his cousins' and aunt's familiars to compare to. He knew what a good familiar should be acting like, and Spencer wasn't it. It's why, when Spencer demanded to be let go, he didn't argue. He regretted it—deeply—but he didn't fight it."

Nico knew how much that must have cost Bel. Hell, just imagining the reverse—Bel ever asking to be let out of their bond—made Nico want to curl up under a blanket and sob his eyes out. Not that Bel ever would, nor would Nico ever give him cause to, but still. The only benefit to that shitshow was that Bel left behind something toxic. Nico knew he and Garen were so much better for their mage.

Low bar to clear, granted. Spencer hadn't exactly set a high standard to beat.

"You can see Spencer's kicking himself," Zia noted.

Nico quirked a brow at her. "What?"

"I've seen it cross his face a few times. He keeps looking at Bel like 'damn, he grew up fine.' Victoria, was Bel one of those gangly teenagers?"

"All knees and elbows," Victoria confirmed with a nod. "Awkward duckling. You could see he'd be cute in the future, he just hadn't quite grown into his own body yet."

"And he's hella cute now," Wicky confirmed. "Oooh, that must be salt in an open wound for Spencer. That sparks joy."

Nico was sadistic enough to admit that Spencer regretting past decisions sparked joy for him, too. As long as he realized it was a past mistake he couldn't get a second chance on, all was well. If he tried to get Bel back, Nico would react with extreme prejudice.

Really, he felt like extreme prejudice might be called for anyway.

Wicky leaned into his side again. "You know...this is a crocodile tour boat we're on."

Why was Wicky stating the obvious? "Yes...?"

"Which means there are crocodiles in this river. With all that body armor he's in, I doubt Spencer can swim well. If you need my help accidentally bumping him over the side,

I'm here for you, buddy. It's all I'm saying."

Nico almost knuckled a tear from his eye. "Wicky, you're really an awesome friend."

"You know it." Wicky winked at him. "Wanna do it?"

Zia pointed a stern finger at both of them. "No. Behave."

Wicky pulled a face, looking sour and dejected. "Why are you such a killjoy?"

"I live to disappoint you."

"Clearly."

Nico ignored the banter as Garen had caught his eye. After so many years, Nico had learned how to read him well. Garen silently conveyed to him his agitation, the concern he had for Bel. Nico shared this utterly.

With a jerk of the chin, he indicated Douchebag and gave a hopeful tilt of the head toward the railing. *It'd be easy to disappear him. Problem eaten and gone, yeah?*

Garen gave a slight shake of the head. *No.*

Dammit, don't be a spoilsport. It's just a little murder.

Garen gave him another shake of the head. *No.* Then he tilted down to press a kiss on top of Bel's head.

Yeah, granted, Bel wouldn't take it well. Initially. But Nico was sure he'd agree eventually that Spencer would do the world a favor when he stopped breathing. Really, he'd be more use as crocodile food than walking around taking up valuable oxygen.

Garen indicated Bel again with a meaningful uplift of the brows.

Yeah, agreed, they'd need the full story from Bel. Nico would insist on that, at least.

Bel growled out something before turning, extending a hand to Nico. "Will you just come here and stop having this elaborate conversation over my head?"

Pointing a finger at himself, Nico silently protested his innocence. He'd never.

"Oh, stop. Like I'm oblivious to that silent conversation

you and Garen were having."

"Bel Bel. Confess." Nico came to him, taking his hand but still giving him a Scroogey look. "You really can see through the back of your head, can't you?"

"I confess nothing." Bel wrapped his fingers around Nico's hand, keeping him firmly planted at his side. "And no disappearing Spencer."

"Dammit, and now you read minds?" Nico could just feel his and Wicky's excellent plan getting shot down in flames. Ah, the best laid plans of mice and men, or so the poem went.

"I'm talented that way."

"So you do confess to that, at least."

"No, you're just that predictable."

Nico would protest, but, well, he kinda was. Protective instincts were to blame.

Sergeant Lee came up to stand on Garen's other side. "Mage Adams, I understand we can only be out here for a few hours?"

"My eyes can only stand to search for about three hours," Bel explained to her, eyes still trained on the river. "After that, I start to get a migraine. I have to break and rest. We'll search as much as we can today before turning around. I hope, honestly, to do nothing else but pick up a trail today."

"Understood. That's why you wanted to do training with us later this afternoon."

"Correct."

Matt joined in on her other side. "It's something we've learned to do. You Marines aren't trained to fight in our manner, and if we're working together on something like this, it's best that we learn how to face the enemy as a unit before we're in active combat."

"I'm all for it," Lee assured them. "I like to have a handle on things before they go to shit. That said, can we pull another squadron to train as well? I have a feeling we'll need the extra support."

Nico personally thought that was a great idea.

Matt shrugged in agreement; clearly no objection there. "Sure. No harm in that."

"Excellent. I'll call that in while he's searching, get it set up. Just give me a shout if you do find something interesting," she requested of Bel.

"I will, Sergeant," Bel promised her. He gave her a brief glance and smile that was obviously forced before his eyes went to the river again.

The next three hours kinda dragged. Nico took turns with Garen slathering more sunscreen on Bel, making sure he kept hydrated, and glaring at Spencer if he even twitched toward the front of the boat. Eventually, Bel gave up as his eyes were starting to hurt and he hadn't picked up even the barest hint of anything large and hungry. He signaled to turn around and finally retreated to where everyone else sat in the shade.

The atmosphere was tense, no one could describe it otherwise. With the team arrayed in seats around them, Nico stayed planted at Bel's side, daydreaming about how to kill Spencer. The initial plan of dumping him over the side of the boat and letting the crocodiles have him might be too simplistic. Not enough suffering. Also, there was the sad possibility that someone might feel the responsibility to fish him out before the local wildlife got him.

This was Australia, land of things that wanted to kill you, right? Surely Nico could arrange an unfortunate training accident without too much trouble.

Over the sound of the motor, Nico could hear Spencer's voice. Not all of the words, maybe one in three, but he was no doubt trying to tell his side of the story and spin it so he didn't look like such a loser. Good luck on that. Nico frankly didn't care what the man said, but every time Bel heard his voice, he flinched and clung a bit tighter to both him and Garen. Every time he did so, it sent a surge of overwhelming emotion along the bond.

Nico felt his own familiar instincts rise to the fore every time, urging him to protect, to touch. He couldn't solve this problem immediately for Bel, damn it all to hell. He wished he could. The best he could do was send reassurance along the bond, to keep his thigh and hip pressed up against Bel's so he could stay in physical contact.

I'm right here, love. I'm going nowhere.

Bel must have felt it, as he smiled up at Nico, a shadow of his normal expression. He leaned against Nico's shoulder for a moment, cuddling in. Nico dropped a kiss on top of Bel's head, catching Matt's eyes as he did so. Matt looked about as worried as Nico felt.

Spencer got louder, saying something derisive, judging from the tone.

Bel flinched all over again.

Fucking hell, this was a vicious cycle they were all in. Nico watched as Garen pulled Bel back into his side, cuddling him without apology, and Nico was fine with that. Garen could soothe and defend, as he liked to do.

Nico would go on the offensive.

Right, so what was the deadliest creature in northern Australia? That Nico could use for an assassination attempt? Google surely knew this answer. He pulled out his phone and input the question. Google-sensei, do your magic.

Oooh, so many possibilities.

The saltwater crocodile, of course, Nico had figured on those. But there were also box jellyfish...and something called a taipan snake? Nico liked the idea of a snake. Easy to put in the man's bed.

Wicky leaned in to take a look at his screen, nodded approvingly, and then tilted Mobius so Nico could see he was doing his own search.

What a friend. Truly. Nico beamed at him, so glad Wicky was still on the same page.

Nico scrolled down and tilted his screen for consideration. *Blue-ringed octopus*?

Wicky shook his head, lips pursed. *Too hard to get the fucker into the water.*

That was a valid point.

Tilting Mobius, Wicky offered with uplifted eyebrows, *redback spider*?

Now there was a good idea. Not sure where he'd find one, though.

Nico scrolled down a bit more. *Oooh, brown snake*?

Wicky pointed helpfully to the caption under the picture. Anti-venom existed.

Well damn, that was out, then. Tiger snake?

Shaking his head again, Wicky pointed again to the caption.

Same problem: anti-venom existed.

Come on, Australia, do your job. Nico needed something killed.

Wicky's brows scrunched together in deep thought, but he gave Nico an encouraging look. *They'd figure this out. Wicky was in this with him.*

"What," Garen asked mildly, "are you two doing?"

Nico blinked at him, the picture of innocence. "Deciding what to have for lunch."

"Oh, really." Garen had known him too long to be fooled by this. His eyebrow arched an nth degree in challenge.

Wicky gave him a defiant look in return, a hand over his heart, appalled Garen would doubt their sincerity. "Nico wants local cuisine, I'm in the mood for steak."

Nico nodded primly. "We should take advantage while we're here, after all."

Bel turned to look their direction, eyes glittering with unspoken laughter. He was not fooled. Smart man. He was also relaxing steadily under this nonsense, briefly distracted by the shenanigans.

"And what, you're having this conversation exclusively via eyebrow?"

"We didn't want to be loud," Nico explained modestly. "Are we too distracting? Wicky, let's change to something else."

"Air guitar work for you?" Wicky inquired, the very soul of helpfulness.

Nico perked up. Now they were talking.

Victoria rolled her eyes, muttering, "Who talks via air guitar?"

With a strong strum, Wicky shredded a pretend guitar and finished with a pleading pout, and *where* had Wicky been all his life?!

It was hard to keep a straight face as he shook his head sadly.

"Too oily," he explained. Then Nico played out his own riff, really getting the energy into it.

Wicky's face fell. "I don't want *vegetables*."

Nico played him a sad *wah, wah, wah,* earning Wicky a sympathetic pat on the shoulder from Zia (who, by the way, had been trying valiantly this entire time not to laugh, but the way her lips kept twitching up rather gave her away).

"Holy shit," Matt muttered in awe. "If I didn't know any better, I would swear the two of you were separated at birth. Nico, you sure the right mage summoned you?"

"*Excuse* you!" Bel latched on to Nico's arm, glaring at Matt. "Mine."

Matt held up both hands in surrender. "Just asking, cool it. It's just crazy how much these two are in sync."

Really, Nico considered Wicky a gift from the universe. He gave Wicky another riff, this one complicated and with a few extra strums in there, trying to get his point across.

Wicky gave him a fist to bump. "Right there with you, man."

Bumping, Nico beamed at him. He had known Wicky was

the sane one.

Bel leaned into Garen's side to mutter, "Do I want to know?"

"Probably not."

"Do I need to know?"

"Unfortunately, one of us does. Just to be able to call for an ambulance."

Nico jerked away from them, appalled, eyes wide with disbelief. "How dare you! I haven't once lopped off anyone's appendage doing that!"

"Okay, I wasn't concerned before," Victoria commented rhetorically to the air in general, "but now I am. How did we move past the topic of lunch to chopping things off?"

"After-lunch exercise," Wicky explained helpfully. "Stabitha and Slashley are bored and want to play. We'll just take them for a quick sparring match."

"Stabitha," Victoria repeated slowly, as if she was trying to put this particular puzzle piece into an overall picture but was utterly failing, "and Slashley?"

Wicky tapped the magical saber hanging off his belt. "Stabitha."

Nico gestured to its twin on his own belt. "Slashley."

Looking between the two of them, Victoria seemed to wait for the punch line. Then gave up. "Of course you named them. Of course you did."

It was a magical lightsaber that was awesome and stabbity. What else was Nico supposed to do? Let it languish about being nameless? For shame!

That was his story, and he was sticking to it.

"I'm so glad we're doing training after lunch," Bel muttered.

Yeah, so was Nico. They were all focused on being good and training, but him? Well, he was reasonably sure he could convince Wicky to call up Godzilla again.

The man was a buddy that way.

Oooh, he could accidentally stab Spencer while they were training, surely.

After lunch training was definitely looking on the up and up.

CHAPTER THIRTEEN

BEL

The three of them retreated to their room while the rest of the team handled training the Marines. Bel would really rather not talk about Spencer, but he knew there was no escaping it. Honestly, it was a miracle Garen and Nico had waited until they were back at the hotel room that afternoon before demanding answers. As much as he wanted to avoid the topic, he owed them, and with Spencer unfortunately close, they had to know. They had to know what they were dealing with.

Nico's idea of feeding him to the alligators was damn tempting, though. Damn tempting.

Bel toed off his shoes near the door, shed the windbreaker and draped it over the nearby chair, then collapsed face first onto the king-sized bed. What a fucking day.

He'd had nightmares about confronting Spencer before. He'd dreamed of being on his own, of just bumping into the man randomly and having to deal with it without any support. Those had been panic dreams, true enough. The worst dreams were the ones where he'd called for a familiar and gotten Spencer all over again. *Those* dreams could bring him bolt upright out of sleep, crying and covered in sweat.

Although they'd stopped after he'd called Nico, thank god.

He couldn't decide if the nightmares were better or worse than what had actually happened. Better, in the sense that Nico and Garen were right there to support and defend him. Worse because he still had to deal with the man tomorrow. Bel didn't know which god he'd offended to be handed this situation, but he'd figure it out and make as many sacrifices as necessary to straighten the matter out.

Right now, he had to deal with his lovers. Their emotions were strong along the bond. Anger, concern, love—love above all else. It echoed along his own emotions because Bel felt the same way. He wanted to reassure them, first and foremost, but wasn't sure if he was in the right mental or emotional state to manage it. Seeing Spencer like this...well, it had done its damage. No lie.

The mattress dipped at his side, a gentle hand brushing through his hair. "Bel, do you want to shower before we talk?"

It was so like Garen to give him a minute if he needed one. The shower was tempting, because he smelled strongly of sunscreen, but no. He couldn't enjoy a shower with this hanging over his head. He turned enough to nuzzle against Garen's hip.

"No. I want to get it over with."

"So, you do understand that we want all the details?" Nico sat at his other side, a hand resting on his thigh.

"Yeah. I figured. I don't want you going up against him without all the facts, either. It's not fair." Bel twisted, just enough to look up into Nico's face. The concern was obvious there in those hazel eyes, as was the love he had for Bel. That, more than anything, gave him the strength to say what he needed to. "It's not like I want to keep secrets from either of you. It's just really painful to talk about."

"We know," Garen assured him, running his hand over Bel's head again in a soothing way. "It's why we never pushed for the full story. If you want to just give us the highlights of what we have to know, that's fine."

Bel thought he might default to that. It would depend on how hard this broke him. Old scars were already wide open and bleeding, after all. Bel hadn't felt this fragile in years. He was determined, at least, to try for the full story first. He couldn't force himself to sit up, as he was too comfortable lying in between them like this. After everything that had happened this morning, he felt exhausted down to his bones. Sitting up took too much energy. It didn't matter how he was oriented, anyway.

"You know how my parents are, how disengaged they are from my life. Matt and Victoria are awesome foster parents. I couldn't ask for better, but it still hurt. To know that my parents weren't invested enough in me to weather the storm. It's why, I think, I was so invested in summoning a familiar. I could call someone to me, someone who would love me to pieces despite everything, and I dreamed about that. I maybe dreamed and fantasized too much. When my cousins started summoning their familiars, I got to be at each summoning. I watched as they were called. They did it so I could see the process, get familiar with it, but also so I could greet a new family member. That's how they saw it. It's how we all saw it."

Nico's hand on his hip tightened. "It never crossed your mind that he would reject you."

"No. In the history of my family, it's never once happened. We've always called amazing familiars to us. It seriously never occurred to me to brace myself for that possibility. When my own time came, I was so nervous. I prepped harder for that summoning than I did for the entrance exams for MAD. I asked my cousins a thousand questions, their familiars a thousand more, and I was giddy with the idea that finally, finally, I'd have someone to call my own. I prepared his bedroom—like I did for you, Nico—and all the paperwork he'd need, everything I could think of so he'd be comfortable in the house. I was sixteen, so I was still living with Matt and Victoria at the time, but they let me do whatever to the house to prepare for him. Chantelle actually flew in for the summoning."

It was getting harder to talk about this. He could feel tears burning in his eyes, and his hands were starting to shake a little. Bel latched on to Nico's arm. He wasn't sure whether he was trying to anchor himself to the here and now, or trying to futilely still that trembling. It didn't matter, either way. He just had to touch Nico in that moment.

Bel took a second, swallowed past a constricted throat, and forced words out of his mouth. "The summoning itself was textbook perfect. It came together so well that it was almost ironic. The minute Spencer arrived, though, he was upset. He didn't seem to get that this wasn't like a normal job. He kept trying to put it in terms of a work contract or a salaried position, asking things like how much time off did he get, why did he have to live with me. He didn't get it. I explained over and over. Chantelle stepped in several times and explained as well, but it was like he didn't want to understand that this wasn't a job—it was a life. When it finally did click, he couldn't believe I'd dared summon him. He kept lashing out, spitting out questions, not letting me answer him. He raged, threw things, demanded I portal him back—like anyone has the power to portal over that kind of distance. When he finally put it together that he wasn't meant to be just a protector, but my lover, he..."

A memory of his expression then, of the disgust and outrage on his face, flashed through Bel's mind. He shoved it back down, pressing his forehead tight against Garen's hip as if to help quell that flash. He couldn't dwell on that memory if he had a prayer of finishing this.

"He hated the idea. He couldn't believe he'd been summoned as a familiar. He called it slavery. He called it sex trafficking. He had a lot of words for it."

Garen maneuvered so he was flat on the mattress, cuddling Bel against his chest. Bel went, burrowing into that embrace, feeling it as Nico wrapped around his back. Their arms around him felt like a balm on an open wound. God above, he needed it just then. Bel could feel the tears leaking out of his eyes even though he tried so hard to fight them back. It had been more than the words Spencer said to him then. It had been the dashed hopes, the rage he felt along the bond, day in and day out. It had been all of that combined into a gestalt of pain and the bleak realization of what he'd be forced to do.

It took more than a minute for him to find the strength to continue. "I tried, so hard, to explain to him that it was none of that. He was meant to be my partner, my equal, he'd never be considered less. It didn't work. The idea that in the future we might become lovers or husbands, it sickened him on some level."

"Is he homophobic?" Nico asked quietly.

"No. He's not that. But he looked at me and thought me too young. I think our age gap made him feel like a predator? You have to understand, at sixteen, I didn't really look my age. I looked more like thirteen or fourteen. I was just so incredibly skinny and awkward looking, I wasn't really appealing. It was a hit to the ego that he didn't think me at all attractive, but in retrospect, I could understand it. You two never had that problem with me."

Garen put a smacking kiss on his forehead. "That's because you're criminally cute."

Bel really liked those words. He liked even more the emotion that came along the bond, the sincerity of it. Garen meant every word.

"Victoria mentioned that you didn't fight it when Spencer asked to be let out of the bond." said Nico.

It wasn't really a question, but Bel answered it anyway. "Yeah. Two weeks in, I knew it wasn't right. The whole situation wasn't right. I had my cousins' familiars to compare to. They'd reacted like you had, Nico. They were curious, flattered, interested. The bond was there and growing day by day. They didn't talk about leaving or express frustration about being summoned. It was a clear black-and-white picture. I didn't...God, I didn't want it to fail. I would have given my left arm for things to work.

"On the other hand, I couldn't figure out how to make the situation better. Spencer wasn't cooperative in any sense. I finally called Chantelle, told her what was happening, and asked what to do. She said Spencer was being verbally and emotionally abusive, he was toxic, and he had to go. I couldn't disagree with her. The one use Spencer had for the bond was making sure I felt just how unhappy he was with me."

Those words sounded simple, but Bel had suffered under the agony of it during Spencer's every waking moment. It got to the point, in the end, that he'd stay up late so he could have some peace while Spencer slept. That deliberate separation, where he avoided his own familiar, had been too clear. It had been one of the signs he couldn't ignore.

"She flew down again to help me break the bond. Spencer had his bags packed, a plane ticket bought. Because he hadn't invested anything in the bond, it didn't affect him as badly as it affected me. He was functional enough to call for a cab and take himself to the airport. It was the last I heard of him. Frankly, I wasn't in a position to track him after the bond was broken."

The memory of that agony shot through Bel, tearing a gash in his chest, or at least that was what it felt like. White-hot pain, there and gone again in a flash. Bel hoped it hadn't transmitted across the bond. The hope was in vain, as both Garen and Nico flinched.

He pulled them both tighter with a wince. "Sorry, sorry."

"I don't even want to know how bad this was that the memory of it, three years later, is still this vividly painful."

Garen pulled him in impossibly tighter. "How did you even live through this?"

"I went catatonic after the bond was broken. Chantelle panicked, called Grandpa, and he came in a snap. He stayed with me for three solid months, just an unwavering presence of love and support. He wouldn't leave my side for more than five minutes. Really, I don't know if I'd have recovered if not for him. It just...it did a lot of damage to me. It seriously took a year before I felt like I was back to myself again. It took another year to even think about summoning another familiar. I really would have put that off until the end of time if not for the brass demanding I had to have a familiar. Still, I dragged my feet and put it off until I couldn't any longer. Of course, when I finally gave in, I got the best surprise of my life."

Bel turned his head enough to kiss Nico's jaw. "If I had known I would get you, I'd have been a lot more enthusiastic about the whole thing."

With a thumb, Nico wiped away the traces of tears from Bel's eyes. There was nothing but love and understanding along the bond, the warm gesture full of affection. "All things considered, I understand why you reacted the way you did. And why you were so cautious with me. Hell, Spencer gave you PTSD."

Bel really couldn't refute that. Nico had basically hit the nail on the head.

Garen rumbled in his chest, almost as if he were pondering. "I'm surprised your family wasn't there the day you summoned Nico."

"I kind of did that on purpose. After the shitshow that went down the first time, I wanted to be able to just send Nico back immediately if I saw the same red flags. The more time you give a bond, the more it takes to break it. If Nico was going to be as angry as Spencer, I would have broken the bond within an hour of the summoning and just flown him back home. I was also kind of afraid of what Grandpa would do if I did, somehow, summon another Spencer."

"Ah. Valid concern. He would have roasted them immediately."

No question there.

Garen kissed his forehead again—all these gentle kisses were quite lovely—before asking, "Were you really convinced it might go to shit again? Familiar rejection is incredibly rare; surely you didn't think it would happen twice in a row."

"It was a fear I couldn't shake," Bel whispered against his chest. "Probably the PTSD talking, but...I just didn't have any confidence it would go right the second time. Nico, you really were a breath of fresh air to me when you came. You were just so...so *true* to what a familiar should be. You were engaged, curious, affectionate. You were adamant that you didn't want to leave. The more time I spent with you, the more settled I became, because it was obvious that my magic really had summoned the right person this time. The only thing that stopped me from taking you in fully was that I could tell you and Garen still loved each other."

Garen snorted. "Although in the end you took us both."

"Best decision of my life. Second only to summoning Nico to begin with." Bel almost didn't tell them, but in the end felt like he had to confess this too. It was bitter to say, though. Bel damn near choked on the words, and if not for their grip on him, the firmness of the bond between them, he wouldn't have been able to say it at all. "The irony of the timing, though, is just...evil. I think it's evil. Today is the anniversary of the day I broke the bond with Spencer."

Both of them went stock-still for a moment.

"Oh, shit," Nico breathed against the top of his head. "Oh, shit, is *that* why?"

That question didn't make sense. "Why what?"

"You've been on edge and trying to act like things were fine for weeks, now. We couldn't figure out what was wrong."

Ah. Fuck. Damn bond communicated that to them, eh? Bel growled wordlessly at the traitorous thing. How dare it give him away when he'd been trying not to worry his men.

"Bel," Garen scolded, "next time just *tell us*, alright? Don't feel like you have to handle this on your own."

"I didn't want to worry you. It's senseless, anyway. It's not like he has any power over me anymore. He can't hurt me like he did."

"Fears and trauma aren't rational. It's alright to admit when you're hurting. I would vastly prefer that over you pretending you're fine. Okay?"

Bel wanted to protest more. He already took up so much of their attention, their time, anything more felt like being a burden. It was a feeling that rankled.

"Yeah, that didn't work," Nico muttered. "Alright, perspective time. Bel Bel, if I'd injured myself while running, but chose to just wrap it and not tell anyone I'd hurt myself, would you be upset?"

"Well...yes. I'd rather know so I could help you. But this is different—"

"How the hell is it different? Because it's a mental wound and not a physical one? The pain's the same, isn't it?"

You know, put like that, Bel really didn't have a sound argument. He was right. It hurt all the same. Could Nico or Garen magically solve the problem? No. But then, a physical ailment couldn't be easily remedied either. It took time and a steady application of love and medication for it to heal. Same as any psychological damage. It wasn't different.

So, why was Bel acting like it was?

"This is the PTSD talking," Garen warned him. "When you have thoughts of 'I don't want to worry people' or 'I don't want to bother them,' that isn't really you. That's the trauma talking. I want you to kick those thoughts to the curb. We want to know. Bel, my heart, we always want to know. Next time, don't hide this from us. Don't try to pretend it's fine.

It won't work, anyway, we'll feel something off through the bond."

Granted, that seemed to be the case. Nico's example made something clear to Bel, too. He wouldn't take it well if they tried to pass something off, to hide something from him. If Bel wanted open communication from his men, that street went *both* ways. Also, the last thing he wanted to do was to carry Spencer with him for the rest of his life. Getting rid of trauma meant facing it, right?

Determination flared in him. He used a hand to orient himself enough to kiss Garen soundly, then turned and caught Nico's mouth in an equally firm kiss. "I promise both of you. No more secrets. If I'm hurting, I'll say so."

Nico kissed him back, smiling against his lips. "Good. And next time the bastard does something, I'll introduce him to the native wildlife."

"No, Nico."

"I'm sure I can persuade you otherwise."

This man. So incorrigible.

Bel wouldn't have him any other way.

CHAPTER FOURTEEN

GAREN

After the ups and downs of the day, it was no wonder Bel fell asleep quickly. The emotional whirlwind alone demanded rest to process all that had occurred, not to mention the fact that he'd been using his eyes for the better part of the morning. When Bel curled up in the middle of the bed and fell soundly asleep, Garen didn't even think to disturb him.

One look at Nico told him that his lover was not settled enough to quietly pass time in this room. Garen felt the same way about it. After everything Bel had told him, he didn't think he could sit still. Hitting something, though, that had appeal.

In silent, unanimous agreement, they pulled on workout clothes and slipped out of the room, heading down to the hotel's gym. Garen stretched first, as it was stupid to do otherwise, taking the measure of the place. It had the usual lineup of exercise equipment on one side, with weight machines and such lining the wall of windows. In their area, the mats were thick, the mirror on one wall meant no doubt for yoga or some such. All Garen saw was room to spar.

"Spar?" he offered to Nico.

"Yeah. If I get too physical, though, I'm taking this out on a punching bag."

"Same." They didn't want to hurt each other, after all. It was just that tempers were stretched tight.

"If we're sparring, I'm stretching a bit more."

Probably wise. Garen on the best of days couldn't really keep up with Nico's speed. He could give the man a run for his money, but he had to be really warmed up and limber first.

As he stretched, he breathed. Deep, steady breaths meant to control his temper. This wasn't the first time he'd ever seen Bel cry, but it made him no less homicidal. His Bel was incredibly kind in nature, and there was no reason for him to be put through the wringer like Spencer had done. Garen couldn't even fathom being intentionally cruel to Bel. It made Garen wish fervently for a time machine so he could go back to that moment, before Spencer's summoning, and just take him out of the competition. Surely Bel's magic would have called for Nico if Spencer had been conveniently dead.

With all the magic in the world, why didn't they have the ability to time travel? Dammit. This was a severe oversight.

Nico was in something close to a split when he finally slammed a fist against the mats, face drawn into a scowl. "I can't believe this. I just can't. How can anyone look at Bel and not see how precious he is?"

"I don't get it either," Garen confessed. "How can anyone look at him and not see him as he is? He's sweet and gentle by nature, and intelligent, god."

"Makes us look stupid, and I don't mind admitting that, either. He's seriously the cutest thing I've ever seen. That might be the bond talking, though."

Garen shook his head in disagreement and shifted to stretch his left arm. "No, I thought the same when I first met him. No bond to influence me at the time."

"See!" Nico looked vindicated. "If you thought so too, then shouldn't anyone bonded to him be absolutely convinced? I don't care how awkward he looked as a teenager, you can't overlook his personality. If he was anything with that asshole like he was with me in the beginning, then I really don't get it. Bel bent over backward trying to make sure I was comfortable, that I had everything I needed. I adored him just for the effort. He was so earnest and sincere. How could anyone spew hatred at him?"

"I don't get it either. But Nico, I don't think we want to understand it. Only assholes would."

Nico looked at him sideways, and Garen knew that look. Nico was calculating at high speed. "You know, with a little thought, I'm sure we can find a way to disappear that bastard."

"I'm absolutely sure we could. I'm also absolutely sure Bel would know it was us."

"Dammit. Pitfalls of having a superbrain for a lover."

"Yup. It's damn tempting, though. I really don't like how Spencer reacted to him. It's obvious that he wants to antagonize Bel even now. For what? Can't the man let bygones be bygones?"

"No, that would take maturity he clearly doesn't have. You heard what his sergeant said. No one likes Spencer. Big surprise there if all he does is go around picking fights." Nico shook his head. "I'm just speechless over this whole thing. No wonder Bel's been stressed out."

"We need to be better about supporting him." Garen was determined to do that. He had a better chance now that he knew what the hell was going on. Showering Bel with love and doing all of those little thoughtful gestures Bel liked was a good first step in making sure Bel felt loved while he dealt with the asshole.

"Now that we know what the hell's going on, I think we'll have a better chance of doing it. But yeah." Nico bounced up. "Let's spar. I need to work some of this energy off before I go hunt that fucker down."

Garen was all for that. He accepted the hand up Nico

offered him, squared off, and started sparring.

The thing with Nico was, he wasn't like your usual partner for sparring. Most of the time, people moved with a touch of caution in order to avoid injury. Especially since they had no protective gear on, they should have been taking precautions. But Garen could barely keep up with Nico as it was, so really, he was operating under a handicap of sorts. He went full out, doing his best to land any kind of a blow, Nico's reflexes enough to parry him.

To anyone watching from the outside, it no doubt looked ferocious, like they were trying to kill each other.

In a blur of speed, Nico managed to get past Garen's guard and pin him to the ground, where Garen landed in a sweaty smear against the mats. Dammit. Had this man somehow, impossibly, gotten faster? Or was it rage that fueled him?

A throat cleared nearby, and Garen craned his eyes that direction to see Wicky standing just on the edge of the mats.

"So...looks like you guys are taking this about as well as I expected. That is to say, with murderous calm."

"That about covers it," Nico growled before letting Garen up. "Did I hurt you, G?"

"Only my pride." Garen took his hand once again and used it to pull himself up. To Wicky he asked, "You here to check on us?"

"I came down to soak in the hot tub, actually, but now I think I need to take you both drinking." Wicky looked them over with some sympathy. "Did he at least talk to you about this?"

"Yeah." Nico's jaw worked with strong emotion. "Yeah, he told us the full story. I think, honestly, the only reason he did was because he didn't want Spencer to have the upper hand."

Astute of Nico. Garen's opinion was the same.

"After hearing everything that asshole put him through..." Nico shook his head. "My God, the courage it must have taken to summon me. I can't fathom it."

"Hell, the courage it must have taken to bring me in with you." Garen wiped sweat off his forehead, and despite the fact he was sweating, he felt oddly cold for a moment. What would his life have been like if Bel possessed less courage? Less backbone? Garen would be back at his old job, slowly having the life sucked out of him, instead of here. Damn, that was a chilling thought. Garen didn't really care for it, either.

Wicky shook a finger at both of them. "Don't dwell on what-ifs. Doesn't do anyone any good. Now, I'm not asking for the full story, as it's really not my business. Just answer a few questions for me. Do we need to disappear the bastard?"

Nico sighed. From his toes. "Bel will catch us if we try."

"Damn. Good point. Okay, second question—you need to go drinking? You guys can get drunk, I'll take you back to Bel and pour you into bed."

Garen looked at Wicky as if he'd just sprouted wings. He really was a good friend. "Drinking sounds great. Honestly, I need alcohol to process all of this."

"Then that we can do."

Nico made a noise of disagreement. "I'm all for getting drunk, but I need to unleash some anger first. I just...can't sit still right now. Wicky, can I have Godzilla first?"

"You want me to conjure him again?" Wicky shrugged in assent. "Sure. Not in here, obviously."

No, there wasn't nearly enough room in here for a twenty-foot movie monster to stomp around.

"Back to the parking lot we go, then." Wicky gave Garen a look askance. "You want to borrow Stabitha?"

Honestly, hacking away at a mythical creature and expending some anger sounded like a good idea to Garen. Would it solve anything? No. Would it make him feel better? Yes. It might also keep him from caving Spencer's face in tomorrow when they inevitably got back on that river boat.

"Yeah." Garen let out a breath. "Yeah, let me borrow it."

Wicky got an arm around both of their shoulders, leading them out of the gym. "You two get as drunk as you like later, okay? I have awesome hangover cures that will get you back to functional in a half hour. If we can think of a way later to get rid of Spencer without it looking suspicious, all the better."

Seeing that this would likely take most of the evening, Garen grabbed his phone and scheduled a text for two hours from now, telling Bel what they were doing. Just so he wouldn't worry. Who knew, Bel might join them for the drinking portion of the evening. Not that Bel could drink, but Garen could speak from experience. Nico drunk was highly entertaining. Better than television.

He blew out a breath. First, though, he wanted to beat something up. Since he couldn't do that to the person who'd actually caused the problem, Godzilla would work as a substitute.

CHAPTER FIFTEEN

WICKY

Wicky admittedly had done some dumb shit in his life, but letting two of his best friends go drinking, on foreign soil, without someone sober to pour them into bed afterward? He wasn't that dumb. He designated himself as the sober one for the evening without saying a word.

Besides, someone had to record choice events of the evening. For posterity.

The bar they ended up at was on base, and it looked like every other Army dive bar in existence. The interior was dim, all wooden walls, dart boards in every other corner, a pool table lurking off in the back area, with lots of simple tables and chairs dotting the open room. The place didn't look all that packed, about half capacity, and the two bartenders seemed to be as occupied playing therapist as they were pouring drinks. About as expected at this time of the day. No doubt it would start really hopping later on in the evening.

Anticipating that these two were going to get beyond plastered, Wicky steered them to a corner table, well out of the way of the other patrons, then fetched shots and a beer from the bar for all three of them. Walking back to the table, he observed the two. Nico looked torn between doing damage to something and cuddling an obviously upset Garen. Garen, usually a rock of logic and calm, had sunk in on himself, just staring at his folded hands and giving off the vibe of murder.

Oh yeah. Wicky was so glad he was smart enough to take these two drinking.

"Oooh, flamethrower," Nico crooned with an expression of homicide on his face.

Wicky eyed him sideways as he put the man's shot on the table. "Out of context, that was terrifying."

Nico didn't blink. "I'm sure I can orchestrate an accidental flamethrower incident where Spencer gets it right in the face."

Downing his shot, Garen informed him, "You're reaching, Tig."

"Dammit, you're such a killjoy."

"I still think your first idea was your best. Bash him over the head and let him accidentally fall into the river. Let the crocodiles take care of him."

Yeah...so the usual Garen had obviously decided to take a vacation. Homicidal Garen was now in the house. Wicky made with the distraction. Besides, he was curious and honestly wanted to know.

"I promised not to ask, but damn, you guys are making serial killers look friendly right now. Do I need to pull back up the list of indigenous creatures that can kill?"

Garen shot him a suspicious look. "That's what you and Nico were really doing on the boat, isn't it?"

"It's a very nice list," Nico offered, tone hopeful.

"That's Plan B."

So, still on the table, huh? Granted, Bel and his familiars had no chill when it came to each other. People looking in from the outside thought Garen and Nico were the protective ones, and Bel was the cute thing they protected. Really, they were all equal in that regard. Bel would absolutely throw hands (magically speaking) if anything dangerous came near his men. He adored them to pieces, and it was obvious to anyone around them for more than thirty seconds. There had been many a time when Wicky had watched these three in action and thought #relationshipgoals.

Wicky tried to put himself in their shoes for a moment. If he'd learned that someone he loved more than anything had been in a toxic, abusive relationship while still young, a relationship bad enough to give them PTSD, how would he react? Especially when that person showed up in their life with the intent to do harm again?

Wow, yeah, looked like murder was the only answer.

Garen sighed, taking another shot before speaking. "Basically, Spencer was a bastard—"

"I mean, I didn't expect anything different." Wicky took a seat and pretended to sip at his beer.

"—and didn't even try to wrap his head around what he'd been called to do. He threw an absolute fit, blamed everything on Bel, and kept throwing his fit for three weeks until Bel finally let go of him. I just...can't imagine this." Garen rubbed at his head, the pain on his face clear. "Mobius, back me up here, but when that initial bond starts between familiar and mage, it's like falling in love. You see the other person through rose-colored glasses."

Mobius beeped in question from Wicky's front pocket.

"Your perception is a bit skewed, Boo Bear," Nico corrected him. "'Cause you loved Bel before he even called you. He and I were complete strangers when I was summoned, so it wasn't like that for me. Still, you feel very positively toward the person when summoned. You are inclined to like them. I was really curious and confused when I first came, but nothing made me antagonistic toward Bel. I can't imagine that. Bel's too much of a sweetheart to make people hate him on sight."

Garen nodded, supportive of this sentiment. "And we feel what Bel feels. Not always exactly, but with the really strong emotions, we do. You know he had to have been in turmoil because of Spencer's verbal abuse. So Spencer deliberately hurt himself by hurting Bel, over and over, and didn't care. Hurting Bel took priority. I'm almost scared to ask if Spencer deliberately used the bond to send hate along it. I can't...how can someone be that cruel?"

Wicky didn't get it either. Then again, no one at this table was the kind of abusive asshole who got off on causing other people pain. Wicky didn't want to understand that mentality. He had a different question altogether.

"I want to know how Bel summoned this guy to begin with. What was his magic even *thinking*?"

Nico jabbed a finger at him. "That. That's my question. Wicky, you're the only magician at this table, you figure this out."

"Dude, did you forget that I posed the question to begin with?"

"Naw, c'mon, I'm not smart enough to figure this out. I've tried. Your turn."

"I'm sitting here answerless, man," Wicky said, but his back brain was already churning, running through facts. "Well, on the surface Spencer meets the criteria. It's not like magic is foolproof when playing matchmaker, it doesn't always match personalities right. It's not normally this off, though. Bel's case might be that one in a million."

Garen looked horrified. "Wait, if he does meet the criteria, does that mean he could possibly be called *again*?"

"Spencer called again? No, highly doubt it. He's already rejected a bond. No familiar who's rejected a bond is considered a candidate after that." Wicky tacked on, still thinking, "Besides, Bel's family is full up with familiars, right? He was the last one who needed to call someone."

"Well, yeah, but Bel's family isn't the only one with demon blood," Nico corrected. "There are a few others scattered throughout the world."

Wicky blinked at him. Now, he had not known that.

Although it made sense as soon as Nico said it. It wasn't like demons were bound just to the United States, after all. Of course they'd visit other countries and get into shenanigans. Curiosity overcame him.

"How many others?"

"Bel told me." Nico's face scrunched up, the wheels and cogs turning. "Er..."

Garen eyed him sideways, mouth kicked up on one side. "You've already forgotten, haven't you?"

"In my defense, I've slept since then."

Wicky could not throw stones at that glass house. He forgot things overnight all the time.

The two of them had basically drained all of their shots, so he hopped up and fetched them more, which they took without a word. They were clearly intent on getting drunk as fast as possible. It was then that the obvious reared its head.

Garen was not a lightweight. Nico and Wicky were about the same size. In other words, there was no way in hell that Wicky could manhandle both of these men all the way back to the hotel. Garen alone might squash him in the attempt.

Aww, damn. He did not think this through.

Which was basically the story of Wicky's life, right there.

Stealthily, he pulled Mobius out of his pocket and texted Zia.

Hey, come drinking.

Her response was immediate: *You are not getting drunk on foreign soil.*

I am not, no.

...then?

Nico and Garen are.

Oh shit.

I'm being good and babysitting but there's no way I can get them to the hotel later.

Omw

And this was why he and Zia were friends. She was a good

bro.

Nico stabbed a finger in his direction. "You're playing games, aren't you?!"

"Nope," Wicky said cheerfully as he put Mobius onto the table, propped up so he could enjoy the show. (The show was incoming, Wicky could tell, because they were six shots in and already starting to lean a little.)

"Yes, you are!" Nico's bottom lip pushed out in an adorable pout.

"I bought you booze. I am not to be corrected."

Garen at least was sober enough to still ask the right questions. "What were you doing?"

Clearly, Wicky needed to work on his stealth skills. "Texting Zia. She wants to join us."

Nico sighed and slumped against Garen, nursing what was left of his beer. "I love Zia. She's the bomb. The bomb diggity. Is that why you're friends with her?"

"That is one of the many reasons why we're friends, yup." Apparently, they were sloshed enough the show was on. "You two are looking empty. Let me grab more shots."

Wicky stood and used the movement to cover up the fact that he was whispering a quick command to Mobius, in French. "*Record.*"

Mobius gave a little flash of light in confirmation and switched to camera mode.

Such a good little familiar. Wicky might reward him with a special voice package later.

The patrons were packing their way in now, and it was getting more and more busy. It took Wicky longer this time to get the beers, and he snagged an ale for Zia, as that was her poison of choice. By the time he made it back, he could see through the front window that she was walking up. Oh, good timing.

Also, clearly while he was gone, the conversation had completely gone off the rails.

"What's wrong with touching a ding-dong?" Nico demanded of Garen.

"In the middle of combat?!" Garen said, voice rising to a truly unfortunate volume.

"Well, when else are you supposed to do it?"

Wicky really, desperately, wanted to know what they were talking about. "Whatzit?"

Nico accepted the shots with a winsome smile. "I was talking about my chocolate ding-dong."

"Yours is chocolate?" Wicky demanded, trying very hard to keep a straight face and not laugh.

"Is there a way to share with the class?" Zia drawled as she approached their table.

Garen shook a finger at her. "No. My ding-dong."

"And Bel's," Nico reminded him, going back to leaning up against Garen.

"And Bel's," Garen agreed in that truly serious way that only the absolutely drunk could manage.

Zia dropped into the chair next to Wicky's and leaned in to question in a low tone, "Are we having a deep conversation here?"

"No," he said in the same confidential tone. "But they're no longer talking about murder, so I'm taking it as a win."

Zia shrugged in agreement and sipped at her ale. Then she looked down at her glass with approval. "Not bad."

Holding up his shot glass, Nico eyed it suspiciously. "Am I drunk?"

"Maybe a little," Wicky consoled him. The man was seven shots in—it was no wonder.

Apparently missing the fact that this was his seventh glass, Nico was still staring at the glass in his hand. "This thing holds a lot."

"But you don't," Zia pointed out in amusement. "Now, one of you tell me how we got on the subject of ding-dongs."

Yes, Wicky was rabidly curious about that as well.

"We were talking about babies!" Nico answered, his broad smile stretching from ear to ear.

Wicky just about choked on the beer in his mouth. Say what?

Zia just blinked at Nico, that slow blink which indicated she had tried to process this, failed, and was now in a reboot. "I'm sorry, how do you think babies are born?"

"Well"—Nico's face scrunched up in deep thought—"you put a penis next to another penis—"

"Okay, no, put those down," she ordered, face rippling with the effort of not laughing. "Wicky, he needs to spend less time with you."

"Why, am I rubbing off on him?"

"Clearly."

Wicky mock-reeled in his chair. "I just took two damage from vicious mockery."

"Your first mistake," Zia informed the other two, "was following him into a bar."

Wicky hoisted his beer in a salute to himself. "Follow me, and you'll never be hungry or sober again!"

Zia gave him that judgmental look that she had not only created for him, but honed to perfection, and let that comment slide.

Tipping his glass up, Garen downed the rest of his shot, then looked into the bottom of the glass with one eye comically screwed shut. He gave a forlorn sigh before setting it down on the table with a much harder clink than he'd likely anticipated.

"What's wrong, bud?" Wicky asked with absolutely no idea what Garen would say next.

"It turns out the answer to my problems wasn't at the bottom of the glass," Garen informed him seriously.

Oh, god. Don't laugh, don't laugh, don't laugh. Zia almost lost it, and Wicky knocked his knee against hers under the table. Stop it.

Doing his best to match that serious tone, Wicky tried to commiserate. "But the important thing is you tried, right?"

"Yeah," Garen agreed.

Then promptly passed out, sending glasses clattering in every direction as his face hit the table.

"Annnnd we're done drinking for the night." Zia took another sip before standing. "Wicky, you get the bill."

"Yuppers." Wicky popped up and went to the bar, checking out and giving a nice tip to the bartender as well. It took a minute, but as he came back, he saw Zia putting a feather spell on both of their drunkards.

Wicky almost stopped dead in his tracks, in awe of her brilliance. The feather spell would make it beyond easy to lift and carry both men out. *Why* hadn't he thought of that?

Zia, unfortunately, knew him too well. She could see from the look on his face every thought that flitted through his head. A hand on one hip, she demanded of him in exasperation, "You really did call me here thinking you'd have to manhandle them both, didn't you?"

Skipping in close, he bussed her on the cheek. "You are as wise as you are kind, my darling friend."

"You're such an idiot," she grumbled but was clearly pleased with the praise. "Alright, you grab Nico, I've got Garen."

"Gladly!" Wicky skipped around the table to grab his friend, reaching for Mobius as he did so. To his familiar, he requested, "Save that video and send it to Bel, okay?"

Mobius gave his usual two-tone beep of acknowledgement.

The phone rang a second later, Bel's name flashing on the screen. Ahh, he was finally awake and missing his men, eh? Good timing.

Wicky swiped Answer and put the phone to his ear so he could hear better. "Hey, Bel. I have them."

"*Oh.*" Bel audibly changed tracks. "*Are you guys out somewhere? It sounds noisy where you are.*"

"Yeah, we were drinking. But I'm bringing them back now."

"*...drinking? Wait, Nico and Garen are drunk?*"

"Plastered, my friend. They are plastered. Have you never seen them drunk?"

"*Uh, no, they generally don't dare because they want to keep tabs on me. Oh man, this must be a sight.*"

"I recorded it all for you. Well, Mobius did. He's saving and sending you the file now."

"*Wicky, the way you say this concerns me. Or intrigues. I can't decide which. What kind of drunks are they?*"

"Don't eat or drink anything while watching," Wicky warned him, still hauling Nico out of the bar, his arm tight around the other's waist. "This is your official spew warning. We'll be back in fifteen. Maybe thirty if this one keeps dragging his feet. Nico, don't you want to go back to Bel?"

Nico blinked at him sadly, tears in his eyes. "Miss Bel."

"Well, I'm taking you to him. Try to put more effort into walking, will you?"

"Going to Bel?"

"Yes, going to Bel," Wicky repeated patiently.

Nico lit up, smile supernova bright. "You're such a friend. BEL, I'M COMING!"

And that was his eardrum. Oww.

Garen snorted as he woke up, looking down at Zia, then around in confusion. "Where's Bel? Nico, where's Bel?"

"Going to Bel," Nico reported happily.

It was in that moment Wicky decided he would never, for as long as he lived, let these two live this down.

That was what true friends were for.

CHAPTER SIXTEEN

NICO

You know, feeding Spencer to the crocodiles looked more appealing every second.

Nico eyed Bel sideways, trying to judge how much trouble he'd be in if he accidentally threw Spencer overboard in this moment. From Bel's dark expression? Not much. All Spencer had to do was put his foot in his mouth one more time.

Thankfully, Spencer seemed intent on doing that.

They were back on the boat, once again heading upstream along the river. Their goal was to pick back up where they'd left off yesterday, to avoid covering the same ground all over again. No one was excited about this. It would have been much worse if not for Wicky's incredibly effective hangover cure. If Nico didn't know better, he would have sworn he hadn't been drunk last night. He didn't feel even a twinge this morning. Still, even without the hangover, Nico was not enthused about being on this boat.

On a scale of one to ten, one being a root canal with no anesthesia, ten being on a boat with Spencer, today was a ten.

Not for the first time, Nico had to ask the universe, what the fuck were you thinking three years ago, trying to pair these two together? For that matter, why the hell wouldn't you arrange a fatal accident for Spencer instead?

Unfortunately, no answer.

Spencer was keeping his distance, sort of. He was a whole ten feet away from Bel, but on a boat of this size, that wasn't really saying much. Also, the man was damn loud. Only a toddler demanding something had that kind of range.

"Can't believe we're stuck on this damn boat again," Spencer said to anyone who would listen. Most tried to ignore him, but he didn't seem to realize that. Or care. "Seems our hotshot expert isn't so qualified."

Bel didn't flinch, but the way his mouth turned down at the corners, his face tightening as he clenched his jaw, suggested he was thinking of mayhem on some level.

Mayhem was good. Nico stared at him hopefully, waiting for mayhem to materialize. Slashley was absolutely ready to go. A little bonking, a hip check over the side, Spencer ceased to be a problem. Please?

Spencer impossibly got louder. "So, how many people are going to die while he gets his act together, that's my question."

Oh, he did not. Bel had been here a whopping three days. How fast did Spencer expect a miracle?! Nico's eyes cut to the asshole. What did this idiot expect Bel to do, magic up the giant lizards somehow?

No, he didn't expect anything. He was just poking at Bel in any way he could.

One of his own squad mates muttered at him, "Man, just chill. We tried tracking these things for weeks, remember? No way he can find them in a single morning."

"Yeah, let's talk about how he's only good to work for three hours. Like a fucking pansy. Too delicate to actually work a full day, huh?"

Yeah, that tore it. Nico knew he was being baited, but at the same time, he had no more fucks left to give. He turned and got into Spencer's face, meeting him toe to toe.

"You know good and well what his limitations are," he snarled, his anger a high heat in his face, a quick tempo in his chest. "Oh, or maybe not. Maybe you were too busy throwing a tantrum to learn anything about him. You like to throw tantrums, after all."

Spencer's lips curled back, revealing teeth. "Hit a sore point, did I? Don't like it when someone pokes at your delicate little princess?"

"My mage can decimate you down to dust with a single spell, asshole. *No one* would call him delicate."

"That why you fuss over him all the time?"

"Wow, you don't even know how to care for someone else? Really? I feel sorry for anyone who tries to date you, then. Maybe you should stop talking, you keep putting your foot in your mouth."

"What, like you're some kind of standard for how a man should be?" Spencer scoffed. "You're smothering."

Bel turned and with the mildest, most threatening tone ever to be voiced, pinning Spencer with a look that could see right through him, said, "I happen to enjoy the smothering very, very much. Nico, *carus*?"

Nico was hardwired to obey that summons as Bel held out a hand to him. He just really wanted to do something to Spencer first. Dammit. With an internal sigh, he gave that up and went back to Bel. He was right; if he stayed close to Spencer any longer, something horrendous might happen. He might catch cooties or something.

"Wow, talk about whipped," Spencer muttered not-so-under his breath.

"Sonuvabitch, this man has three feet," Wicky growled. "Hey, asshole. Let's get this straight. It's clear to all of us that you're a sore loser."

Spencer went rigid, a hot retort on the tip of his tongue.

Wicky stabbed a finger at him. "Don't even try to deny it. They don't see it—their backs are to you most of the time—

but I fucking see it. You're wishing now that you'd stayed, that you hadn't been such a hothead all those years ago. Bel turned out fine, didn't he? Cuter than you imagined. Watching the three of them, seeing how in tune they are, how in love they are, I'm sure it's like sandpaper under your skin. But you need to put a fucking lid on it. You're not doing yourself any favors by spewing stupidity with every other word."

Nico beamed at Wicky.

Spencer wasn't about to admit to this, of course. "Who the hell are you to say that? Huh? And who would even want to be tied to him like that? I mean, look at them, Bel calls them like he would a faithful dog. It's *sickening* how they revolve around him."

"I would give my eye teeth to have a relationship like theirs." Wicky's smile was wicked and sarcastic. "So would you. Can't be the bigger man and admit that, can you?"

"I don't have to admit a damn thing!" Spencer darted for him, fists clenched. "This isn't your business, anyway. Stay out of it."

"Wow, you don't know how friendships work either? Listen, these three are my brothers from another mother—"

Aww, Nico felt loved. He'd hug Wicky for that statement later.

"—and I'll defend them from anything. Including you, fucker."

Garen cleared his throat. When he spoke, it was in that voice that heralded doom. It sent chills up Nico's spine, as he had only heard it a few times, and shit had gone down shortly after. Every time.

"Marine, back up. To the other side of the boat. You're done for the morning."

"You're not my CO. I don't have to do a damn thing you say." Spencer made for Garen, or tried. Nico immediately moved to block him.

Spencer shot Nico a glare, but there was a vicious mockery to the twist of his lips. "You protecting him, too? Wow, so all three of you doing the nasty, huh? You're sick, man."

"Do you not get polyamory? Really?" Nico's hand itched for the lightsaber on his belt. A little bonking, that's all he needed to do here. Problem solved. He was fairly sure everyone on this boat would swear it was an accident. They were all pretty fed up with Spencer at this point.

"DAVIS!"

Nico glanced up and saw Sergeant Lee descending on them like an avenging angel. Even she'd had enough, eh? Oh good, she could put this idiot in line better than anyone else.

Spencer's expression was sour in the extreme, but he turned to respond to her. "Ma'am."

"Davis, the order I gave you yesterday to keep your distance at all times from Mage Adams did not expire at midnight. You will *continue* to keep your distance from him." She glared at him with heat. "To the other side of the boat. Now."

He hated to do it. That was obvious. Spencer didn't have a choice, though. He muttered to himself as he stalked to the other end of the ship, stomping like a three-year-old the entire way.

Seriously, universe. What the hell were you thinking trying to pair him up with Bel? Nico absolutely did not see how that would have ever worked out.

He breathed a sigh of relief when the douchebag was finally gone. Now, maybe, Bel could concentrate enough to get some work done. As much as Nico wanted to fight a kangaroo, he was also very ready to get out of Australia.

"Thank you, Sergeant." Bel gave her a tired smile.

"I'm so sorry about that idiot." Lee pinched the bridge of her nose with thumb and finger, looking absolutely done. "He scores well on everything, which is why they thought it was a good idea to send him overseas, but...he needs an attitude adjustment. I'm afraid you called it, earlier, when you said it was a case of sour grapes. He obviously regrets leaving you. He's just too immature to admit it."

Bel's expression turned thoughtful. "Are you so sure of that?"

"I know it's hard for you to see, as he only looks at you that way when your back is turned, but yes. It's very obvious. He's not subtle."

Bel's eyes flitted between Nico and Garen, and there was a hint of something there. Introspection, maybe? His expression was hard to read just then. He shrugged and said to her, "I wouldn't have Spencer back for love or money."

"I don't blame you. You definitely got the better familiars on the second try." Lee blew out a breath and turned to glare at Spencer's back. He was sulking near the other guard rail now. "I'll try to keep him away from you. He's good at slipping past me every time my back is turned for more than thirty seconds."

"I appreciate the effort." Bel turned and looked at the river again. "I think we're almost at the same spot we stopped at yesterday."

"You're correct."

"In that case, I'll get to work." Bel really focused and oriented himself so he could sweep the river and the banks all at once.

Nico left him to it, as this wasn't something he could help with. He did sidle up next to the sergeant, though, and asked her in an undertone, "How would you feel about an accidental murder?"

She eyed him back, eyes twinkling. The expression was promising. Her response was not. "As tempting as that might be, don't. The paperwork for a death on foreign soil is no joke, or so I understand."

"Damn."

"That said, thank you for your forbearance. I know he's

testing your patience every second he can. Frankly, I'm amazed you haven't punched him already."

"I am too," Nico admitted. "I came really close to it just now."

"I saw that. It's why I was quick to intervene." Lee shook her head, like a parent done with their kid's shit. "I, unfortunately, have this idiot for another year. Then I can ship him back. I will mark in his record, though, that he's being a little shit."

"Please and thank you." Nico knew it wouldn't do a lot of good until Spencer did something truly unthinkable. But it was good to document stuff like this, so she would have a clear paper trail to point to.

Nico went back to Bel's side, leaning against the rail and watching the banks go by. It was interesting how the land around them changed as they moved. Parts of it were grassland, barely any trees at all except what lined the river itself. Other parts were dense forest, and the change between the two was drastic, with a clear tree line. It was like random land masses had been shoved together willy-nilly. Although some geologist or botanist could probably explain it so it made sense.

Just watching the landscape gave him time to think. Getting drunk last night had helped Nico process things a little. He didn't like it, what had happened to Bel. He hated that he wasn't the one called on the first try. Nico hated to think of himself as the second choice for Bel but...hang on. He and Garen had been together still at that point. So, technically, he hadn't met the criteria because he hadn't been "free." He'd been in a relationship with someone else.

Ahhh shit, why hadn't he thought of that before? Damn, that made sense now.

For the first time ever, Nico was actually glad he and Garen had broken up. It had given him the opening he needed to get them both to Bel. In retrospect, that was a good decision.

It didn't change anything, although it made him feel better. Nico chose to focus on what he could do now.

Time went by. Nico took turns pushing a water bottle into Bel's hand—he didn't remember to hydrate when focusing like this—slathering sunscreen on him, and chatting with Wicky. Wicky was of the opinion that maybe two Godzillas to train with was better, since they were training two squads, but of course holding the spell for two Godzillas at once was a bit much. They had to gang up on Zia a little to convince her to do it, instead. She wasn't really keen on the idea for some reason.

Matt was, though; he was intrigued by the idea. Also a bit giddy, his inner five-year-old coming out. Wicky went into the spell mechanics, which went straight over Nico's head, but that was fine. As long as he had another spellcaster on board with this plan.

Bel made an intrigued noise. It grabbed Nico's attention as nothing else could, and he zipped back to Bel, leaning over his back to put his head on the shorter man's shoulder. "You see something, Bel Bel?"

"I do." Bel sounded relieved to say those words. He pointed ahead and to the left. "There. One of the lizards we're tracking landed there."

Everyone was interested now, and Victoria asked, "How long back was this?"

"I think...about five or so days? So not recent, but the trail is there and goes further upriver. I see the influence of it."

Victoria flicked over her wrist to check her watch. "You've been using your eyes about two hours now."

Bel growled in vexation. "Has it really been that long?"

"Yeah," Garen confirmed. "So we can only track this for another hour before we need to give you a break."

"Shit."

Zia made a noise of dissent. "Not necessarily. If I can pinpoint the trail, I can pick it up and use a tracking spell.

We can switch out that way, keep going without relying on his eyes."

Oh, now there was a good idea. Nico liked it a lot. It took some of the strain off Bel, which he was always in favor of.

Bel turned and gestured her in closer. "Tell me how to highlight it for you. Do you need a physical imprint? There's not much there."

"No, more the energy signature, I can work from that."

"Oh, perfect. Nico, ask the captain to pull us in tighter to shore so she can visually see what she's tracking."

Nico was all for this and skipped to the back of the boat. Progress!

May this mean something to kill in his near future, amen.

The sooner they got away from Spencer, the better.

CHAPTER SEVENTEEN

BEL

Bel gladly handed Zia the tracking spell. It wasn't that he was tired after two hours of work. It was more the culmination of being mentally and emotionally bombarded for days on end. If he wasn't trying to ignore Spencer, then he was trying to ignore all thoughts and memories of the man. It wore on his spirit, on his mind, and left him with nothing but exhaustion as a result. He hadn't slept well last night, either. Yesterday's nap could only do so much.

Garen caught him around the waist and urged him to the nearest chair under the metal roof. "Come, curl up next to me for a moment. Rest."

That obvious he wanted a nap, huh? Bel didn't fight it, just went along and curled into Garen's lap. Nico took off his windbreaker and draped it around Bel's shoulders. Bel shot him a quick smile of thanks before tucking his head in against the crook of Garen's neck. He just smelled so nice, like warm male skin and wind. It soothed the raw edges of Bel's emotions.

He knew that his men didn't like this situation. He knew they'd gone off yesterday afternoon and pounded out their frustration against something before Wicky took them drinking. Bel hadn't chastised them for drinking while on the job. Of course this situation would disturb them. Any familiar being faced with a former one would feel uneasy. Spencer had the talent to make anyone mad, too, so there was also that to contend with.

Maybe all three of them needed naps.

Bel really had to find these damn monsters. Just to get them out of here and away from Spencer.

A warm hand soothed him up and down his spine in a gentle caress.

"Shh," Garen murmured against his forehead. "Relax. You're too tense right now."

Bel relaxed steadily into Garen's chest, eyes closing. There was something so inherently soothing about Garen holding him. Nico, too. It was this gestalt of things, really. Bel felt his skin, heard his breath, and finally, for just as long as he was within these arms, found peace. Quiet. Refuge. Home. For Bel, love was the person who made the world stop and listen.

How fortunate he was, then, that he had two such men who held that power for him.

Garen could feel it as he relaxed completely, and there was this sound from Garen's chest. Rather like a purr of contentment, a noise of satisfaction and pleasure. It made Bel wrap an arm around his waist and snuggle in even further, making his own noise of happiness.

He felt Nico's hand on his shoulder before his other lover leaned in and kissed the top of his head. Awww, he felt loved.

"The fuck, man!"

Bel snapped upright at hearing Spencer snarl those words, the volume enough to carry up to another continent.

"You can't even act professional?"

Bel could see him, stomping his way around to the front of the boat again. He started to rise, to deal with it himself, as sitting on Garen's lap while telling Spencer off didn't feel right. Garen pulled him back in, though, not letting him up.

"Nico's got it," Garen murmured. "Relax."

He would have protested, but it did seem like Nico had it, as his other familiar was already halfway there, meeting Spencer head-on. The look on Nico's face—not to mention the feeling along the bond—was pure disgust and frustration. Nico's eyes were spitting fire.

Spencer jabbed a finger toward where Bel still sat. "You keep telling me to put a fucking lid on it. How about you assholes start? Huh? It's *sickening* how you three behave around each other!"

"You sure you're not a homophobe?" Nico drawled in return. "You sure do spit venom often enough for it."

Spencer responded, but Bel didn't really pay much attention to the words. Instead, he watched the man. He looked at Spencer, at the rage on his face, crawling up his neck and turning his skin almost purple. No one looked mature while throwing hands around and screaming at the top of their lungs. Spencer had regressed to somewhere around the age of two. Maybe one.

It had taken a year of therapy, close support from friends and family, and time for Bel to really heal from Spencer. He could admit that freely and not feel any shame about it. There had always been a part of him that had wondered, though, what it would have been like if he had somehow been able to get through to Spencer back then. If he'd possessed the right words to turn his attitude, just a little, or to calm him enough to listen, how would things have turned out? If Spencer had agreed to stay, to be his familiar, would it have all worked out in the end?

Now that he saw him toe to toe with Nico like this, Bel realized he was asking the wrong set of questions. Rather than ask what could he have done to make Spencer stay, he should be asking something else entirely: What would Bel have done if he had stayed? What would his life have been like?

The only answer he could think of was: not good.

Look at him. Raving like a lunatic, almost frothing, Spencer was beyond mad. Just because he wasn't getting his way. Nico stood there like an iron wall, deflecting him, refusing to let Spencer even an inch closer. Nico wasn't calm, not by a long shot, but he looked like the picture of discipline and control in comparison. If Spencer had stayed with Bel, *this* would have been his life, wouldn't it? Spencer losing his temper. Spencer not getting his way. Bel having to soothe, fix, compromise in order to calm him down again. He'd not have the care he needed, a familiar at his side. Instead, he'd have been the one forced into the role of supporting the other. It might well have either gotten him killed, because he didn't have the support he needed, or ended his career.

He could have been stuck with this man-child for the rest of their lives.

God, what a terrifying thought.

He had been so fixated on the idea that Spencer must have been called to him as a familiar for a reason, he'd never really looked at the man like this before. Spencer was so incredibly lacking as a person. Never mind as a familiar—because Bel was sure he'd never compare to Nico and Garen in that, ever—but even as a man. He was just so...wanting.

Why the hell had his magic ever summoned Spencer to him?

No, seriously, why? Seeing him like this, in front of his own familiars, knowing what his magic could have brought to him instead, Bel really begged the universe for an answer. This made absolutely no sense. He'd never been mad at his magic before, but by all that was unholy, he was horrified with it right now. How could it have matched him with *that* when he could have had Nico instead?

If Bel had possessed the ability to sit his magic down and have a talk, he'd have done it in that moment.

Sergeant Lee marched around and got in Spencer's face, throttling him down and sending him to the other side of the boat to pout. Again. She looked ready to help Nico disappear him overboard.

Hell, Bel might let them at this rate.

Lee threw him an apologetic look, then went after Spencer, no doubt to give him a proper tongue-lashing. Bel left her to it.

Coming in, Victoria touched a hand to Bel's shoulder, the fingers light as she leaned in and asked him quietly, "Alright?"

To her, this might seem like something that could trigger one of those dark depressions Bel had suffered through. She didn't understand how illuminating the past two days had been.

"I am. Victoria...was he always that immature?"

She blinked at him, her head coming up a tad. "Well... honestly, Matt and I always thought he was. It's why we were so confused about why he was brought to you."

"I guess I was so fixated on making him happy, I never really got the man's measure." Bel shook his head slowly, those memories coming back but at an entirely different angle. "Looking at him now, he's not someone I would ever choose to associate with. Or even want to call dear. What the hell was my magic thinking?"

"Seriously." Garen snorted before throwing a dark glare over his shoulder. "That one wouldn't have been a good familiar. He might have the fighting skills, but he's too self-absorbed. I shudder to think of what dangers you would have faced on a job just because he wasn't paying enough attention to you."

Now there was a pleasant thought. Urk.

Nico slung himself into the chair next to Garen, tucking Bel's legs over his own thighs in a casual, possessive manner. "You're telling me that even three years later, he hasn't matured any?"

"Well, he kinda has," Matt corrected from his position at

the rail. "He hasn't thrown things this time."

"Seriously?" Nico rolled his eyes. "Wow. Remind me to give him a thank-you card later. The man did us all a favor by walking out like he did."

Garen's voice was desert dry. "Yes, I can see that going over well."

"What? He did!"

Victoria just shook her head and left them to their banter, returning to stand at Matt's side.

Bel knew that Nico was mostly kidding—although the evil glint in his eyes suggested he'd enjoy giving that thank-you card and watching Spencer explode afterwards—but the words struck him.

Spencer had done him a favor.

You know...the more Bel watched this man, the more he thought Nico was right. Spencer had done him a favor. Bel didn't have to walk around on eggshells because of his familiar's temper. He didn't have to spend every day compromising, bending, erasing parts of himself just to make his partner comfortable. He didn't have to wrestle with feeling unwanted or unloved.

What had Spencer ever given him, to make him want the man back?

Bel couldn't think of a single thing.

Instead, he had this. He had two men who loved him. Two men he loved to pieces. He had support he could trust, a team he could depend on, laughter and camaraderie, even when challenging situations arose. This present was so much better than the future he'd faced three years ago.

Nico was right. Spencer had done him a favor.

That thought was freeing, liberating enough it felt like someone had lifted the world off his shoulders. For the first time in days, he felt a genuine smile grow on his face.

He cuddled in against Garen again, one of his hands lightly gripping Nico's where it rested on his thigh. Some part of him was aware Spencer was arguing with Sergeant Lee back there, but he didn't really pay it any mind. It was no longer important to him what Spencer wanted, or said, or anything. Why should he care?

Spencer was the past.

He wanted to live in the present.

He just had to get used to ignoring the man, that was all. For those scars to stop twinging when he faced his once-familiar, it might take practice and a bit more time. Bel was determined on this point, though. He'd give nothing more of himself to a man who couldn't properly treasure him to begin with.

"Oh," Garen murmured, lifting a hand to touch over his own heart. "Bel?"

He surely hadn't felt that along the bond. Had he?

Nico tilted his head to look at Bel's face too, though, eyebrows lifted in question. "That tension of yours, the unhappy buzzing we've had along the bond, that just faded. Like, zip, almost gone. What happened?"

Ahh, right. Garen had said he'd felt something off with Bel. Well, it wasn't like he minded explaining it to them. He did keep his voice low, though, so it wouldn't carry past the three of them.

"I realized you were right. A future with Spencer would have been a disaster. I'm actually much happier now about him leaving because I was able to have both of you, instead. I can't be upset about the past anymore."

Both of his lovers relaxed noticeably at those words, their shoulders dropping as the tension they had been carrying lessened. Nico's expression was one of pure joy and relief. He pressed in close to kiss Bel, just an affectionate brush of the lips.

"I'm really glad, Ruby."

"Me too." Bel felt strangely like laughing, the sound a bit strangled in his mouth. "All that therapy and what I really needed was to see how badly Spencer acted as an adult. Now you couldn't threaten me into taking him back."

Garen hugged him, strong enough to make ribs squeak. "Good. We can tell you're happier right now."

"Yeah. I mean, I might keep flinching just because he's being really awful, but I don't regret the past anymore. So, both of you stand firm, okay?"

"Always," Nico promised him, kissing him again.

Mm, these kisses were nice. Bel would find a way to get them private time later, so he could properly thank his men for being so amazing and patient during all of this. Right now, though, he could just bask in being with them.

Eventually, the yelling at the back of the boat stopped. Bel actually did doze off against Garen's shoulder for a while. When he woke back up, he felt refreshed enough that he thought he could switch out with Zia. Returning to the railing, he picked up the trail easily enough with his eyes, saw how steadily her spell held. She had this, no question. Still, it would be nice of him to ask.

"You want to switch back?"

Zia waved him off. "I can hold this spell for days. It's not draining."

"Okay."

"I am worried about the light, though. We're losing daylight pretty quick."

Yes, so they were. It was mid-afternoon now, the sun already heading toward the horizon in a wash of orange and gold. "I don't want to face this thing in the dark. And going further as we are now doesn't make sense. Its trail is in the middle of the river, it clearly doesn't land anywhere nearby."

"Right? I think we should drop a marker, stop for the day. Come back and pick its trail up again tomorrow."

Yeah, it made more sense to do that. Bel gave her a nod. "Do that. Matt?"

"I'll talk to Sergeant Lee, tell her the plan." Matt pushed

off the railing and moved toward the back of the boat. "I think we might discuss actually camping out here tomorrow, though. We can't afford to lose time by traveling back and forth like this. No point if we have a trail to follow, too."

Good point. It made logistical sense to do so. But... camping out here in a national reserve? Without backup? With two territorial lizard-things that ate people?

With Spencer?

Yikes.

CHAPTER EIGHTEEN

GAREN

Garen eyed the Godzilla stomping its way toward them. Had Wicky made this thing bigger? He could swear it was bigger than last time. Nico had said it was something like thirty feet tall but this looked more like fifty.

Wicky was cackling like a loon off to the side. That rather answered the question. He definitely had. What had happened to two Godzillas?

This was supposedly for training, as they wanted to get a feel for how to fight the lizards now that they had a trail to follow. Garen was all for training, and doing so in this grassy field was alright by him, but Godzilla was lit with nothing but overhead spotlights to track him by.

Still, there were things to bonk, so he wasn't complaining. Just a little worried, because along with Wicky cackling like a demented rooster, Nico was giggling. Never a good sound, Nico giggling.

Not to mention Bel was standing at his back, a low whistle out of his mouth. "Wow, Wicky's really done an amazing job with the spell work."

And then there was this one, whose mind wasn't on the job at all.

Garen threw a glance over his shoulder. Sure enough, Bel was not in a combat stance, just looking over Godzilla like it was some creative art project. "Bel? Focus, please."

"For this, I shouldn't," he replied readily. "I can dismantle all of Wicky's hard work in about fifteen seconds—"

Wicky let out a noise of pained protest.

"Calm down, I won't, I'm just saying I could. So, for this, I'm going to hang back and cover you and Nico."

Ah. Probably for the best. It was good practice, either way. Bel often had to stand still and really look over things anyway, so doing so now would get everyone used to it. Garen suspected that was the cover story, though. Bel actually wanted to just watch the show. Granted, Nico in full monster-attack mode was quite the show. It was like the grownup version of playing combat against action figures.

Sergeant Lee had spoken with Matt and Victoria on the way back yesterday, getting an idea of how to arrange her own people now that they had a second squad to train with, and they were in a vee formation now with the mages in the back. Zia had given enhanced personal shields to every soldier, just in case—Godzilla could do damage, after all, just not critical damage—and their weapons were modified paintball guns, so a hit would register with their magical enemy. Good thinking, there. Friendly fire was definitely an issue with this group.

Mostly because of Spencer.

Godzilla let out a roar—wow, that sound was straight from the old '60s movies—and stomped ever closer, impossibly making the earth tremble under Garen's feet. Damn, seriously, how had Wicky managed to pull that off? Godzilla had "weight" to him? He'd seriously put too much thought and effort into this.

Godzilla turned and let out a mighty swing of his tail, forcing people to scatter. Well, most scattered. Nico, of course, didn't. He charged like the loon he was, letting out a happy war cry as he sprinted, his lightsaber held high over his head like a samurai warrior.

Garen turned as well, orienting just in case Nico didn't get that tail to completely stop, turning his arms stone. Unlike the soldiers, he knew the weight and strength of Zia's shields, knew what they could stop and protect against. He held firm, feet planted, a living shield at Bel's side.

Nico did manage to get a good cut into that tail, making Godzilla roar in pain, but the momentum was there. No stopping it now. Nico had to duck and roll to the side to avoid being squashed, although he was up within a split second. Garen could spare him little attention, as he had the tip of a tail to deal with. Just a little thing, maybe twenty feet long, with the mass of a small bus. No big deal.

Even through Zia's shield, he felt the impact as it hit, a grunt of air escaping his mouth. The force of it reverberated up his arms, right into his bones, and he skidded back a good foot along the grass. Garen gritted his teeth and held firm. He could hold it and have nothing but bruises to show for it tomorrow.

Bel, though. Bel would be knocked over flat and end up unconscious if this thing hit. He just didn't have the body mass to contend with something like this.

In a flash, Nico was back at his side, and the next hit of his lightsaber cut off the tail completely, severing it from Godzilla in a neat slice. Of course, being a magical construct, it just dissipated into harmless lights in the air, instead of a mess of blood and flesh.

Nico and Garen's minor victory proved a morale booster for everyone else. The soldiers opened fire, some bracing on their knees to get a good fixed position. Godzilla roared again, mostly in pain this time, and staggered back a few feet.

Calm as day, Bel called out, "Aim for the inside of the mouth!"

Oh, was that a weak point?

"Bel," Wicky whined at him. "Don't give them hints!"

"My job is to provide the cheat code, remember?"

Wicky muttered and grumbled but subsided into a pout and let it be.

The mouth, eh? No armor in there, which made sense. Garen drew the paintball gun hanging on his back and also dropped to one knee, gaining a good position before levering the gun up to his eye.

Godzilla was thrashing around so much, trying to hit the people shooting at him, that it was hard to get a good shot lined up. Garen waited patiently. No use rushing a shot, it would just waste ammo. Wait for it...wait for it...

For a moment, just a moment, Godzilla paused in place to let out another roar, this one sounding like a challenge. Garen double-tapped the trigger and let out a burst of quick fire.

It hit perfectly, dead center of the gaping red mouth ridge. Garen could see the impact as Godzilla staggered backward, this time with the incoordination of a creature who had just taken a serious injury.

Nico, at Garen's shoulder, fired again. The shot must have hit near the same place, as Godzilla staggered again, groaning as it fell to one knee.

In smooth coordination, Matt and Victoria got their own shots off, a few soldiers also getting good shots in. Godzilla let out a death rattle, then a sigh, pitching forward in slow motion. He dissipated into magical lights, like glitter, before impacting the earth.

Just as well, too. He'd have landed square on Garen's head if he'd actually fallen.

"Well, that took fifteen fucking minutes," Wicky said cheerfully. "Well done. I'll make the next one harder."

Bel turned to him and mildly rebuked, "This isn't a video game. We don't need to make the bosses progressively harder to level up."

"I beg to differ." Wicky slapped both hands together and rubbed them with evil glee. "I'll make the next one more agile. I know just how to do it."

Oh, god. Wicky had now taken this as a *challenge*.

They were doomed.

Spencer's voice carried from fifteen feet away, the snide tone clear. "We'd have gotten that down a lot faster if Mr. Delicate over there had done his damn job."

Garen lifted his eyes to the heavens and prayed for patience.

One of Spencer's own squad mates, Green, turned to him and growled, "Davis, shut it."

"I'm just saying!"

"We're practicing *exactly* what it's going to be like in the field. He told us point blank he has to examine something for a full minute sometimes without moving. He's being upfront about how his magic works. Stop acting like this is all a surprise or like he isn't pulling his weight."

Bel turned to him and gave a slight smile. "Thank you, Corporal Green. I'm glad someone was paying attention."

Green gave him a nod in return. "No problem, sir. Sir, can I ask a question?"

"Of course."

"Will the lizards we're fighting be of this size?"

"No, but close to this. I estimate from their energy signatures and footprints they're at least twenty feet tall. They're longer, though, their tails more like a true lizard's tail." Bel waved to where Godzilla had stood a minute ago. "We chose this form because Wicky already had the spell made up for it and we thought it would add some fun to the training."

"For training accuracy"—Spencer was already heading for Bel, intent on making trouble—"you really should make us face something that actually looks like the monsters. That too hard for you, little mage?"

"Davis, for the love of god!" Green looked ready to punch him. "He's already said he doesn't know what these things are. Of course he doesn't know exactly what they look like. How can he form up something he's never seen?"

Wicky's brows were drawn into a dark frown. He looked ready to throw hands. "And *I'm* the one who created this spell, thank you very much. You can leave Bel out of it."

Bel gave an instant nod, expression so bland it bordered on being painfully neutral. "True, I had nothing to do with it. Wicky came up with it on his own. We're just capitalizing on it."

Spencer had his mouth open again to say something— who cared what—when Sergeant Lee intervened, sounding tired. Just absolutely done with his shit. "Davis, do us all a favor. Shut up."

Spencer did not want to shut up. That was clear from the expression on his face. He looked like a toddler told to take a nap who wasn't in the mood to be even remotely obedient.

His sergeant's expression firmed, and she gave him The Look. All subordinate officers knew this look. It meant: Defy me and see what happens.

As antagonistic as Spencer was, even he didn't dare to cross her in that moment. He subsided, although the way he glared at Bel hinted that he'd find a way to hassle him again soon.

Garen could almost empathize. If he had lost Bel, he'd have been sore about it for years, too. His empathy stopped short of hassling the man he wanted, though. That was such a grade-school level. If Spencer really wanted him back, wouldn't it be a better tactic to try and seduce him? Charm him? Bullying never won anyone's heart.

He wasn't about to say so, though. If the man was intent on putting both feet into his mouth, let him. It wasn't any skin off Garen's nose.

Lee turned to her own people and called, "Ten-minute

water break, then reset!"

That was probably wise. It was a warm day, and they needed to stay hydrated. Garen let his skin relax back to its usual state and went for the water bottle he'd left at Wicky's feet. Bel and Nico followed him, retrieving their own, gulping some down.

Interestingly enough, Lee followed them and tapped Garen's shoulder. "Dallarosa, let me ask you something. You and di Rocci move like you're a unit. I know you and he haven't been Adams' familiars all that long, so what kind of training did you do? To achieve this kind of rapport, I mean."

"Oh, Garen and I go way back," Nico corrected. The look he gave Garen was warm, full of history and affection. "We were in boot camp together, in the Army. We served together, too, up until this traitor went and changed careers on me."

"I offered to take you with me," Garen reminded him. Again.

Rueful, Nico made a face. "Yeah, in retrospect, I should have probably gone with you. Wait, no, what are you saying? You hated that job in the end."

"Well, yeah, but it would have been more fun if you'd stayed with me." Not to mention they wouldn't have suffered the same heartbreak. It was history now, that scar no longer twinging when he thought of their separation. Garen was ever so glad how things had worked out in the end.

For her sake, Bel filled the sergeant in. "Nico went Army Ranger. Garen left the Army and became Secret Service, mostly in a bodyguard capacity."

Lee's voice rose. "Wait, what? Army Ranger and SS? Are you serious? I've seen some pretty crazy familiars, but what kind of spell did you use to call *them*?"

Garen was rather flattered by that reaction. He could tell Nico was too.

Eyes twinkling, Bel drawled, "The right one, apparently. Well, I say that, but when I summoned Nico, I used the standard spell. Garen's was the tricky one, as I wanted to specifically call him. Which, far as I'm aware, has only been done one other time in history."

Her eyes flew wide, mouth dropping open a notch. "Well." Eyes darting to Garen's face, she took him in. "He was very determined to have you."

"We were all very determined," Garen assured her dryly. "I'm fortunate he was smart enough to figure out how to do it. Bel knew it could be done, but no one could actually tell him how."

"Ah. Well, anyway, I have my answer for why the two of you work together so well. Years of experience." Lee gave a shrug. "I'd kind of hoped for a different answer so I could get the same kind of rapport with my own people."

"Yeah, sorry, no way to speed that process up." Garen did see why she was asking, though. Good rapport between members of a squad was sometimes more important than extra ammunition in the clip. It could make or break a bad situation, no question.

Lee turned and looked around, then groaned. "How is it that I say 'take a ten-minute break,' and the second my back is to them, people go missing? What is this, kindergarten?"

Garen looked around at the same crowd, most of them sitting on the grass, and realized precisely who she meant. Spencer wasn't in sight. He could just be lying down, though, it wasn't like Garen could see every face from here.

In a voice meant to carry, Lee demanded, "You guys seen Davis?"

Nothing more than shrugs of ignorance.

Nico's expression was pure mischief as he told her, "I got this." Raising his hand to cup his mouth, he called, "Who's been a useless slacker and hasn't hit anything?"

"FUCK YOU!" Spencer snarled back, popping out from behind the nearby building. He'd apparently been resting in the shade.

"Found him." Nico was the picture of evil satisfaction.

Garen just shook his head. As expected of Nico. He was not one to take the high road when he could have a little fun instead. Also expected of him that he'd been tracking Spencer through all of this and realized the man hadn't made a single good shot.

Leaning in, Bel muttered to Nico, "Aren't you the least bit ashamed of riling him up? He's such an easy target, after all."

Nico pointed a finger at himself in mock-confusion. "Can I feel shame?"

"No," Wicky replied. "That's a bonus action."

"I thought so."

Oh god, these two were already on a roll. Garen tried to divert them. "How about we try for some diplomacy?"

Nico *tsk*ed him, wagging a finger. "Reject diplomacy. Embrace bonk."

Right on the same page, Wicky nodded in approval. "This falls under the heading of bonk, so I must support."

Yup. As expected, no help from that quarter. Good thing he hadn't been looking for it.

Bel, proving that he could resist being sucked into their pace, poked at Nico's side. "Why don't we get back to what we were doing."

"Killing things?" Nico bounced on his toes. "Excellent suggestion. Wicky, make it more agile. It went down too fast."

"Roger that."

Garen tried to intervene. "Remember, you've fought against Godzilla multiple times now. These guys haven't. Let them have more of a trial run."

"Hmm, sounds like a Spencer problem to me."

Yeah, Garen gave up. The most anyone would suffer today was bruises and injured pride.

Okay, he might also like to see Spencer struggling to keep

up with them and failing miserably. He'd never claimed to be a nice person.

CHAPTER NINETEEN

NICO

Something about sparring and training always got Nico a little horny. Probably because it got the blood pumping. At least, that was his story, and he was sticking to it. With two very sexy lovers at his disposal, it was rare that he now had to take a shower and deal with such impulses himself.

Right now, though, might present the only opportunity he would have for several days to get his game on. They'd be camping and tracking in the Australian swamps for the foreseeable future, after all. Who knew when they'd make it back to the hotel room? And they had the rest of the night to themselves. Why not capitalize on it?

Alright, truth was, he was feeling not only horny but also mischievous. So sue him.

Shower time had become this kind of free-for-all unless stated otherwise, where they all kind of just came in and out as they wanted, washing off before leaving. Unless sexy times ensued. Which was often. Anyway, this time Garen just went in, washed off the sweat from that day's training, and went out again.

Bel was set to follow suit, but Nico caught him before he got further than wrapping a towel around his waist.

"Hey, Ruby. Want me to teach you something fun?"

Bel eyed him with frank suspicion. Which was hurtful. Nico hadn't done anything to deserve that look (yet). "Does this fun thing involve danger and/or destruction of government property?"

"Nope," he said, popping the *p*.

"Will it end with one of us in traction or a cast tomorrow?"

"Uh...hope not."

"Alright, I trust you enough to let you continue. What's this fun thing?"

Nico would mourn the loss of trust from his mage but... well, history rather backed up Bel's caution. He dismissed this and went back to the important matter at hand. "Want to learn how to turn Garen on in two seconds?"

Bel's expression flipped from cautious to intrigued. "Oh, so it's a sexy fun thing. Oooh, is there really a secret button?"

"There really is. Just like your ears." Nico leaned in and kissed Bel's neck softly, right under his earlobe. "There. Kiss him just there. Something about that sends a signal straight to Garen's brain that says, *I want you.*"

That small pink tongue flicked out over Bel's lips. "I'm all for this. Umm..."

Nico's interest perked. That was quite the expression on Bel's face. This mix between lust and uncertainty. "What, Ruby?"

"I know I don't normally ask to top you guys..."

"That's true, you don't." Not that either Nico or Garen minded flipping roles, it was just that Bel expressed wanting to be bottom most of the time. In fact, this might be the first time he'd ever suggested otherwise.

"I'm kinda in the mood to top tonight?" Bel paused before admitting, "But I kinda want to be taken, too. I'm not sure which mood is dominant right now."

Ahhh. "You can totally do both. You're welcome to take me, you know that. Garen can always top you."

"Bel sandwich, huh? Well, actually, I was thinking we

could flip this. Garen always seems to dominate or control things when we get into bed."

That was true, he did. Mostly because Nico got distracted easily and Bel was usually too lost in pleasure to make any higher-functioning decisions. Nico saw where Bel was going with this.

"So, you want to first turn Garen on, then turn the tables on him and make him lose his mind?"

"In a nutshell. Um, we haven't really played around with much, so I don't know. Is Garen okay with being tied to the bed?"

The only reason they hadn't done a lot of experimentation was because Bel was too new to things. Granted, he'd had experience before coming to them—he hadn't been a virgin— but it didn't compare to Garen and Nico's. Just being in a threesome blew his mind most days. They'd been taking it rather slow for his sake. Nico could answer this question with authority.

"He's perfectly fine with it. In fact, on days that have gone to shit, he prefers it. One less place he has to make decisions."

"Got it. In that case..." Bel's expression turned naughty. Beautifully so. "There are maybe handcuffs in my duffel bag at the foot of the bed."

Nico put a hand over his heart, so happy he might well perish on the spot. "Bel Bel, you did *not* prepare for kinky sex on this trip!"

"I didn't, actually. I keep the cuffs on me because we are technically law enforcement."

Oh, yeah. Nico had forgotten about that.

"But hey, if they come in handy for non-legal reasons, who's to complain?"

"Not me," Nico agreed cheerfully. "Okay, action plan: You go turn on Garen, I'll grab the cuffs."

Bel put a hand palm down. "On three."

Nico slapped his hand over his, like they were a team

ready to take the ball field. "One, two, three, break!"

From the bedroom, Garen's voice called, "What are you two doing in there, and do I need to be worried?"

Bel skipped out, still only in a towel, and caroled, "No need to worry~"

"See, when you answer me like that, and when Nico's got that shit-eating grin on his face, I doubt you. All the doubts." Garen was propped up on the bed, legs crossed, only boxers on. He had his reading glasses perched on the tip of his nose and his phone in hand, clearly already settled in for the evening with no intention of going anywhere.

He put the phone aside as Bel climbed onto the bed, straddling Garen's lap without a by-your-leave. The towel got lost somewhere around the edge of the bed during this maneuver. Bel leaned in and kissed exactly the right spot.

The reaction was visceral and unmistakable. Nico knew it well because he'd pushed that button many times. Garen grabbed Bel's head with both hands, his fingers tangling in Bel's hair as he kissed him.

See? Two seconds, all it took.

Nico fetched the handcuffs and zipped around the side of the bed, not worried when his own towel dropped in the process. Before Garen could flip them—and he was already turning, his body angling to put Bel underneath him—Nico caught a wrist and tugged it up. The hotel bed fortunately had a slat design, and Nico took full advantage, slipping the cuff around it so he could hook both wrists up.

Garen pulled from the kiss to watch as Nico got one wrist cuffed. "Oh. Oh, is that what you two were scheming about in there?"

"Objections?" Bel asked as if this did worry him on some level.

"Pfft. No. You can cuff me any time."

Nico knew that'd be his answer. He didn't blame Bel for double-checking, though.

Bel set to kissing Garen again as if making love with his mouth. Nico had to stop and just appreciate the view for a moment. Bel's porcelain skin was in high contrast to Garen's darker skin, almost like an artist's charcoal drawing. It was full-on erotic art with them stretched over white sheets, entangled in each other. They were so incredibly sexy when they were like this, kissing as if they couldn't get enough of each other. It wasn't just the view, but the noises, the sound of kissing filling the air.

He got a little hard from it. Not going to lie.

Garen's head dropped back to the pillows, eyes slipping shut as Bel moved down his neck, teasing that spot under his ear again, lingering there like the teaser he was. Nico let him play for a minute while he found the lube. It was determined to hide, and for the life of him he couldn't figure out where it had escaped to.

"Bel," he whined toward the bed. "The lube's run off again."

Bel lifted his head and briefly glanced around before pointing to a spot near the corner of the room, under the small, circular table. "There. It's lurking under the chair."

Really, those demon eyes had several perks to them. Being able to find absolutely anything in a glance was just one of them. How the lube got over there, Nico left to the heavens to answer. He didn't frankly care as long as he could lay hands on it.

He turned back toward the bed and for a second, honestly forgot to breathe.

Damn. That was hot.

Garen had both legs spread for access, and Bel had his head down, working Garen's dick with a long, steady bob of his head. He pulled off only to move further down, hands lifting and spreading Garen's cheeks. If Nico didn't know Bel was rimming Garen, then the man's strangled groan of pleasure would have told him everything.

He absolutely wasn't content to stand there and watch, though. In fact, Nico was of the opinion Bel needed a dose of his own medicine. His little blond liked being rimmed. Loved it, in fact. Time to eat some ass.

Nico crawled up onto the bed. Bel's ass was already in the air as he bent forward, so it was at the perfect angle. Nico gave him no warning as he dove in, getting his mouth right where Bel liked it best. He used the tip of his tongue to trace first, feeling Bel's shudder wrack his body from head to toe in reaction.

Bel didn't lift his head, but he did make delicious noises as he enjoyed the attention. It fueled Nico further, and he fucked Bel with his tongue.

It was apparently too much. Bel lifted his head on a gasp, arching. "Shit. Ni-Nico!"

Nico made an inquiring noise but didn't lift his head. He was frankly having too much fun driving Bel crazy.

"Get in me, dammit!"

"I echo that," Garen growled, sounding past his limit. "Get in *me* before I do something to this very nice bed."

Threatening the bed's integrity, eh? Nico mentally cackled. Aww, these two were so much fun to rile up. Sex with them was amazing because of it.

He pulled back long enough to prep Bel, a very quick prep, because no one was patient right now. While he prepped Bel, Bel prepped Garen. Judging Bel was ready, at least, Nico grabbed the lube and used it on himself, three good strokes enough to get him hard and ready. Nico put a hand to Bel's waist, guiding himself in with the other, and felt the clench and reaction as Bel took him in. Mm, so hot and tight, as always. Bel was a delight.

Almost as soon as he was settled, Nico paused, giving them a second to adjust. There was plenty of lube left on his hand, so he reached around, readying Bel's dick with several thorough strokes, fingers teasing the tip, just because.

Garen lifted his head to watch, eyes intent on the action. Even though he was clearly enjoying the show, he protested, "Nico, stop teasing Bel. You're both driving me crazy."

"You know that's a favorite pastime of mine, G," Nico riposted.

"I will do something absolutely mean to you later."

"Looking forward to it."

Bel turned his head just a little, and he did look right there on the edge. His face was flushed, pupils blown wide. He was past words, his hand grasping Nico's hip and drawing him in as he pushed backward.

Following that silent instruction, Nico pressed close as Bel tilted Garen's hips up, entering their other lover with a slow and steady push. Garen sighed in satisfaction, head tilting back as Bel filled him.

Nico tried to be patient, he did, but he really couldn't. His blood thundered in his ears, body demanding movement. He pulled back an inch and thrust in, the motion not only sending him into Bel, but also forcing Bel closer into Garen. Both men gasped in reaction, which just fueled Nico even further. Hell yes, he loved that. Nico pulled back again, further this time, fucking in harder. The domino effect was perfect. So perfect, he did it again, with even more force, making the whole bed rock.

Bel's hands spasmed, locking onto Garen's arms as he sought purchase. Nico felt the same need for it, as he kept an arm around Bel's waist, turning his head to suck a mark into Bel's neck as he fucked into both men. This was perfect. Too perfect. He wouldn't last much longer at this rate.

The thought no sooner crossed his mind than he felt that telltale tightening in his groin. Nico held Bel tightly as his hips erratically thrust in, climaxing hard inside that hot, tight channel. He might have checked out for a moment, as he sought to catch his breath, just lingering over Bel's back. The other two had come near the same time, apparently, as they were just as blissed out and boneless. Mm, good sex.

Garen shifted a little restlessly. "Okay, you two are cute, but move."

It probably was an uncomfortable position with both of them pressing down on him like this. Nico pulled out first, then assisted Bel, as he looked ready to just curl up and pass out. Then again, he had been getting it from both ends.

Nico uncuffed Garen first, as that was the nice thing to do, then went for a washrag to clean everyone up with. By the time he tossed it into the bathroom and returned to the bed, Bel was already wrapped around Garen's side, both of them under the covers and situated for sleep. Nico came in to curl up on Garen's other side, snuggling in. Garen greeted him with an affectionate kiss against the forehead and wrapped an arm around him to bring him in closer.

Perfection.

"You taught him that trick, didn't you?"

"I did," Nico admitted without an ounce of shame.

"Good job."

"You're welcome." Nico kissed his shoulder before snuggling back in.

Proving he wasn't as asleep as he looked, Bel muttered a request against Garen's bare skin. "Teach me Nico's magic spot next."

With a leer, Garen promised, "You got it."

Well. Looked like Nico had started something.

He looked forward to the next part very, very much.

Wait a minute. He had a spot?

Nico would've asked, but Garen was already asleep and of course Bel didn't know. Huh. He had a turn-on button.

Well, this should be educational for all three of them.

CHAPTER TWENTY

BEL

After a very satisfying romp last night with his men, Bel was in a much better mood the next morning. He boarded the boat, this time with both trained squads, ready to get these monsters knocked out and done. The sooner, the better. They had camping gear with them so they could stay on the trail this time instead of having to double back every day.

Not that anyone was looking forward to camping in monster-infested swamps. Still, not much choice in the matter.

Bel just wanted to know what the hell they were. This had to be a first, that he'd tracked something for several days without even knowing what the creature was. He'd forgo repeating the experience in the future. It was definitely a zero-stars, not-recommended situation.

Zia picked her spell back up at the marker she'd left, and they continued tracking along the river. Bel didn't actively use his eyes, but he couldn't help but see what she did. He stood beside her at the rail and stared hard at the traces of energy left behind.

"I think..." He trailed off for a moment, eyes squinting in concentration. "Yeah. I think this one is from the second house I studied."

"Oh? Are you sure?"

"I'm pretty sure." Bel pursed his lips as he leaned a little more over the rail, studying the signature on the river's bottom. "This one apparently likes to take naps on the river bed from time to time. He rested there a good hour before coming back up and continuing on his way."

"So...truly amphibious?"

"Apparently."

Zia made a noise of interest. "I really wonder what this is."

"We all do. Jack has made me promise that when we find him, we'll report immediately to him so he can send a team to retrieve the creature. The research department wants all the deets on these things."

"I can't blame him. On the off chance this happens again, there should be some kind of file for the next agent."

"Yup."

She cast a quick glance around. Bel wasn't sure why. Garen and Nico were on the chairs a few feet behind them, relaxing and letting the river flow by. Wicky was stretched out nearby, hands on his stomach, taking a nap. All the familiars had decided this was a good idea and were using him as a pillow. Victoria and Matt were in the middle of a call back to the agency, updating them on the situation. The Marines were all doing the same, either relaxing or taking the opportunity for a nap.

Leaning in, Zia spoke in a confidential tone. "Things seemed to have eased up? Nico and Garen aren't hovering over you anymore."

Ahhh, that's what caught her interest. "Yeah. Once I explained everything that was going on, it helped. It's not like they're not worried about Spencer—because he does seem intent on causing trouble—but they're not as worried about his effect on me. Really, I wouldn't have that man back for love or money. Without the bond in place to influence my view of him, I can look at him without blinders on. He's toxic as fuck."

"He really is. I know it was hard on you getting rid of him, but it really was for the best." Zia glanced forward, making sure her spell was still doing its job, before continuing. "I really wonder what your magic was thinking, calling him. I know he fit the requirements. Strong fighter, not bound to anyone else, etcetera. Still, he doesn't really have familiar potential to me. Familiars have to be willing to be devoted to someone. He's not selfless enough for that."

"He must have had it, though. My magic wouldn't have called him, otherwise. He just chose not to devote himself to me." Bel shrugged, as frankly, he no longer cared. "Water under the bridge. I'm quite happy with how things turned out."

"I would be, in your shoes." Zia's attention turned back to the river, and her dark brows drew together in a frown. "Hmm. Seems like our prey made a turn here."

"Oh?" Bel tuned in and gave the trail a better look. She was right, he had taken a left at the river's fork and gone further in. "The energy of the trail is older, though."

"Is it?"

"Yeah, by a few days. I kind of want to investigate it anyway. I want to know what it was doing over there. Is there a den? Did he strike and leave victims we don't know about?"

"All good questions."

Bel put a hand to her shoulder. "You keep tracking him. I'm going to alert Sergeant Lee and the boat captain that we want to make a turn up ahead."

"Please and thank you."

Bel trotted toward the back of the boat, acquiring a Nico as he moved. He'd rather expected that. Curiosity alone would make Nico pop up and follow him. Besides, Nico had been sitting for a whole fifteen minutes, which was something of a record for him.

"Where we going, Bel Bel?"

He wasn't really willing to repeat himself, so he encouraged Nico, "Keep up, and I'll explain it to all of you at once."

"Cool beans."

Sergeant Lee looked up from the phone in her hand as Bel approached, then stopped leaning against the railing altogether. He went up the short three steps to the top, where the pilot's nest was, stopping on the top step.

"Hey, so, update for you. There's an older trail that leads to the left at the fork. Zia and I both want to follow it for a bit, see what's there."

The pilot, a grizzly man with perpetually sunburned skin and hair bleached white by the sun, turned his head to speak. "Lake is that direction."

Oh? Oh right, the map showed that. "How big of a lake?"

"Pretty big. Doesn't lead to anything else, though. Dead end."

That was good to know. Bel rubbed at his jaw, thinking hard. "I don't know if there's a den in there or not. The trail is a good day older than the one we're currently following. I mostly want to make sure there are no other victims in that direction. People shouldn't be out here, right?"

"Shouldn't be," the pilot agreed laconically. "Doesn't mean jack shit, though."

Yeah, as Bel knew from personal experience, people loved to ignore warning signs. Sometimes he was convinced humanity as a whole couldn't read. "Do you mind if we deviate and take a look?"

Sergeant Lee shrugged. "I don't see the harm. It won't take much time, and I'd rather make sure."

"Yeah, me too." Satisfied, Bel retreated the way he'd come and headed for Zia.

Nico fell into step with him. "If it's an older trail, though, odds are there's not a den back there."

"I agree, but I don't want to assume anything at this point. Frankly, I don't know enough to make assumptions."

"Fair enough. When do you plan to call the hellhounds? Tonight?"

"Yeah. They'd just cause chaos on the boat." Bel knew very well why he'd asked, and his eyes cut up to Nico's face. "You and Wicky are dying to play with them again, aren't you?"

"Maaaaybe."

"Maybe meaning yes. I'm onto you." Bel just shook his head. "Some of the fiercer guardians of Hell, and you guys treat them like friendly puppies. You realize I can't guarantee I'll pull the same batch you made friends with last time, right?"

Nico did not look bothered by this possibility. "I can make friends with the new guys too."

Somehow, Bel didn't doubt that.

They deviated as planned, and the pilot was correct that there was a large lake there. They puttered around the perimeter of it, Bel sweeping the banks with his eyes. He didn't actually want more victims, and judging from the signs, there weren't any. The lizard seemed to have come in here more for the fishing, as there was no sign of humans at all. Good.

Sergeant Lee came over to them. "Anything?"

"Not a thing," Bel said. He idly waved a mosquito away from his face as he spoke. "I do see hints that the other lizard has been in this area too, but that was several days ago. As far as I can tell, these two don't cross paths."

"Interesting. Then again, there's only so much hunting ground to go around."

"True enough."

Pointing to the sky, she indicated the failing light. "We've got maybe an hour or so before dusk hits. How about we stop here, make camp? Since there's no obvious sign of them being nearby, it should be safe enough here."

Bel couldn't find a flaw in the logic. They were running out of daylight, and another hour wouldn't get them much further along, so why not? Besides, if they were really lucky, the lizard might come back and save them the trouble of hunting it down. "I'm for it."

"I'll just drop a beacon where the trail was." Zia flapped a hand toward the river. "Easily enough done."

"Good. I'll tell Mick." Lee turned and headed back for the pilot's nest.

It was easy enough for them to pull up near the bank, extend a ramp, and offload everything. The area right near the water was thick with trees, but another ten feet in, it cleared some and gave them enough area to put down tents, create campfires, etcetera. Bel let them focus on that as he and Zia marked a defensive perimeter so she could put a ward up for protection. They'd all sleep better for it.

That done, he went with the second task for the evening, namely summoning hellhounds. He stepped away from the camp by a good fifteen feet, then put both hands over his heart, focusing on the demon blood within him. This was a little different from summoning his grandfather. "*Ich rufe Euch, sechs Höllenhunde herbei.*"

Six hellhounds rose from the ground in a circle of summoning and fire. Normally a sight to put fear into lesser mortals, their ferocious snarls immediately turned to happy tail wags when they saw Bel. Which was normal; all lesser demons liked Bel on sight. They recognized his blood.

"Hello, hello, yes, come and get scratches." Bel leaned down and gave them lots of love under their chins and behind their ears, avoiding the little spits of happy—and acidic— drool. "Such good hounds. I want you to guard the perimeter of the camp tonight, alright? Come, I'll walk it with you so you know where to be."

The only thing better than a summoning was to have a fun

task, which this qualified as. The hounds were quite happy to trot at his side as he walked around the camp, keeping them just inside Zia's barrier so they would know to stay inside it.

His phone pinged with a text. Bel pulled it out to find that Naamah had just texted him.

Ok? Grandpa said you summoned hounds.

Bel was incredibly impressed he'd gotten enough signal to get that message. His phone reception had been hit and miss since coming to Australia. Bel texted back, *Ok. Just camping out in the swamp, called them to guard.*

Cool, she replied.

From absolutely nowhere came a high-pitched call. "PUUUUUUUPPIES!"

At least one hound had been with them at the cave because its head snapped around, and the body wag was immediate. In five bounds, it crossed the distance to Wicky and then jumped, flattening the mage to the ground without care or apology. Wicky went down laughing, hugging the hound that dwarfed him by a good fifty pounds, ruffing the scruff.

"Who's a good puppy? Who's a good puppy? Is it you? Ahh, such a love. Let's go play fetch, yeah? Yeah? You want to go play fetch?"

Seriously, why was Wicky like this? Did the man not have any trace of fear? Self-preservation? Bel gave him an exasperated look. "Wicky. I called them here to work."

From the depths of the tent Nico had just put up, his head popped out, and he looked around with excitement. "Oh, you called the dogs already? Awesome! Here puppy, come here, want some scratches?"

Then again, Nico was just as bad. Survival instincts? What are those?

Bel gave up. The new hounds, the ones not yet charmed by these two crazy people, were already turning and looking interested. Scratches? Fetch? Apparently, they were the fun buzzwords. He could tell, he'd already lost their attention. Bel sighed and shooed them on. "Go, go play. We'll do perimeter later."

They didn't even hesitate. Just bounced off, one of them even snagging a handy stick on the way.

Was it because they hung around with Bel so much that nothing from Hell fazed them anymore? Was that it? Or was it just Wicky and Nico being Wicky and Nico? Somehow, he felt like it was the latter.

Shaking his head, Bel went toward their tent. Might as well help Garen sort their sleeping bags and such while Nico played. When he ducked into the three-man tent, he found Garen had organized their bags off to the side and had one sleeping bag already out of its holder.

"Nico's playing with the dogs, I take it." Garen's green eyes sparkled with amusement.

"Of course he is."

"If we didn't travel so much, we'd have a dog. You know that, right?"

"If by 'a dog' you mean at least four, then, yes, I'm aware. We'll probably be inundated with dogs once we've retired and can stay at home more."

Garen put a finger to his lips. "Don't say that too loudly. He'll take it as a promise and we'll never, ever get him to forget it."

Bel shrugged. He really didn't mind. He liked dogs. Cats, too. It was just that with his career, keeping a pet was completely impractical.

He went with the typical set-up chores, activating the cooling charm at the top flap of the tent so they wouldn't swelter from the heat, then activating the floor charm to give them some cushion. Well, he was going to just activate it, but this thing was military grade—i.e., completely inferior. Bel frowned at it, thought of a sleepless night with a crick in his neck the next morning, and deactivated it again. This was minor magic, so he didn't bother to call for Victoria or Matt for a boost. He just took a Sharpie to the stitched-in design, redoing it to give it more oomph. There, that was better. He slapped a hand on it and activated it again.

His efforts didn't go without notice. Garen knelt off to one side, head canted in question. "Now, that seems different than before? What did you do?"

"Gave us more cushion. Original design would have only provided an inch of air padding. This will give us five."

Garen leaned in to smack a kiss on his mouth. "Bless you. Alright, who's cooking?"

The rest of the evening went by in anticlimactic fashion. Bel finally got the hounds to do a perimeter walk with him so they could do their job. He introduced them to the Marines as he went so the hounds knew to obey them and the humans didn't crap their pants. Bel personally found the hounds to be reassuring in a different way. The noises in an Australian swamp didn't match what he thought of as typical night noises. Things here made different sounds and it was just different enough to be unnerving.

People cooked dinner, cleaned up, some settled in with a book to pass the time before bed. Lee set up a watch rotation despite the ward, but Bel didn't argue with her about that. It was fine to have extra security. This place didn't promise safety, after all.

Bel finally made it back to the tent and placed his boots inside it, to keep anything creepy crawly from getting in them. (He's made that mistake only once.) Then he checked his sleeping bag, giving it a few pats and a thorough look to make sure nothing had crawled in during his absence. Reassured, he curled up in what was fast becoming his spot, with Garen pressed against his back and Nico tucked in against his chest. Never mind that Nico never stayed in one spot throughout the night, he always started curled up with Bel. Which was nice, honestly. These cuddles before sleep sucked him under.

He was almost asleep when he heard that god-awful sound. If a lawn mower could be congested and snore, it might sound something like this. He felt both Nico and Garen startle, coming partially up onto one elbow as they tracked the sound.

"Ignore it," Bel advised, eyes still closed. "It's just local wildlife."

Nico sounded a touch incredulous. "That's local wildlife? That sound like a chainsaw bemoaning its fate into a beer? What the hell makes that sound?"

"It's koala mating season. That's their mating call."

There was a digestive pause.

"That is a koala," Garen repeated. "Those cute little animals with the funny noses? Those?"

"Those," Bel confirmed.

Nico was not satisfied with this explanation. "How the hell do you know?"

"Been to Australia before. Suffered through koala mating season before. Trust me, there's no way to mistake it for anything else."

Another digestive pause.

"I think I'm scarred for life," Nico muttered. He flopped back into position.

Bel smiled into his pillow. "Welcome to Australia."

There were disgruntled groans from both men. He could hardly blame them. The koala was loud. Obviously-not-getting-laid kind of loud. No wonder the female was ignoring him, if he was being that obnoxious.

He had no memory of his eyes closing, but Bel felt it when Nico jerked awake, scrambling for the tent door. Prying both eyes open, he mentally scrambled, trying to make sense of what had alarmed Nico. Wha—?

Howling from the hounds, snarls of bloodlust, people shouting in alarm, gunfire—and above it all, the roar of something he'd never heard before, sounding guttural and inhuman.

Shit.

They were under attack.

CHAPTER TWENTY-ONE

GAREN

Garen was right on Bel's heels as they both tumbled out of the tent, his feet bare and a gun in hand. One of the modified ones, fortunately, because they were indeed under attack.

And *that* wasn't going to go down easy.

Garen had three seconds to get his bearings as Bel stopped and took stock. Those three seconds made his mouth run dry. He'd heard Bel describe the two things they were hunting often enough he could remember the words without trying. Amphibious, lizard-like, twenty feet or so tall with long, whip-like tails. This beast that was roaring and trying to break through the barrier fit the description to a tee.

But it was so much more in person, too. The large red eyes, glowing in the darkness, seemed inherently threatening and evil. Its skin was green, or seemed that way in the dim lighting, and when it opened its mouth, Garen saw nothing but teeth. Just rows and rows of teeth, like a shark that had gone on steroids. Garen was horrified by the sheer size of this thing, standing so much taller than himself. He felt like he was facing down an ancient dinosaur, that was how stark the danger levels emanating off this thing were.

"It seems," Bel said in an oh-so-calm voice that heralded shit going down, "the hunter has become the prey."

Garen couldn't help but ask, "Is this the thing we've been tracking?"

"No, it's Monster One. Dumb luck sent her our direction, I guess." A shit-eating grin passed over Bel's face, his red eyes gleaming. "Saves me the trouble of hunting her down."

Sometimes, Garen forgot Bel could be absolutely ruthless. His book-loving lover was gentle by nature and not one to start a fight. Against something like this, though, he had no mercy.

Hopefully he saw a weakness because, despite the impressive amount of firepower being unleashed against this thing, she didn't look in any danger. Just pissed off. The lighting was bad, only a campfire at their back and the LED lanterns casting little illumination, but she definitely wasn't in danger of going down any time soon.

With a whirl, the green lizard turned and slammed her tail against the ward. Garen could feel the vibrations right down to his bones, and he instinctively put himself between her and Bel even though they were a good thirty feet away. She hadn't gotten through Zia's shield, but—

"Another five good whacks, that thing might get through Zia's ward," Bel observed. He sounded upset but still unnaturally calm. "We'll need to be quick about this."

Nico dodged back to them, barefooted like the rest of them, Slashley in a two-handed grip. He didn't even look winded, a wild light of pure glee in his eyes. Nico, at least, was having fun.

"Hit this thing at least three times and she barely flinched. I might as well have been using a wet noodle."

Spencer passed them at a jog, gun out. There was a sneer in his voice as he threw out, "Your little toy won't do any good here, *former* Army Ranger. Step aside, and let the men handle this."

Nico stared after him, flabbergasted. "He did not just diss my lightsaber."

"He did, which is funny, because if he thinks traditional bullets are superior, he's in for a rude awakening." Garen shook his head. Why was Spencer still trying to show himself as superior? There was no point. Seriously none. The man had such a fragile ego.

Also not his problem, fortunately.

Garen kept one eye on Bel, waiting for his lover to analyze this thing and give them the information they needed to take it out completely.

The Marines were stacking right up at the edge of the ward, firing at the lizard as much as they could, most seemingly aiming for eyes or mouth, which was fair. It was what they'd done in training, and those spots were probably weak points. It didn't seem to work well because the creature kept jerking her head this way and that, not allowing anyone a clean shot. The modified bullets weren't working as well as they'd hoped.

Another whirl, and the lizard slapped the ward again with her tail, sending people tumbling back. Damn, even Garen could see the effects this time, an obvious crack right along the side.

That...was not good.

Victoria jogged back to Bel, although carefully staying out of his line of sight. "Bel?"

"I'm not seeing an obvious weak point," he admitted, still staring hard. "This thing is covered in this slimy coating that's acting like armor. If we can get through it, I think fire would be effective, but getting through it is the trick. Don't aim for her tail, no weak point there."

"Belly?" Matt called from the ward line, clearly able to hear something from there.

"If you can!" Bel called back. Then added in a lower tone, grimacing, "I think. It's so low to the ground, it's hard to hit there, though. I'm not sure how viable a target that is. Mouth might be our best bet."

"So, just like we practiced with Godzilla." Victoria gave him a nod. "Got it. Let's aim for that."

She had some idea of what to do as she ran right back to Matt's side, a spell glowing and ready in her open palm.

"Nico," Bel requested urgently, "Grab Wicky. I've got an idea."

Nico spun on his toes and was gone in a flash, fetching as requested.

It was on the tip of Garen's tongue to ask what Bel was planning when several things went wrong all at once. Spencer decided to act both stupid and rash, charging the creature, firing rounds as quickly as he could squeeze them off, his modified M27 rifle shooting bullets etched with runes of fire. Why he thought that was more effective than the M240B machine gun one of his squad mates was using made no sense to Garen. In terms of firepower, they couldn't begin to compare.

Unfortunately, his bravado took him outside the protections of the ward. He was a sitting duck as the lizard turned her full attention to him. If he realized the danger, he gave no indication, as he kept advancing.

Aw shit, the idiot was going to get himself killed.

His squad mates realized it and advanced too, trying to cover him long enough to pull him back in. Garen swore as they did so, knowing they were putting themselves at real risk of being hit in seconds.

Bel growled out something that may have been a curse and sprinted forward, calling to the hellhounds as he moved, "GUARD!"

The dogs leapt to the defense of the soldiers, but they were a few seconds too late. Even as Garen ran at Bel's side, that incredibly powerful tail whipped around again and crashed into the nearest soldiers, sending three of them flying. They flew several feet into the air before skidding on the ground, one of them fetching right up against a tent and taking it down.

"Damn fool," Bel snarled.

"RETREAT!" Lee snapped to the others, moving forward herself to snag people if they didn't move quickly enough.

The hounds were busy distracting the lizard, snapping and howling, harrying her feet so her attention went to them instead. It provided enough cover for the soldiers to pick up those injured and not moving, dragging them back into the protection of the ward.

It was an injustice that Spencer was not one of those injured. Garen considered that a damn shame and an oversight.

Wicky appeared with Nico, Wicky at least breathing hard and looking outraged. "What was that idiot doing?!"

Bel just shook his head. "Ignore that. Wicky, can you pinpoint a spell inside that thing's mouth?"

"Sure, why?"

"I have a particular spell I want to try with you." Bel whipped out his phone and typed in something quickly before showing Wicky the screen. "Yes?"

"Fire *and* brimstone?" Wicky's evil smile stretched from ear to ear. "That's amazing and, yes, absolutely, let's combine magic and do this thing."

Thank god, finally, something of a game plan. Garen was distracted for a brief moment as Matt called out to Zia, requesting she renew the ward. Zia waved in acknowledgement, but it looked like she was already in the process. Then again, she was the type to think well on her feet.

They absolutely had to take this thing down before real aid could be given to those injured.

Bel called out in quite possibly the loudest voice Garen had ever heard him use, "Matt! BAIT!"

This meant something to Matt, as he waved a hand and then combined powers with Victoria to fire off two quick spells. The lizard's head snapped down in their direction, and she gave a roar of challenge, tail lashing like an upset cat. If a cat's tail was the size of a telephone pole, at least.

The distraction was what Bel and Wicky needed. They fired off their own spells, the German and French mingling in a weird synchronicity, a nasty-looking fireball of gold and white heat hitting hard and fast. Garen harbored a split second of hope that it would hit as intended, but the lizard jerked her head up at the last second and it didn't go cleanly in, instead scraping along the inside of her jaw.

It might not have hit the intended target, but it had caused real pain. The lizard let out a scream, thrashing her head from side to side in an effort to get it off.

"Well, that worked—" Wicky started, only to cut himself off. "Oh, shit. She's heading for the water!"

Shit. Granted, that was common sense. Something burning, put it in water, but Garen really, really didn't want the lizard to head for the river. It just meant escape and would force them to chase her down again later.

Bel was already a step ahead of him, urging Matt and Victoria, "Lasso spell!"

They didn't visually acknowledge him, but their hands rose, a rope of light coming out of them and shooting around the lizard's neck, pinning her to the ground. Wow, that was handy. Garen wasn't sure how long it would hold, though, as the lizard was already jerking hard against it, the soft earth tearing up. The spell might need a better anchor to be truly effective.

Bel took off running, Garen, Wicky, and Nico right at his side. It was only thirty feet to the edge of the ward, where the lizard was pinned, but it felt like three hundred yards to Garen, as he could see the lizard was really minutes away from tearing free and disappearing into the river.

"Back of the head," Bel rapidly relayed to Wicky. "I see a weak point at the base of the skull, let's hit the back of the head next!"

"Got it."

They skidded to a stop and fired again, the spell leaving their hands in a deadly burst of flame just as before. It hit dead on, from what Garen could tell, right at the base of the skull.

The lizard let out a roar and thrashed some more.

That was *not* a death rattle, dammit. Just how tough was this thing?

"Once more," Bel urged.

"No, wait," Nico corrected. "I can see where you've taken off the protective slime. Let me try something."

Eh? What the hell could Nico try that would outdo fire and brimstone?

Garen had no chance to trot the question out. Nico was already gone, sprinting across the distance at a speed that few other mortals could even begin to keep up with. He leapt lightly onto the lizard's back, racing forward along its spine, Slashley at the ready.

Was he—?

With both hands, he lifted the lightsaber high and then jammed it full force into the base of the skull, his entire body weight thrown into the action. Then, smart man that he was, he jerked it free and leapt right off, retreating back into the ward. Which was good for Garen's heart, as he really didn't like Nico in that kind of danger. At all.

The lizard let out a long sigh and slumped, going unnaturally still. No one could fake true death, the stillness that came with it as the soul left the body without any chance of return.

Finally, the fucker was dead.

Nico threw up a fist into the air. "Ha! I thought so. I figured I could get through the slime coating and penetrate deep that time."

"You crazy man." Bel snagged him by the nape of the neck

and drew him in for a quick kiss. "Only you have the speed to pull that insanity off. I just about had a heart attack watching you do it, though."

"For shame, Ruby. You know I wouldn't attempt something like that unless I knew I could dodge if things went wrong."

Bel just shook his head and kissed him again.

Now didn't that just put the matter into perspective? Garen couldn't help but reflect on Nico's words for a moment. Spencer had charged out to prove a point. Nico had done it only as an assist, fully planning to duck back into the ward if it didn't look viable. How incredibly different the two attitudes were.

And the results showed.

Garen stepped in to kiss Nico's forehead as well. "Good job."

Nico's grin was electrifying and satisfied. "I know."

"You're such a brat."

"I know that too."

So incorrigible, this man. Garen looked around and took a mental tally. They may have won, but it had come at a cost. They had at least four people injured, some of them cradling limbs as if they were broken, two of the tents were smashed in because of flying soldiers, and that was just what Garen could see from here.

"I'll go help stabilize people." Wicky moved in that direction, muttering as he went, "It'll take hours to get them to a hospital."

So it would. It might be better to call in for an air lift, all things considered.

Bel ran a hand through his hair. "First, shoes. Then I get to call this in. Garen, can you take pictures for me, email them to the research department? Jack's going to want details on this."

"Sure."

It looked like they were in for a long night.

CHAPTER TWENTY-TWO

BEL

Matt called in an airlift for the injured, with Victoria calling MAD to set up carcass retrieval. Airlift was being sent in to help with the wounded, but it meant the rest of them got to retreat to the base via boat. It was also on them to pack everything back up. Bel didn't mind the work, per se, but he was worried about Garen, Victoria, and Matt. They kept yawning and frankly looked dead on their feet. It didn't help that Jack kept calling Bel, asking for more details. He'd have been able to sleep if not for those calls coming in every thirty minutes.

Unfortunately, with Bel's mind, he couldn't really just turn it off. It was constantly thinking on one level or another unless there was a sexy distraction on hand. Standing in a swamp in northern Australia did nothing to keep his mind from clicking along at high speeds.

Bel had suspicions. Many suspicions.

Garen was a shadow at his side, no need to collect him, but Bel wanted to run this by Matt. He flagged down his foster father with a wave of the hand, drawing him away from the cleanup.

"Matt. Evil thought."

"Oh, god." Matt did an exaggerated slump, head hanging

for a moment. "I hate your evil thoughts. They tend to be right. What?"

"Couple of things are bothering me. One, this isn't the creature Zia and I tracked in here."

Garen made an intrigued noise. "That's right, it wasn't."

"Two, this thing approached from the north. Over the land. Every other time we've seen them, they've used the water to travel about. If she's coming from that direction, there has to be a good reason. I think maybe her den is over in that direction somewhere."

Matt and Garen both froze before turning and looking where he'd indicated. As if they could possibly see anything in the dead of night in a swamp.

"Oh," Matt said, drawing the sound out to be twelve syllables. "That...makes a lot of sense. Shit, we can't just not check that out. Didn't you say that these were female and male? It's possible there might be a nest in that den, if it exists."

"Her den is *somewhere*, that we know. I'm just saying, high possibility it's near here." Bel looked around, knowing there were whole sections of thigh-deep water, tree roots, and unsavory things for them to trip over, and regretted what he was about to say. Very much. "I really don't want to leave a nest behind if it's close by."

"Shit, I don't either. The idea of leaving it here does not spark joy. But on the other hand, tramping through all of this at night also does not spark joy."

Bel shrugged, as he couldn't comment. Darkness was not a deterrent for him like it was for other people.

Matt mock-growled at him. "Yes, I realize that you can see fine. The rest of us mere mortals will struggle."

"Mage lights?" Bel offered helpfully.

"Definitely. No question. Let's fill in Sergeant Lee."

Bel let him do that and went through a mental checklist of what he'd need to bring with him. Hopefully not much more than a canteen and a first aid kit. Just in case.

Lee came back to him with heavy concern written all over her face. She did not look happy about this, and Bel honestly couldn't blame her.

"Mage Adams, how viable is this possibility of a den nearby?"

"I give it fifty-fifty."

"Shit. I don't like those odds. How far?"

"I honestly can't say. I won't know until we get closer, if we get closer to it."

She put hands on hips and blew out a stressed breath, looking in that northward direction. "I don't like this, but I really don't want to come back to this spot and repeat work if we don't have to."

"Zia can put a moving shield around us as we march," Matt offered. "That way, we can't be surprise-ambushed. Well, not badly; we'll have protection up and the dogs as extra protection."

"That does make me feel better about this. On the other hand, I don't want to go far, either. Mage Adams, let's do this. If we can't find this den within half a mile, we'll mark the location and come back in daylight. I don't want to venture too far, all things considered."

Bel completely understood and agreed. They'd already been hit hard tonight and, really, she was generous to give him even this much. "Thank you. I think, honestly, that if it's not within a half mile then I'm probably wrong. Let's at least take a look, that's all I ask."

"Alright. I'll get everyone ready to move in ten minutes."

"Okay."

Lee was true to her word and had everyone ready to go in short order. Bel and Nico took lead, with everyone else flanking in a V formation behind him. Bel was used to taking point; he was the one that could see where to go, after all. Nico fundamentally couldn't let him go ahead when there might be danger, so he was two steps ahead and slightly to his left, lightsaber up and at the ready.

The trail was clear to Bel's eyes, stretching ahead, the energy of it unmistakable. He followed it and only winced a little as mud seeped over his shoes. Damn, maybe he should have worn boots instead of tennis shoes. These might well be a loss. Hard to get swamp mud out of things like shoes.

Nico, of course, still had energy to spare. His head kept panning from left to right, vibrating with the eagerness to hit something. "Bel, which way?"

"Left."

Nico paused at the base of the tree and peered around it.

Seriously, he was far too hyped up. Bel had to tease him. "Guess what happens next?"

"Bronze dragon?" Nico was all childlike hope.

"No, you go left!"

"Dammit."

Garen, at least, appreciated this, as he was snickering. "Now, Bel, don't tease."

"He just gives me so many openings."

Nico turned and stuck his tongue out at both of them.

Bel could hear at least one person in the back complaining about him taking things too lightly. Bel ignored him. When things went to shit like they had tonight, that was precisely when you had to keep your sense of humor. Laugh while you can, that was his philosophy.

They kept tracking through the muck, with the far-too-large insects buzzing around their heads, everyone making mud-slogging noises as they moved. It was a miserable hike, no question there.

One that paid off rather quickly.

"Well, shit." Bel stopped dead in his tracks and turned, pointing ahead. "There it is."

Everyone else stopped as well, peering ahead. Victoria flung a mage light in the direction he was pointing, illuminating the squat, cave-like structure made of mud, wood, and who knew what else. A beaver's dam times a hundred in size would resemble this.

That wasn't really what caught Bel's attention, though. It was the seals around the den. They were beyond old, something he couldn't identify at a glance. It was a type of magic he didn't really have much experience with, either.

Lee and Matt were right at his side in a second flat, peering ahead with him.

"That's the den?" Lee asked, a trace of doubt in her voice. "It's pretty short for that."

"Opening is deceptive," Bel answered absently. "The floor of the den goes deep immediately."

"Oh. Gotcha."

"What are you seeing, Bel?"

Of course Matt would know to ask that question. "I'm seeing a lot of old seals wrapped all around this thing. Not something I recognize. I assume they're from the aboriginal tribe, whoever that is, but this is from a good four or five hundred years ago. Closer to five hundred. Remarkably well done, from what I see. The seals certainly kept the creature asleep and caged here until very recently." Bel really wanted to study them and give a thorough report on it because seriously, that was some of the tightest, most efficient seal design he'd ever seen.

"What happened, why the escape?"

He turned to Lee to answer. "The seals just wore out. Seals aren't eternal, they'll eventually fail. It's a credit to the creator that they lasted this long."

"I'm almost relieved to hear it. At least it's a local problem, not something that's coming out of another area." Victoria blew out a breath. "Alright. Bel, do you see eggs?"

"I see...something that might be eggs?"

That was too much for Nico's fragile willpower and he darted ahead to go look.

Bel rolled his eyes and prayed for patience. If he could just borrow some of Nico's energy. Like, even a ten percent boost, that would be amazeballs.

"Nico, get back here!" Garen called after him, exasperated.

"I'm just looking, I won't touch!" Nico called back. Which would have been reassuring if he hadn't tacked on, "Probably."

At least he was honest about it.

Nico apparently got frustrated rather quickly by the lack of proper light, and his flashlight could only illuminate so much. He half-turned to call back to Bel, "What's past this opening?"

"Down," Bel drawled, deliberately not being helpful.

Nico was not fazed. "How do you get to the Down?"

"Hole."

"How do you get up from the Down?"

"Climb."

"You're not letting me climb in here, are you?"

"No."

"Dammit. You're such a killjoy, Bel Bel."

"Forgive me for liking you whole and hearty. Now, come back here. Wicky, batter up."

Wicky was all for that, although he didn't move with the usual bounce in his stride. Too tired for that, as they all were. Nico returned to Bel's side and leaned lightly against Garen, listening.

"What am I doing?" Wicky asked.

"Fireball," Bel suggested.

Wicky slapped his hands together and rubbed them in glee. "Oooh, a classic. I'm game. You really think there are eggs down there?"

"There's something gooey and nest-like, at least, that strongly resembles eggs. Maybe unfertilized eggs? I dunno, not an expert on monster-lizard breeding habits. All I know is that it's suspicious and I want it gone."

"Fair enough. I'll make this extra spicy and hot, then."

"Do." Bel wasn't in the least worried about a fire spreading, not with this much water around them.

Zia apparently was, as she put a protective ward around the area with an opening in the front for Wicky to shoot through. He cast with flair—apparently not tired enough to drop the theatrics—and the fire that shot out and down was so hot it was nearly white. The den didn't stand much of a chance. It went up like kindling in short order, Zia's ward keeping it contained nicely. In three minutes flat, nothing but a ruined, smoking husk remained.

Perfect.

Bel heaved a breath of relief. "Gone. Thank you, Wicky."

"The enemy of my enemy is dead." Wicky grinned with wicked delight.

Zia cocked her head at him. "That...is not how that saying goes."

"Isn't it?"

Bel was too tired to correct him. He frankly didn't care. He just wanted a shower and bed, in that order. "Sergeant Lee, I'm satisfied we've done our job."

"Let's return to base, then. I'm more than ready to call this day quits."

No one was about to argue with her.

CHAPTER TWENTY-THREE

NICO

What with tracking down the den, destroying said den, packing up the rest of the camp, and the boat ride back, it made for a very long night. Tempers were short, to say the least, everyone grouchy from the lack of sleep and caffeine. Bel kept the hellhounds around as an extra guard until they finally got on the river. There was much sadness as Nico didn't even get a chance to properly play with them before they were sent home.

Nico, personally, was glad to be back on base since it was nearing seven in the morning. Mostly because, despite washing his feet off in the river three times, he still felt like there might be traces of lizard slime on the soles. Which, eww. Or maybe it was swamp mud. Either way, eww. As they offloaded in the parking lot on base, Nico poked Bel's shoulder.

"Bel Bel, you promise there's no slime left on my feet?"

Bel shot him an exasperated look. "They're sparkling clean and smell like cinnamon. You can't do anything more."

"Can't I?" he bemoaned. "I still feel the sensation. It was icky."

"Well, who asked you to run up a monster's back with your bare feet?"

"I didn't have time to put on shoes!" Nico pointed a victorious finger at him. "You didn't, either! You were running around without shoes too."

"I also had the common sense to stay inside the ward."

Yeah, okay, Bel had him there. Damn smarty-pants. Nico wanted to protest that he'd done it all for a good cause, but the truth of the matter was, Bel and Wicky probably could have killed the lizard without his help. 'Cause they were cute and dangerous that way. Nico just hadn't been able to resist stabbing that thing viciously. It was predator instinct or something.

Well, he could have a nice, hot shower when they got back to the hotel. Bel and Garen would sleep until late in the afternoon; he knew they would, but Nico was still hyped up from the kill. He'd manage a few hours of sleep before running or hitting the gym. Oooh, pool. They had a pool here. He could swim for a while—that would be fun.

Nico shouldered his bag, turning to keep an eye on Bel. No reason why, just the instinctual need of a familiar to track his mage. Nico often did this, and he didn't try to fight the urge. Besides, Bel was cute and fun to look at. No problem.

He saw it when Bel overbalanced, one toe catching his other heel, fatigue making him clumsy. Nico's hand shot out, catching him around the shoulders and hauling him in against Nico's chest. Bel landed with a soft *oomph*, clinging to Nico's waist as he sought to orient himself.

Not wanting him to be embarrassed, and unable to help himself from teasing, Nico waggled his eyebrows and drawled, "You can just say you want a hug, Ruby. No need to accidentally-on-purpose trip into me."

Bel gave him a grin in return, taking the teasing in stride. "I'll remember that next time I play damsel in distress and turn my ankle."

"Good, do that."

"He's tired." Garen took the duffel's strap from Bel's

shoulder, tugging it free.

Bel tried to snatch it back. "We're all tired. I can carry that."

"I'm not tired," Nico pointed out. He wasn't, really.

With a groan, Bel leaned further into him, abandoning the attempt at wrestling his bag back from Garen. (Which was wise. In this mood of Garen's, he would not win.) "When I grow up, can I have Nico's energy?"

"No," Garen informed him firmly, although his eyes twinkled with laughter. "I refuse to have two of you."

"Aww, c'mon, G." Nico shifted to allow Zia past so she could reach the trunk of the SUV and get her bag. They probably should move so other people would have easier access to the vehicle. He'd do so after he teased his men some more. "I'm a bundle of fun!"

Garen ignored him and looked to Bel. "Can you make a Nico-sized straitjacket? No reason."

"I'll get right on that. After I sleep for twelve hours."

Nico wasn't worried. He could totally outrun these two before they could even get the jacket's sleeve on him. Besides, they were just grumpy and sleep deprived right now. A lot of sleep, a little food, and they'd remember why they loved him again.

It was the tone that caught Nico's ear. That ribbing tone people used when poking fun in not-nice ways, meant to rile up another.

"—thanks to a certain someone, our squad is out of commission for weeks now and we're probably stuck on desk duty. Thanks for that, Davis," a woman sneered from somewhere near the other SUV.

"Fucking shut it," Spencer snarled back.

"I still want to know what the hell you were thinking, going outside of the ward. I mean, seriously."

"You're not saying that to the hotshot familiar over there!"

"Well, yeah, obviously. He took it down. He gave it the

final blow. All you did was bait it and then let everyone else take the damage for you. Great job, there."

Nico one hundred percent understood why all of the Marines would be mad at Spencer. Hell, he was upset with the man, too. But to them, it was worse than that. Semper Fi—you never left a man behind. That meant, flipped, if one person went out, everyone else had to follow in order to protect their own. Having a reckless idiot like Spencer who charged first, thought second, would endanger everyone else. Nico really, truly understood why they wanted the man to grow up and learn some common sense.

On the other hand, he didn't want to be anywhere near Spencer when someone was poking at a sore point. That was just an explosion waiting to happen.

He turned his head, just to track the situation, as it sounded like the female Marine and Spencer were getting closer to them. It turned out to be the wrong move at the wrong time. Just as Nico turned his head, Spencer rounded the butt end of the SUV and saw him standing there with Bel tucked under his arm.

Spencer was already red in the face, a mixture of anger and embarrassment warring in his expression, but when his eyes landed on Nico and Bel, his eyes narrowed in pure hatred. Nico could almost see the switch when Spencer targeted him to blame.

Aw, shit. Fireworks in three, two, one—

"You just fucking can't keep your hands off him, can you?" Spencer pulled something from a pocket and threw it, hard as he could, toward the back of Bel's head.

Nico's hand flew up and caught it, instinctively not allowing anything to touch his lover. His hand closed on something sharp and metal and he winced but didn't let it drop. It stung, though. In fact, it hurt like a bitch. His nerves lit up with fire, and he could feel the wetness of blood.

Bel turned sharply, a noise of alarm high in his throat.

"Nico! Spencer, what the fuck do you think you're doing throwing a knife at him?!"

Ah. Knife. That explained it. Nico let it drop and it clattered to the pavement with a loud ring. Especially loud as everyone in earshot had stopped dead, staring, their mouths gaped open in realization. Even Nico was a bit stunned by this. Of all the stupid things to do—this truly was a whole new level of stupidity. Had jealousy and anger driven Spencer mad? Who threw a *knife* at the back of someone's head? What if Nico's reflexes hadn't been fast enough to catch that? Bel would have taken it full force.

The mental image of that alarmed Nico so much he just couldn't stand still under the force of it. His bond flared, beyond enraged, beyond angry, like bottled lightning in his chest. It demanded blood. *Now.*

Never in his life had he moved so quickly. Hand-to-hand combat training kicked in, and he was on Spencer before the man could even properly drop his duffel bag, losing the burden. His first hit struck squarely in the solar plexus, doubling Spencer right over, the air knocked out of him in a tortured gasp. He caught the man around the waist, throwing him sharply to the pavement, not at all satisfied when Spencer landed hard. It just fueled him. He caught the man's arm next, jerking it upright, keeping him pinned to the ground as he kicked him three times hard in the back, forcing Spencer to jerk under the blows. The one time the man tried to lift his head, tried to get onto his back and up, Nico punched him hard in the face, bloodying his nose.

Two strong hands he knew well caught him around the chest, pulling him off. Nico almost fought Garen off—wanted to, as this piece of shit needed more of a beating than this. With Garen restraining him, though, he could finally hear Bel's voice.

"—Nico? Nico, come back to me, *carus.*"

Nico felt the tug along the bond, too, felt Bel magically

pulling him off. Shit. He didn't want to. He really, really didn't want to. His familiar side called for blood still. He wouldn't really be satisfied until Spencer was in a shallow grave somewhere.

But Bel called for him. Garen was pulling him off, too. He had to trust their logic. He was too mad to really think straight in this moment. Growling out a curse, he gave Garen a nod before looking to his Bel, his soft-hearted Bel.

"I want this damn punk under the jail." Nico was not joking.

Sergeant Lee stepped forward, and the glare she gave Spencer promised a world of pain. "I promise you three, it'll happen. This is outside enough. Davis, not only have you disobeyed *two* direct orders I gave you, you're now throwing weapons at allies? On top of the shit you pulled tonight? You're heading for a dishonorable discharge. The Marines don't need someone like you."

They really, really didn't. Nico absolutely agreed with her on that.

Lee looked up to Nico, eyes full of sympathy. "I'm so sorry. Thank you for not killing him. How bad is your hand?"

Oh. Right. He'd gotten injured. Nico had honestly blanked on that for a moment, his own rage too intense to register something paltry like pain. He opened the palm and looked down, realizing the gash actually was deep enough to require stitches. Damn, now that he looked at it, it really did hurt.

Wicky, brother that he was, was already at his side, taking Nico's hand in his. He muttered some kind of spell in French, which knitted the wound back together and stopped the bleeding. Enough it would only need a bandage, at least.

"Thanks, man." Nico gave him a grateful smile.

"No problem. Don't actively use this hand for about three days, okay? It's only knitted together on the surface. You still need to let the rest of this heal."

"Okay."

Nico only bothered to glance over as Lee hauled Spencer to his feet and force-marched him off. Absolutely no one offered him a healing spell or even a tissue to stop the nosebleed with. They were all more than ready to let Spencer suffer the consequences of his own actions.

Bel examined Wicky's handiwork too, brows drawn together in a deep frown. "I hate that you were hurt like this. Why would he throw a knife, of all things?"

"Jealousy can unhinge a man," Nico responded quietly. "Not excusing him, but I think he's the type to let his emotions get the better of him. I'm just glad I caught it. I absolutely do not want sharp, pointy objects anywhere near your precious head."

"Well, I don't either, but still." Bel hugged him hard, arms twined around his waist. "Thank you."

"You are, as always, welcome." Nico dropped a kiss on top of that fair hair, hugging him back with relief. Bel was fine. Come on, bond, Bel was fine. Spencer was out of sight, even, his sergeant having dragged him off to place charges on him. With the mood Lee was in, he'd be lucky to get two aspirin for the pain.

Was it wrong of Nico to hope he didn't get any treatment and just got to suffer?

Garen put a hand to the small of Nico's back and urged them all forward. "Come on. To the hotel. After the events of tonight, we all need a hot shower and a chance to unwind."

Sounded heavenly to Nico. He had just one concern. "Beeeeeel~"

Bel put a hand in Nico's as they walked back to retrieve their bags. "What?"

"Do the paperwork for me?"

Bel blinked up at him with absolutely no comprehension. "What paperwork?"

"I just got into a fight on base—there's going to be paperwork." Nico gave him his best winsome smile.

The light dawned. "Oh, *that* paperwork."

Garen eyed Nico sideways. "You're the one who got into a fight. Shouldn't the paperwork be your responsibility?"

Well, yeah, but that didn't mean Nico wanted to do it. Forms in triplicate were a no-thanks in his book. He blinked down at Bel, trying to look as innocent as possible. He had a feeling he was mostly failing, but the point was the effort. "Do you want me to take on that responsibility?"

Bel didn't even hesitate. "Hell no. I don't want you doing it. I'll handle it."

"This. This is why I love you."

Garen grumbled something about Bel spoiling him. Nico didn't even try to correct him. He enjoyed the spoiling very much, thank you. Besides, it was a division of labor. Nico bonked things. Bel wrote up the reports about it. Fair was fair. This did not come under the heading of bonk, thereby was not his job.

Nico absolutely wasn't taking advantage of the situation. Much.

CHAPTER TWENTY-FOUR

BEL

Bel walked back from the commander's office that afternoon with an interesting mix of emotions duking it out in his stomach. What with half of Lee's squad now out of commission for the next several weeks, the commander had issued orders for Bel to take a new squad. Which was fine, and expected, but that did mean they'd have to pause today and retrofit the new squad with the right weapons to give them a fighting chance. They'd learned the bullets from last time weren't as effective as they'd hoped, but with real fighting experience, it was easy to make adjustments.

Well, really, Victoria and Matt were dealing with that. Matt had firmly told Bel that he, Garen, and Nico had the day off today. After the volatile way things had gone down a bare six hours ago, with Spencer being such an unmitigated ass, both Nico and Garen were a bit high strung right now. Understandably. Whenever Bel thought of that moment, his heart tended to leap in his chest, too.

What had Spencer been *thinking*? The obvious answer was, he hadn't been thinking at all. He couldn't have been. No one threw a serrated knife at the back of someone else's head, with that many witnesses, *on a joint Army base*, without consequences. Spencer was about to feel every ounce of those consequences, too. Part of this afternoon's meeting was a review of what Spencer had done. The commander had wanted the full story of every single transgression Spencer had committed. Bel had spared no detail. Frankly, he didn't see the point of trying to cover for the man.

Spencer had dug this grave. Then proceeded to dig some more. He got to lie in it, and Bel refused to get in there with him.

It was quiet this afternoon, most people in their offices or out on the training fields. Bel could hear sounds of someone barking out commands and the tread of feet as people jogged as he walked down the sidewalk, heading for the hotel room. It was white noise washing over him because his mind was fixated on something else entirely.

If Nico or Garen had been in Spencer's position, what would they have done? It was almost ludicrous to ask, really, as neither of them would have let go of Bel to begin with. But what if? What if they had? What if Bel had lost them as he had Spencer and coincidentally bumped into them years later, like he had here?

He could see Garen professionally putting distance between them and trying to avoid him as much as possible, just to keep the awkwardness down. Bel could see Nico coming right up, saying hi, and at least trying to keep things on a friendly basis since they had to work together.

What he couldn't see was either of them acting like Spencer had, with the tantrums, the taunts, the outright attacks. That, he couldn't see at all.

Bel had thought this before, but he was now absolutely confident in the feeling. Spencer had done him a favor by leaving as he had. He wasn't even a tenth of the man Nico or Garen were. It might have hurt like hell to lose his first familiar, but you know, Bel would do it all again in a heartbeat if it meant he would have Nico and Garen in the end.

Spencer was not worth keeping.

The realization brought a smile to his face, and he felt himself letting go of a scar he'd harbored for years. Seriously, facing old ghosts and seeing them for what they really were was better than therapy sometimes. Bel might have hated every second of being around Spencer, but it had really been good for him. It had given him the closure he'd needed.

Bel might have been a bit giddy under the release of those old burdens. He might also be in the mood to reward Nico for such excellent reflexes. He chose not to examine himself too closely as he bounced up to their hotel room, thinking perfectly lecherous thoughts as he went.

When he did enter the room, he found Garen at the table near the window, typing up something on his laptop, glasses on his nose. Nico was in loose sweatpants and nothing else, doing stretches that looked vaguely yoga-ish, with one foot tucked up against his knee, arms over his head, as of course he couldn't just sit still.

Toeing off his shoes at the door, Bel shucked his shirt, then headed for Nico. Nico tracked him automatically as he came closer, a smile on his face.

"Hey, Ruby. What did the commander say?"

"That he's going to throw the book at Spencer and we'll have a replacement second squad."

"So, what we expected."

"Pretty much." Bel wasn't interested in this conversation. He had Plans. He reached down, grabbed Nico by the back of the thighs, and lifted him enough to toss him backward toward the bed.

Bel wasn't really strong enough to haul Nico or Garen around, but Nico, in this case, was cooperative, and the bed was only a foot behind him. He landed with a laugh and a bounce, a wide smile on his face. For a brief moment, he looked like one of those sexy model pictures, all tousled hair and abs, sprawled out on a bed and ready to rumble. Bel immediately climbed up on top of him.

"Hi, Bel. Are we in a good mood?"

"An amazing one." Bel leaned in and smacked a kiss against that mobile mouth. "I'm going to sex you up now. As a reward for laying Spencer out."

"Oh, are you? Far be it from me to suggest otherwise."

The man was such a tease. Bel leaned in again, this time with more purpose, licking his way into Nico's mouth, enjoying the taste of him and the groan of pleasure Nico gave. Nico often took the more active role in bed, but he did have moments, like now, when he let Bel do as he liked. The submission was both sweet and hot as fuck.

Bel trailed down and sucked on his Adam's apple, then down a little farther, trailing toward the magic spot Garen had told him about. Well, he'd told all three of them about it, as apparently Nico hadn't realized he had this button to push until Garen pointed it out. Just above the happy trail, like a tease of things to come, that was what turned Nico on in two seconds.

Bel didn't just touch it, though. He took the flat of his tongue and licked upward, eyes on Nico as he did so. Mischief had him fighting a grin as he liked the way Nico shuddered under him, a gasp strangling in his throat.

"Bel Bel," Nico managed, his good hand tightening on Bel's shoulder like it were latching on to a lifeline, "you're going to push that button of mine every chance you get, aren't you?"

"Is this a question?"

"Mostly a rhetorical one."

Bel had no defense. He liked turning his men on in under two seconds. So sue him.

With thumbs hooked in the waistband of Nico's sweatpants and boxers, he tugged at them, pulling them off. He needed those out of the way so he could properly get this man all riled up. As Bel worked on those—Nico lifted his hips to help—Nico spoke to Garen.

"You're welcome to join us."

"Oh, I probably will in a minute or two," Garen answered, a trace of heat in his voice. "Right now, though, I'm enjoying the show."

"That's fair. I'd probably do the same in your shoes. Bel doesn't get all dominant on us often."

"That he does not. I like it."

So did Bel. Maybe he should do this more often.

Also, Nico had just said far too many words. It was a clear sign that Bel needed to shut his brain off.

He threw the pants and boxers carelessly off to the side and got a hand on Nico's calf, lifting the leg so he could plant a kiss just inside the curve of his knee. Nico's non-injured hand found its way into Bel's hair as he kissed his way up the inside of Nico's thigh, the skin warm under his mouth. There were traces of citrus in his nose, no doubt from the bodywash, but mostly it was the musky scent of warm male skin.

Bel used his nose to bump Nico's leg a little wider, giving him proper access to his balls. He teased them with the tip of his tongue for a moment, just tracing meaningless patterns over the wrinkly skin.

Nico's hand tightened in his hair to the point of pain, his hips moving an inch or so, restless.

"G," he complained breathlessly, "he's over here driving me crazy."

Hmm, still too many words. Bel really had to up his game.

He vaguely heard Garen leave the chair, but that wasn't his focus. With one hand steadying Nico's dick, Bel ran the flat of his tongue along the underside, right on the main vein.

Nico shuddered under his hands, a low groan tearing free of his throat.

Oh look, no words. Much better.

Bel felt hands at his waist, Garen working on getting his pants off. He cooperated, as that would be helpful, but it wasn't his main focus. He kept working the tip of Nico's dick with his mouth, just teasing little bobs that didn't let Nico have what he really wanted while promising him all the things.

Pants went away somewhere, yay. Now, back to driving Nico properly crazy.

Or so he thought until he felt one blunt-tipped finger enter him. Oh! Well, that felt nice. Garen was stretching and lubing him up. Perfect, Bel didn't want to stop long enough to do that. He was so much more invested in the groans, sighs, and aborted thrusts Nico was making into his mouth. His usually hyperactive lover was trying very hard to stay still and not choke him, which Bel appreciated, but the effort alone amused him, too. Nico very obviously wanted to move. Desperately.

Well, he wouldn't get his way. Not yet.

Bel felt two fingers enter him, scissoring and stretching, Garen teasing at his prostate with each thrust. Delightful sensation. Part of him indulged in the little shudders of pleasure that raced up and down his spine, the slight burning sensation as Garen worked him loose. That always felt good.

As distracting as it was, he didn't let himself get sidetracked. Bel indulged Nico precisely once, taking him deep in his throat, relaxing his muscles as much as he could to take the man properly in.

"Fuuuuuck," Nico groaned, the sound almost a growl in the back of his throat.

That sound triggered Bel as nothing else could. He wanted more of it. He wanted to watch as Nico came completely unraveled under him. It tipped Bel over the edge of desperation.

He pulled free of the dick in his mouth with a pop and turned his head enough to tell Garen, "Pull out. I want to ride him."

"Oh, fuck yes, please," Nico whimpered.

Garen pulled free, and Bel lost no time climbing up, straddling Nico's waist, and taking his dick in one hand to hold it steady so he could sink down on it. Despite being prepped, it still burned slightly as he relaxed. More a sensation of fullness, of being stretched by a hot hardness. Bel loved that feeling more than anything in the world. He kept his hands on Nico's chest for balance as his head fell back, eyes slipping closed as he focused on the sensation. Mmm, perfection.

Nico's hand had a stranglehold on Bel's thigh, urging him to take him in deeper. Bel had no problem with that, sinking until his ass rested against bare skin. He leaned in enough to kiss Nico, Nico lifting up halfway to meet him in that kiss. There was nothing gentle about it, just tongues and hunger as they fed off each other's mouths.

He couldn't wait any longer and lifted up, sinking back down in a thrust meant to test his position. Bel felt a spark as the tip of Nico's dick grazed his prostate. Angle was perfect. Awesome.

The next thrust down wasn't at all gentle. Bel had no patience left. He wanted this man. Now. Nico met him on the third thrust, somehow, impossibly sending him in deeper. It was Bel's turn to shudder as his nerves threatened to overload with sensations.

Bel chased that feeling, thrusting faster, working his whole body into the motion. The slapping of their bodies filled the air with sound, mingled with their breaths as they became harsher, quicker.

The bed dipped to the side, drawing Bel's attention to Garen as he climbed onto the mattress to join them. He'd shucked clothes at some point, eyes glued to them, mesmerized. He leaned in first to kiss Nico, the kiss hot and filthy, then lifted up to catch Bel by the back of the head and kiss him in the same way. Bel welcomed the kiss but didn't stop moving. He couldn't. His body demanded release in a very urgent way.

Garen released him, moving down so that he lay half propped over Nico's waist. Bel had no idea what he was doing, watching through heavy eyes as he continued to thrust hard onto Nico's dick. What was Garen trying here—?

He very quickly had his answer as Garen oriented himself so that he could take the tip of Bel's dick into his mouth. Not fully, but enough to give Bel that wet heat to thrust into.

Oh god, that was amazing. It was exactly what Bel had been craving. It might well be his undoing. Bel tried to keep his pace steady—he didn't want to choke Garen at that angle— but it proved hard as he wanted to thrust into the welcoming mouth as much as he wanted to keep the dick in his ass.

Bel could feel the tension growing in his groin, see the edges of his vision going dark, knew he was only seconds away from climaxing. He tried to thrust harder onto Nico, to bring the man with him. Nico must have felt the same as he thrust up more, too, hand almost like a claw on Bel's thigh.

Almost...almost...the climax teased at him, taunting him just out of reach...almost—

Bel tried to get a warning out. His mouth wasn't exactly cooperating, his body more focused on coming, but he tried anyway. "G-Garen—"

Garen hummed an acknowledgement with a mix of permission, and that tipped Bel completely over the edge.

Bel's whole body clenched as his climax ripped through him. He came hard, stars bursting behind his eyes, breath seizing in his lungs.

Bel came to slumped over Nico's chest, feeling all sorts of mellow. Damn, he loved having sex with his men. It really was always a pleasure. In more ways than one, fufufufu. He checked and Nico was just as blissed out, relaxed under Bel now that he'd come. He turned his head enough to look at Garen, who was propped up on his elbow, one hand supporting his head and the other casually working his own dick. He was the only one who hadn't come yet.

"Gimme a minute," he requested with a thick mouth. "As soon as I can properly move, you can fuck me."

"I think that's going to take you more than a minute," Garen observed, eyes twinkling. "You look really done in at the moment."

That was fair. Bel felt so limber he could be rubber right now.

Nico planted a kiss on his forehead and gently rolled them the other direction, pulling out and leaving Bel relaxed on his side. Bel allowed this, as lying still and being a human vegetable for a moment sounded marvelous to him.

Rolling back over, Nico caught Garen by the waist. "How about I suck you off?"

"Now, that invitation, I'll take."

Ooh, he got a show while he recuperated. Awesomesauce. Bel always enjoyed moments like these.

There really were so many benefits to having two lovers. Right now was very much a case in point.

CHAPTER TWENTY-FIVE

NICO

Bel, Zia, and Victoria were talking magical theory. *Again.*
Didn't they get enough of this last time?

Did they have to do it every time they were stuck on a boat and Nico had no real means of escape?

His brain wasn't built for complex magical theorems, dammit. There was a reason he'd gone into a shooting-things type of career.

Garen was over there, off to the side snoozing, the traitor. Granted, they weren't in the "danger" area yet, and Bel's eyes could tell them from a quarter of a mile away if a monster was coming, but still.

Giving up, Nico retreated from the heated debate (something to do with calibrations for weight versus light subjectivity, nothing made sense, absolutely nothing), and went looking for Wicky. You know, the other crazy one who was really the only bastion of sanity on this damn boat.

Wicky stood next to the squad sergeant, showing him some kind of new doohickey Nico hadn't seen before. It looked rather like a shiny silver box with a scope on the end? Like a single binocular. Only more square-y.

"—will not only detect visual spectrum but heat and magical energy as well," Wicky explained to the sergeant, who was all ears. "I only have three of these, but I thought we should pass them around to whoever is on watch. Don't want to be caught again with our pants down just because Bel's asleep."

Nico came around to put his chin on Wicky's shoulder, looking down at it with curiosity. "Whatcha got there, friend?"

"New toy," Wicky explained, tilting it up so Nico could see it better. "If binoculars, thermal vision, and magic had a baby, this would be the result."

"Awesomesauce. How field tested is it?"

"I mean, I used it for at least two hours. I'd say it's good to go."

"Sounds legit."

"In other words," Sergeant Owen translated dryly, "we're going to field test this for you."

"Awww." Wicky batted big brown eyes at him, a hand over his heart. "You're too kind."

"You're a real piece of work, Agent."

"Oh, I'm not as bad as Nico," Wicky demurred modestly.

Nico snorted. "I probably did whatever you're blaming me for, but there's no need to call me out about it in front of a witness."

"You beat down a Marine so fast he couldn't even get his guard up," Wicky pointed out.

Okay. That was fair. But he'd asked for it. And Nico had been mad. Very big contributing factor, there; Nico had been hella mad.

Sergeant Owen had a cautious expression on his wide face, black brows pulled up in a question. "Can I ask about that? We've heard some pretty interesting stories about what went down that morning."

Nico had no problem with it. Actually, he'd prefer to straighten the record out now rather than have outlandish tales being spread around. "You heard that Spencer Davis was Bel's first familiar but chose to leave him?"

"Yeah, that we heard. So, that's true?"

"Yuppers. Happened about three years ago. They hadn't kept track of each other or seen each other until we stumbled across Spencer here. As soon as Spencer saw Bel, all hell broke loose, basically. The man was outrageously upset Bel was near him." Nico was editing this way down, obviously, but the bystanders didn't need every detail. "I think it was jealousy, in part, because he really did not like me and Garen being near Bel. Anyway. With every passing minute, he got more and more in our face about it. More antagonistic. After we got back from the first lizard fight, his temper snapped and he threw a knife at the back of Bel's head."

Wicky muttered under his breath, "Which was the stupidest thing I ever saw that man do, and that's saying something."

Seriously. Spencer had done a lot of stupid things, but that one had to take the cake. Nico finished the story with absolutely no apology in him. "I took him down for that. Part familiar instincts, part lover instincts, but I wasn't about to give him the means to get back up again."

Owen heard him out, sat on it for a second, then shook his head. On his face was an expression of sympathy and understanding. "So, Davis was stupid enough to attack a mage in front of his familiar, is what you're saying. Yeah. Okay, idiot deserved what he got. No wonder Base Commander is intent on burying him under charges. We were warned not to mess with you three when we got our orders. But you've been so easygoing, I couldn't make sense of the disparity between what I was told and what I'm seeing."

"Really, all three of us are pretty chill," Nico assured him. "As long as you're not openly antagonizing us, you've got nothing to worry about."

Wicky nodded in support of this. "Really, they are pretty chill. It's just that the past several days have been like a bad movie. Movie title being: *The Good, the Bad, and the Fuck Spencer.*"

Nico offered him a high-five because that was beautiful.

Wicky smacked his palm against Nico's, a grin on his face. "Liked that?"

"It was genius."

Owen's eyes darted between the two of them. "I get the feeling you two are peas in a pod."

Slinging an arm around Wicky's shoulder, Nico explained, "This man is my brother from another mother."

"It's why I'm moving closer to him," Wicky tacked on.

Nico blinked. Blinked again. Wait, what? His head snapped around so he could demand of Wicky, "What? When did you decide this?"

"Huh? Oh, me and Zia talked it over last night." Wicky gave a slight shrug of the shoulders. "It just makes logistical sense. It was a freaking nightmare getting travel arrangements lined up so we could get on the same plane over here. If we're going to be a permanent team, might as well move closer to you guys. Makes sense for us to move. Me and Zia are renting anyway. You guys actually own your homes."

Oh. Well, when put that way, sure. Nico's excitement rose. "That means you'll be nearby to play with me."

"Hell yeah, man."

Visions of things they could do danced through Nico's head. His voice turned dreamy. "We're going to get into so much trouble together."

Wicky tilted his head to lean against Nico's, and his voice was just as dreamy. "It'll be so much fun."

Owen shook his head. "I feel like someone should warn the rest of your team about you two."

"Shhhh," Nico murmured. "What they don't know won't hurt them."

Matt's voice carried back to them. "We've got a new trail!"

Oooh, that sounded promising. Nico let go of Wicky and bounced back to Bel.

No more magical theory as his mage was focused with laser precision on the river. His red eyes were narrowed and intent on something Nico couldn't begin to see. Victoria was on one side of him, Zia on the other, so Nico came in behind and put his head on top of Bel's.

"Bel Bel?"

"Yeah, it's the one Zia was tracking the other day," Bel answered absently. "It's recent, too. I swear he went through here yesterday."

Now, that sounded promising. Maybe Nico could bonk something sooner rather than later.

A man could dream, couldn't he?

With Bel giving directions, they followed the path, the sun steadily going up and over their heads only to come back down. Nico passed the time by discussing real estate and moving logistics with Wicky, as he really wanted Wicky closer rather than farther. Not a lot of possibilities in Plymouth—small town, after all—but there were a few houses Wicky liked the look of. Zia joined in on this conversation midway through, also intrigued by the real estate listings. She refused to share a house with Wicky for some reason, though.

Nico sensed a story.

Late afternoon, Bel directed them to the right of the river, up a smaller branch of water. Deep enough for their boat to navigate up, but at least a fourth of the size of the river they'd just left. The tree branches were closer to the boat, sometimes scraping the roof as they passed. Not much room to maneuver back in here. It kind of made Nico's skin crawl, as it felt like they were going up a fatal funnel.

This area was far swampier, too, much more lush and green than the other areas they'd passed. He could see why a monster would choose to be in here, as there had to be better game options. All of this mud would make things hard to maneuver through, though. Nico didn't like mud. It totally messed up his speed.

Bel pointed up ahead and to the right again. "That cave! Go in there."

A cave? Did that mean they'd found this creature's den? Nico sent up a prayer that was the case. Finding the creature's home base was a win he absolutely would take, no question.

The captain found a place to pull in tight to the bank, and they tied off to a tree before extending the ramp out. Nico was off in a split second, Slashley out and at the ready but not fully extended yet. He looked all around, getting his bearings. Drier here, certainly, but not really *dry*. Dry enough to not have mud sucking his boots off his feet, at least. Too many trees to make fighting feasible unless they were right at the mouth of the cave. That was the only clear area in sight. Good for an ambush, though. Nico was a fan of ambushes. When he wasn't the one being ambushed, at least.

He turned to Bel, almost vibrating with excitement. "Is the lizard in the cave?"

"No, trail leading in and out is hours old," Bel corrected.

Awww, damn.

"But," Bel tacked on, his head panning back and forth to study the area, "he comes in and out of here regularly. This is definitely his den. The seal on this one is the same, interestingly enough, as the other one. Made at about the same time. Damn, whoever did this was really, really good."

Scooooooore. That was all Nico needed to hear to make his day.

Bel's eyes narrowed at him, and he accused, "You want to go into the cave, don't you?"

"I can check it out for you!"

"You realize this cave is probably not as much fun as the last cave we were in?"

"You don't know that," Nico pointed out hopefully.

"Which is why I really need to go in there. To scout."

Bel seemed to realize the futility of trying to keep Nico out. He had that indulgent look, the one he often wore when Nico was being absurd, but he was willing to let it ride. With his eyes, he could no doubt see right through the rock and all of the interior of the cave. But that took all the fun out of exploring.

With a shake of the head, he sighed and waved Nico on. "Go. You've got five minutes."

Nico darted in and smacked a kiss on Bel's mouth, like the whirling dervish he was often accused of being. See? Bel loved him after all. Even when they both knew he was being ridiculous, Bel let him play.

Bel slapped him on the ass as he turned again and jogged for the cave. It put a smile on his face as he went in, as he liked how Bel had relaxed enough to do things like that in public.

The cave was very cave-y. It was damp inside, the very stones smelling cold and wet, with a trickle of water sounding from somewhere in the distance. The floor was mostly sandy at the entrance, becoming harder stone farther in. Nico saw evidence of shedding, as there were massive skins tucked along the side, but no bones. Strangely clean inside, really. He'd expected something more than just stone and dim light. He had to key on Slashley just to act like a flashlight.

In short order he reached the end of the cave, and there was absolutely no rear entrance in sight. Good. Always problematic if your prey could escape. On the other hand, if the prey could retreat, it would make it more fun and challenging.

Oh, good. Oh, no? Nico couldn't decide between these two emotions.

Well, anyway, Bel had been right. The cave was no fun compared to the last one he'd been in. Not a single arrow trap or dusty skeleton to contend with. Booo. With a sigh, he jogged back out, pulling Slashley back in as he did so.

In the time he'd been inside, people had been organizing outside. Bel had recalled the hellhounds, too; they were happily sniffing about and ignoring the wide-eyed glances of the Marines around them. Nico would totally play with them in a minute. Garen caught his eye and motioned him in closer, filling him in.

"We're going to set up an ambush on either side of the cave's mouth. Zia's got a ward that will mask our scent, so once that's up, we have to stay inside."

"Got it. You're not going to ask me what the cave was like?"

Garen gave him a patient look. "How was the cave, Tigger?"

"Boring as fuck, man. Bel only let me in there because he knew there was absolutely no danger, am I right?"

"Sounds like him."

"You're all killjoys, I hope you realize this."

"It's a grave sin of ours that we'll repent for. Eventually. In the meantime, let's get ready to ambush this son of a bitch. I want out of Australia."

Now that, Nico was completely on board with.

CHAPTER TWENTY-SIX

GAREN

The interesting thing about lying in wait for a monster in the middle of an Australian swamp with people you didn't know all that well was the conversations that happened while waiting. Garen sat on a log next to Bel, listening idly as Wicky carried on a conversation with one of the Marines behind them.

"I didn't build a mouth so it can't complain," Wicky explained seriously.

"No face so it can't bitch at you?"

"Precisely."

Garen thought about getting context for this conversation. Decided sanity was the better part of valor and chose not to even glance behind him. Less was definitely more in Wicky's case.

He thought about leaning in and asking Bel what he thought of Wicky and Zia moving closer to them, but Bel had that look on his face, the one that heralded him seeing something no one else did. The narrowed eyes and furrowed brow only meant one thing.

"What, Bel?"

"I think I see him."

That stopped all conversation around them, and everyone

leaned in to hear him better.

"You sure?"

"He's a distance away, still in the river, and I have a lot of tree roots interrupting my sight lines, but...yeah, that's him. He's coming." Bel sat up straighter, even more focused now. "Give it maybe twenty minutes, and you'll see him yourself. He just turned into this inlet."

Excellent. Exactly the news Garen wanted to hear.

Nico, on Bel's other side, slammed a fist into a palm. "Time to take down President Blub Blub."

Eyeing him sideways—did he really want to know?— Garen pointed out, "We don't know what this creature is or what it's called."

"I don't care what its name is. I'm calling him President Blub Blub."

Yeah, okay, Garen had walked right into that one. He should have just let it go.

With experience under their belt, they had a much firmer plan of attack for this round. Garen might well be useless in this fight, and he was perfectly okay with that. His job was to keep track of Bel and make sure his distracted mage didn't stumble into anything he wasn't supposed to.

Seconds felt like hours as they trickled by, everyone mostly holding their breath as they waited for the lizard to appear. When Garen finally did see a head poking out of the water, it was such a relief. Finally, an end in sight.

They couldn't move just yet, though. The creature was still in the water and making his way to the cave. They wanted this thing on dry ground before attacking. Hold position.

Hold...

Hold...

Dammit, couldn't he swim a bit faster?

Okay, there we go. His front legs were on the bank now. Damn, he was a big motherfucker. Not as green, either, more of a blue-green in his hide. The middle row of legs moved upwards, one of them clearly missing from the second joint down. He moved onto the bank and didn't seem to suspect anything, as he wasn't scenting the air or looking around. Just heading straight for the cave entrance.

Almost there...almost...

Back legs on land! Yes!

Matt and Victoria were quick on the draw. As soon as those back feet touched land, they had a lasso spell around his neck, anchored into the bedrock of the cave this time, leaving him with no possibility of escape.

The lizard screamed, throwing his head up, trying to yank free. When that failed, he thrashed from side to side, desperate and sending water in all directions. The Marines fired on him, keeping him distracted and focused on the front. The hellhounds harried the lizard's feet, snapping and barking, trying to keep him from focusing on any one target. They were doing a fantastic job of it.

Garen had his weapon in hand but prayed he wouldn't need to use it. He wanted the plan to work, first and foremost, as it meant a quick kill.

"Bel," Wicky demanded quickly as he moved up, "base of the skull still good?"

"Yeah, still the weak point," Bel confirmed.

Wicky came right to Bel's side and they worked that spell of fire and brimstone once more, aiming for the back of the neck. It hit, but not cleanly, with all of the thrashing the lizard was doing. Moving targets were a bitch to hit.

Without pause, they did it again, still in sync, the German and French an odd mix in Garen's ears. It hit better this time, taking away the slimy coating on the skin, the air filled with the scent of burning flesh. The lizard screamed in agony, fighting even harder now, and there was an ominous cracking sound from the rocks he was anchored to. He was fighting hard enough that the lasso spell might not last another minute.

Bel turned sharply. "Zia!"

She didn't need the prompting. Zia already had the spell half formed in her mouth, hand lifted, and when the lizard stopped thrashing and tried pulling hard instead, giving her a clean shot, she took it. A solid shaft of hard ice, shaped like a spear, flew through the air and straight into the spot Bel and Wicky had cleared. It penetrated deep, the shaft going straight through the back of the head and out the front before disappearing in a flash of multi-colored fragments, dissipating in the air.

The lizard let out a long death rattle, like a moan and a sigh mixed together, before slumping straight down onto the ground in a boneless sprawl. His eyes were still open, tongue hanging out of his mouth, the tail lifeless in the water.

Dead.

Thank god.

Garen let out a breath of relief, his eyes closing in a silent prayer of thanks. Finally. All they had left to do was report this and then they could go home. Garen could not express how much he wanted to go home and leave this shitshow well behind him.

Soldiers and mages alike put down weapons. There was a cheer from several people, everyone happy that went so smoothly. Garen holstered his weapon and shared a smile with both Nico and Bel.

"Good job," Bel congratulated Wicky and Zia. "We couldn't have pulled that off more smoothly if we'd had several dry runs ahead of time."

"Well, this is what makes us a good team," Zia responded, hands on hips and giving off an air of supreme satisfaction. "We're good at working together. Let's get drinks later."

Nico pointed to Garen. "Is he buying?"

"He doesn't know it yet," Wicky cautioned, an evil glint in his smile.

"I'm right here," Garen groaned. He sensed a certain

inevitability to this. "But sure, I'll buy the first round."

Frankly, he didn't care. And at this point, Garen thought they'd all more than earned a drink. This had been one of those weeks when he honestly wondered why he hadn't started day drinking.

People were already poking at the corpse, wondering aloud what it was. Garen saw at least one group taking pictures next to it. Which was rather inevitable. Garen idly listened as Bel called it in, reporting the kill. While he handled that, Matt called in to MAD to report they had yet another carcass for retrieval.

Nico sidled up next to him, leaning his head against Garen's shoulder. "When we get home, let's take three days to just veg around the house and do nothing more productive than sex each other up."

"Sold." Garen lifted his hand, knuckles closed in invitation.

Nico bumped fists with him. "I knew you would be. Damn, this trip has been hell. I need the next one to not be so emotionally intense."

"From your lips to god's ears."

"I'm going to go play with the hounds. They did a good job. They deserve playtime."

"Uh-huh." Garen honestly couldn't decide who "deserved playtime" more, the hounds or Nico, but whatever. Let him have his fun. They were decorative until it was time to load up and go back to base anyway. Although that should happen soon, as they were nearly out of daylight. They'd lain in wait for the lizard a good two hours before he showed, and it had to be...he checked the clock on his phone...yeah, it was six in the evening already. They'd get in late at the rate they were going.

At least they had no need to return here, though. Garen would take that win.

Garen couldn't see Wicky—he was on the other side of

the lizard's corpse—but he sure could hear him.

"Don't piss me off! I will sing musicals at you."

Someone scoffed. "You can't sing a whole musical. Don't you mean a song?"

"I said what I said."

Zia growled out a curse and *moved*, almost sprinting for her friend. "For the love of god, don't get him started!"

Oh. So Wicky could really do that, huh? Noted and filed.

Garen nipped the problem in the bud. "Wicky, come play with the hounds! Poor Nico's arm will fall off at this rate. And he still has a bum hand. They all want to play fetch at once."

The reaction was immediate. Wicky dropped the argument, whatever it was, and appeared at a loping walk. "The dogs are still here? Oh, they are! Come here, my loves, come play with me. Such good puppies, yes, you are!"

That was better. Distraction successfully implemented.

Zia paused in her attempt to rescue them all, and her shoulders sagged in relief. She came back to Garen and muttered, "Thank you. You do not want to get Wicky started. Last time someone pissed him off, he sang all of Roger and Hammerstein's *Cinderella*."

That must have been an experience. Garen couldn't help but ask, "Is he tone deaf or something?"

"No. He's actually got a good voice. That's half of the problem." Zia rolled her eyes. "The other half is that he'll have Mobius play the karaoke version of the songs for him, loud, and he'll not only sing the musicals, he plays all the parts. The dancing, everything. Full production. Once he gets really started, it's almost impossible to get him to stop."

"So...in other words, don't get him going unless we're all drunk enough to find him entertaining."

"I couldn't have said it better myself."

Bel finished his phone call and gave them a nod. "MAD has the coordinates to come pick this up. Zia, if we can throw some preservation spells on this thing? Then we'll be good to go."

"Done and done," she assured him. "I'll let you handle negotiations to get both boys back on the ship."

Bel looked over the group of men and hounds happily playing fetch or mock wrestling with each other, and blew out a breath. "Why is it my turn?"

"Because it was my turn last," Garen drawled.

"Dammit. Alright, if I'm not back in five minutes, send in reinforcements."

Garen waved at his back, silently wishing him luck. He would need it.

CHAPTER TWENTY-SEVEN

BEL

Bel was very thankful to have the final report in to the base commander. It meant they were free to leave the next day, and everyone on the team was more than ready to do that. With a skip in his step, he headed for the hotel.

Something Commander Martin had told him lingered in his head as he went. He'd started out reassuring Bel that Nico was absolutely not in any trouble. His actions were considered self-defense because, as Bel's familiar, defense of him still counted as self-defense. Bel hadn't thought differently but was still glad for the reassurance.

Then Commander Martin started listing all the stupidity Spencer had done in the past five years. Apparently, Spencer's file contained documented offense after offense, disciplinary action after disciplinary action. Shock! Surprise! His bad temper had landed him in trouble more than once. With this latest attack on Bel, his career was done. He'd be court-martialed for this and not only dishonorably discharged from the Marines, but he'd likely serve jail time for attempted murder. With the use of a deadly weapon, it couldn't be considered anything less.

Frankly, Bel was glad for it. Spencer was a loose cannon with no guide rails. Something needed to keep him in check, and maybe serving some prison time would show him what consequences really looked like. He doubted it—people with self-serving attitudes and bad tempers never seemed to learn—but either way, he deserved the punishment.

As much as Bel didn't like Spencer, something inside prompted him to go see the man. Some need for closure, to stare him down once and for all.

On a whim, he turned and instead headed for the base holding area. The stockades were small, only a single level, in the charming blocky architecture of all other government buildings. Nothing unique here, folks. Bel went through the glass front door and stopped barely three feet in, as that was where the front counter sat. A bored-looking MP sitting behind the desk glanced up, then took in Bel's badge hanging around his neck and the windbreaker with the gold MAD letters on his breast, and abruptly straightened.

"Yes, Agent, how can I help you?"

"I'd like to visit Spencer Davis."

The MP blinked at him, brown eyes looking confused. "Uhh...sure, sir. If you'd like."

"Thank you."

"Just sign in here, with the visitor's log. If you're armed, you'll need to check your weapon in with me before you go back."

Bel lifted his jacket and showed the man either side of his hips. "Not armed."

"Then you're good to go, sir. He's in the third cell on the left. Really, he's the only one we're holding except a drunk and disorderly further down."

That didn't surprise Bel much. He repeated with a smile, "Thank you."

Bel walked past the desk, the man pushing the electronic door to the unlocked position from his controls at the desk. Bel heard the beep and snick as the lock retreated before he tried to open it. Walking through, he passed by another MP, who gave him a nod of acknowledgement as he went through the same door.

As the door closed, he could hear the two talking amongst themselves.

"Who's he here for?"

"Davis."

"That bastard's getting a visitor? Really?"

"Well, I bet it's something official. Davis doesn't seem to have friends."

Bel's mouth quirked in a humorless smile. He wasn't about to correct them.

Three cells down, he found the man, hunched over on the thin metal bed with his head in his hands. Spencer did not look like the boastful, cocksure idiot now. He seemed to realize that this time, he'd really fucked up, and the full consequences rested on his shoulders, bowing them in.

He also looked like an alley cat that had gotten into a fight and lost. Nico really had done a number on him. The right side of his face was just one big bruise, eye swollen shut, and the way he sat hunched indicated pain all along his right side. Stood to reason. It was where Nico had railed on him.

Spencer sensed his gaze on him, and his head came up. Then he jerked upright, his anger returning to his face so quick it was almost jarring to watch.

His jaw worked as he spat the words, "What? Here to gloat?"

"No, in fact. I'm here to thank you."

Spencer's brows drew in heavily. "You being sarcastic?"

"I'm perfectly sincere." His sincerity must have been conveyed in his tone, as Spencer's head drew back in confusion. "Thank you. Thank you for leaving. I would have been miserable with you."

Spencer leapt off the bed, hands grabbing the bars and rattling them. "You fucker! You're enjoying this, aren't you?"

"I'm not you. Your punishment gives me no joy. You put

yourself squarely in this position, and blaming me doesn't bring you any benefits." Bel shrugged. "Blame me if you wish, though. Feel free. I frankly don't care. I just came by to thank you. What you do, or think, no longer matters to me."

Spencer tried to reach through the bars, to grab him, but Bel had been smart enough not to come within that kind of range. Spencer's fingers grasped only empty air. Frustrated, the man fell back to words.

"You loved me then. You still feel something for me. It's why you were so bothered when you saw me again."

"It's called PTSD, Spencer. I was reliving past trauma. I may have loved you, back then, I may not have. I honestly don't remember that time. But I will tell you this. They say the opposite of love is hate. I don't think that's right. It must be indifference. That's all I feel for you now—supreme indifference." Bel gave him a smile. It was not a nice one. "Try to keep your temper in the courtroom, will you? Otherwise, they may never let you out again."

Impossibly, Spencer turned an even darker shade of red, almost maroon from anger. "You fucking *bastard*. You *are* here to gloat."

Maaaybe just a little. It was hard not to when the man was such an easy target. Bel gave a little waggle of the fingers in a wave goodbye before turning and walking smartly back out. He was done here.

"You'll regret this, Adams!" Spencer yelled at his back. "I'm better for you than he is! Either one of them!"

Bel didn't bother to turn, but he did laugh, a deep belly laugh, because that was so absurd it didn't even warrant a response. Better for him than Nico and Garen? Not in a million years.

He signed back out and then went hunting for Nico. Bel knew Garen was at the hotel—he'd said as much—but where were Nico and Wicky? It never boded well, that question.

Still, Bel would take Nico's harmless shenanigans over

the bastard he'd just left any day. He may have even been smiling as he went hunting for his happy-go-lucky familiar.

With six hellhounds and two men playing fetch, they weren't exactly covert. Bel found them without even trying too hard, playing in the parking lot behind the hotel. How they'd managed to get hellhounds to play with was the question, as Bel had sent them back before they returned to base.

The answer was apparent as Belphegor stood right there, watching Wicky and Nico play, chuckling as if this was the best entertainment he'd had all day. Wicky seemed to be playing some kind of tag where the hounds happily chased him, tails wagging, and it involved a lot of laughing. Nico had a crushed metal rebar in his hands he was using as sticks for the dogs to fetch, which they happily did. Only to come back and get belly rubs for their efforts. Nico looked alight with simple joy, a grin stretched from ear to ear. Bel loved seeing that look on his face, no question there. It was just...

Bel surveyed the scene and groaned. Oh god, this was going to be like the cave fiasco all over again. The hounds were going to categorically refuse to return to Hell, weren't they? He didn't even have to ask, he knew the answer already.

Bel came up to join his grandfather, standing at the man's side with a smile of greeting. He eyed the Linkin Park hoodie and plaid pajama pants, the mussed blond hair, and lifted an eyebrow.

"You look comfy."

"I was at Naamah's."

"Ahhh. Still helping with the twins, of course."

"Naturally." Belphegor jerked a chin to indicate the dogs and men still playing. "Nico texted Naamah to ask me to summon the hounds. I was happy to do it."

Of course he had been. Bel wasn't even surprised. "What were you two doing, movie night?"

"Marathoning *Discovery of Witches*. Such an excellent

show."

Bel figured. Grandpa loved being in what he called "human attire" when relaxing with family. Naamah was a new mother now, with twin three-month-old infants. She'd need both backup and a babysitter so she could sleep. Her husband-familiar couldn't help at all with sealing the twin's eyes, although Bel was sure he was trying to do everything else. A good way of keeping her company was providing a distraction, and she loved that show.

Belphegor gave him a hug, then just hung on, head resting on top of Bel's for a moment. "How are you, my child?"

"I'm doing really well." Bel smiled as he said the words because he meant them. "We found the things eating people and defeated both of them. The hounds were very helpful for that."

"I'm glad. Is that why Nico and Wicky wanted to play with them?"

"That, and they have no fear of Hell. Apparently."

"It's why I like them."

Bel just snorted. Still, he supposed they'd all earned the break.

Belphegor tilted his head down and regarded him curiously. "I can't put a finger on it, but it feels as if you have set down a weight you were carrying. You look far lighter and more at peace than I've seen you in years."

Of course his grandfather could tell. Not much got past him. "I ran into my first familiar here."

"What?!" Belphegor tensed, red eyes flashing with an unearthly glow. "My child, you should have said something earlier. I'll go incinerate him for you."

Bel latched on to his waist and refused to let go. "It's fine, it's fine."

"How is it fine? I still have a spot reserved in Hell for him. A very special place I crafted. I'll just go grab him. He's a little ahead of schedule, but it's fine."

Spencer really was going to be in for it when he died. Bel tried to feel pity for him.

Pity? Pity? Yoo-hoo? Damn, he had a runner.

Oh, well. Bel would repent about that later. Maybe. For now, he kept hold of his grandfather. "Wait, Grandpa, just listen. It's turned out to be a good thing."

Belphegor's eyes narrowed for a moment. "How is this a good thing?"

Starting from the beginning, Bel told him everything. His initial reaction, his fears, the journey his emotions took as he compared Spencer with the men who loved him. All of it. He had no reservations about doing so, as he had no secrets from his grandfather.

Belphegor listened patiently, nodding now and again, asking the occasional question, but mostly listening. When Bel finished, he thought about it for a long moment, lips pursed.

"I can see why you're glad things worked out like this," he finally said. "I still want to incinerate him."

"Let him rot in prison first," Bel suggested. "The United States Marine Corps wants a crack at him. You can have him later."

"I suppose that's fair. The way you say that, it declares you have no lingering feelings for this man."

"None. It's really liberating to say that, to mean it. I just realized, at some point, the man did me a favor by walking out. If I had known three years ago what I would have after him? The love, support, and devotion I get from Nico and Garen now? I would have handled that broken bond a lot better."

Belphegor kissed his forehead. "I'm so glad, my child. So utterly relieved you're past that heartbreak. I will have to thank Garen and Nico properly at some point as they are definitely the reason you feel this way now."

"Truer words have not been spoken." Bel hugged him

again. "But whatever you do, no matter what Nico says, you are not to let him keep one of the hellhounds."

Belphegor blinked down at him, his innocence so pure it was absolutely fake. "But, my child, think of it! It would be another added protection for you, and the hounds do love your familiar so."

Bel made his expression and tone firm. "No, Grandpa."

"Whyever not?"

"Because my house is flammable."

"I'm sure we can negotiate this."

"You know, I don't need for you to take Nico's side before he even opens his mouth. That is the opposite of helpful."

Belphegor's eyes sparkled with mirth. "We demons are tricky that way."

"Uh-huh." Turning his head, Bel tried to nip this problem in the bud. "Hey, guys!"

Nico waved an arm at him. "Hey, Bel Bel, come join us!"

"Nooo," Bel said, drawing out the sound on purpose. "It's time for the hounds to go home."

Nico's face immediately fell. "What? No! They can stay tonight."

"Where? In a hotel room with flammable carpet and bedding? No thanks. I'm not cleaning up that mess. You got to play with them, Nico. They can go home now."

Wicky immediately bargained, while still running—man had stamina, had to give him that—and waved a hand in protest. "Two more hours!"

"No."

"One more hour!"

"No."

"Half an hour!"

"No."

"Five minutes!"

What was he, three? Bel shook his head in amusement. "How about until Grandpa's ready to take them home?"

"Deal!" Wicky picked up his pace and returned to running.

He didn't seem to realize that was imminent. Bel wasn't about to enlighten him.

"Now, now," Belphegor pitched in. "They can surely keep the hellhounds."

God help him. Bel meant that literally as, clearly, he couldn't expect any help from Hell. Alright, who could he call in for both backup and to be the voice of reason?

Negotiations had just commenced.

CHAPTER TWENTY-EIGHT

NICO

After all the running around with the hellhounds, Nico had to take a shower that evening before bed. He did so a little under protest, as Grandpa had said he could keep a hound, and Bel was being a total killjoy and refusing to let him keep one. Sure, the house was flammable, but still....

It had been fun negotiating the point, though. Bel had been laughing, his eyes twinkling in that way they often did when he knew Nico was mostly pulling his leg for the fun of it but was playing along anyway. He'd looked a lot lighter these past several days, especially after Spencer was arrested. Nico didn't feel that weighted sadness tugging at his bond anymore, either. It was a good sign Bel had done some healing while here. Still, he wanted to properly doublecheck with him. Most dangerous thing Nico could do was assume.

He got out of the shower, toweled off, and threw on boxers but nothing else. Nico was more or less packed, ready to leave in the morning for home, and he wasn't dragging things out of his suitcase any more than necessary. He had clothes laid out for the morning, and that was all he was doing.

Coming out of the shower, he saw Bel sitting up on the bed, phone in hand, Garen poking around the table in the corner while muttering.

"Whatcha doin', G?" Nico inquired as he approached the bed. Bel looked like a prime target for either tickles or cuddles. His instincts were currently at war about which way to go. Sometimes, Bel looked so tempting, Nico got cute-aggression. It was a thing.

"Looking for my glasses. Damn things disappeared again. I wish I could Ctrl+F for things in real life."

"Well, you can, you just have to open the program first." Nico prodded Bel in the arm with a finger. "Bel, glasses?"

Bel tuned in to his immediate surroundings again, blinked at both of them, then panned his head from side to side. It took him only a second. "On the floor, lurking under the curtains."

Garen huffed out a breath as he bent to search. "Thank you."

"Why is your laptop out, anyway?"

"I have to do an after-action report on the lizard. Bel did yours already."

Nico planted a knee on the bed and leaned in to kiss Bel's forehead. He crooned, "Ruby, I love you."

Bel shot him a droll look. "No one, and I mean no one, likes your after-action reports. It's fine. It's faster for me to do it than to nag you into doing it."

That was fair. Also accurate. It wasn't that Nico was difficult on purpose, it was just...paperwork. Sitting still. He was really terrible at both of those things. "Did Jack ever tell us what they are?"

"Oh...yeah, he did. He had to call a local lore expert here. It's called a Whowie. No one really remembers them, as the Aboriginal tribes sealed them before the white man ever discovered this place. Legend has it they consumed everything in the area and it got to the point nothing could live here. The tribes all banded together to hunt them down, corner them, and seal them away."

"Why do I hear that you get to write extra reports

for finding something no one really remembers?" Garen inquired dryly.

"Because you are as wise as you are handsome?" Bel returned with equal dryness.

Nico snorted in amusement.

Garen regained his seat, glasses perched back on his nose. While he got back to work, Nico decided cuddles were the way to go. Bel looked sleepy, all cute and snuggly, and it tipped the balance. Nico slid in next to him and pillowed his head on Bel's chest, arm around his waist. He smelled nice, too. Nico might have to nibble on him later.

"Comfortable?" Bel inquired dryly.

"I am, thanks for asking."

"Oh good. I wouldn't want you to be uncomfortable while using me as a body pillow."

"You're an excellent body pillow. You even smell good."

"I do try."

Nico snickered at the sarcasm.

From the table, Garen let out a long, aggravated groan. "They're making me change passwords. *Again*. What the hell, I just changed passwords. Guys. I don't know if I have any more passwords left in me."

Nico felt the same way every time MAD's system prompted a password change. He sympathized and tried, for once, to be helpful. "Fuckisutalkinbout."

Slowly, those green eyes lifted and pinned him in place. "That is not one word."

"It's totally one word. Add a one to the end, it'll even meet password requirements."

Garen must have been desperate because he tried it. Then rolled his eyes. "Oh my god, it really did go through. Nico, how many times have you used this word?"

"I can neither confirm nor deny because agency protocol is that we are not supposed to discuss passwords," Nico riposted primly.

The look Garen gave him said he knew very well Nico was being a little shit but he wasn't going to call him out on it. Out loud. Nico grinned back at him, just daring him to actually say something. He was in a fine mood; he wouldn't mind a little sparring. Verbal or otherwise.

Garen chose to just ignore him, though, focusing on the screen once more. Probably intent on getting the report done so it no longer hung over his head like a dark cloud. Nico left him alone so he could focus.

Besides, he really wanted to talk with Bel for a moment. He snuggled back in, putting a kiss on Bel's neck before relaxing.

"How you doing, Bel?"

"I suppose with everything that's happened, that's a fair question." Bel paused for a moment, clearly thinking over his response. He absently carded a hand through Nico's hair. "I'm far better than I anticipated. I'm far better than I ever expected, actually. I used to have nightmares about running into Spencer. Now, it feels like I've healed from him. I don't think I'll ever really think about him much in the future."

This sounded good to Nico. Bel had this thoughtful tone to his voice, no trace of pain or regret to be heard.

Garen might be sitting in front of his computer, but he was clearly listening. "So, you do realize he did you a favor by leaving?"

"Yeah," Bel confirmed. "Actually, I stopped by the stockade tonight and saw him."

Nico jerked upright, surprised by that. He'd done what?!

With a shrug, Bel gave them both a smile. "It might have been a little mean of me, but I wanted to thank him to his face for leaving me. I told him he'd done me a favor. He was really mad that I was sincere about it."

Oh, no doubt there, the man was probably livid. Nico didn't care about Spencer. He did care that Bel was so sure of his feelings he'd actually confronted the man one-on-one without either Garen or Nico at his side. He'd really grown past a lot of that trauma if he could do that.

Well, that explained why Bel looked so much lighter than before. He'd really moved past the trauma of three years ago.

Thank fuck. Nico felt like celebrating.

Bel looked between the two of them, smile tugging up in a rueful manner. "I feel bad for both of you because this trip was really hard. I know you were struggling and worried about me most of the time."

"It was," Nico admitted without apology or hesitation. "But Bel, I think it gave you the closure you needed."

"It did, yeah."

"Then it was worth it." Nico meant every word. Hell, he'd do this again next year, every year, if it meant putting Bel's demons to rest. Effort and care on his part to take care of this amazing man was never a hardship.

"It was worth it," Garen echoed firmly. "Don't apologize to us for this. It's not like you set any of this up. If facing that man gave you a way to let his ghost go, then we're glad he was here."

Well, glad might be pushing it. Nico couldn't see how anyone would be glad to see Spencer. But he wasn't about to argue the sentiment.

"You guys are really night-and-day different from him." Bel tugged Nico back down so he could hug him, tight enough to make bones squeak.

Nico hugged back, perfectly content to lie there with him for a moment.

Garen snorted and went back to typing. "It's not like the man gave us that high of a bar to clear."

Yeah, truly. Spencer was one of those people who hit rock bottom and then proceeded to dig.

It wasn't that Nico was boasting, per se, but Bel really had done better summoning a familiar the second time. The universe had been a lot kinder on the second try. Nico just wished he'd been summoned the first time and spared Bel all that pain and heartbreak. He couldn't have been, of course, he and Garen were still together at that point so he wouldn't have met the criteria. Still, he wished. He had Bel now, and that was what really mattered.

A hand slid down his back and over his ass, fingers playfully squeezing. It perked Nico right up. Oh? Oh, was Bel in the mood to do something fun?

Bel put a kiss against his forehead, then traced his way down a temple, to Nico's cheek, coming in closer and closer to his mouth. Nico tilted his head up to encourage this, meeting him halfway in a slow, sensual meeting of lips.

"You two are *not* starting something while I'm stuck writing a report!" Garen whined.

Bel lifted his mouth long enough to instruct, "Type faster."

Then he went right back to kissing Nico.

My *man*. Nico did love it when he got all sassy and bossy like this. Teasing Garen was just an added bonus.

Garen swore at them both. But his typing also picked up speed.

See? They were just providing motivation.

Nico would have made some snarky remark to Garen, but Bel's fingers found their way under the waistband of his boxers, and that really did take all of his attention.

EPILOGUE

GAREN

Four months later

Garen woke up by lazy degrees, his consciousness rising from the depths, in absolutely no hurry to join the waking world. They were home, there was no emergency on the horizon, nothing on the to-do list, and all was right in the world. It was a rare moment, and he indulged in it. He was so comfortable in bed it felt almost sinful. Waking without wallowing in this luxury was blasphemous.

A slender hand came up and around his back, lips finding his bare shoulder blade and working their way up in a trail of light, teasing kisses.

Well, Garen had wanted to wake slowly. Apparently, Bel had other ideas.

Not that he minded lazy morning sex on a Saturday. Far from it.

The debate between sleep and sex didn't even take a second to process. Sex won. Especially when Nico leaned in against his chest and nibbled that spot right under his ear. Garen's body lit up with immediate interest. Oooh, sexy times incoming. Got it. Firing brain up now, eyes opening!

Garen caught them each with one arm, pulling them in

closer and catching Nico's mouth first since it was at the right angle. He indulged in a long kiss, his tongue darting out to trace the other's lips, enjoying the heat and firmness of the body pressed against his. Nico was always a delight to kiss.

"Now he's awake," Bel declared with satisfaction.

Oh, he was definitely that. No question there.

Garen broke the kiss only so he could kiss Bel, taking his time with it. Bel hummed into the kiss, settling in against him, that slender body half-draped over his. Someone worked at removing Garen's boxers, which he cooperated with without doing anything super athletic like actually getting up.

Bel lifted off, just an inch, and there was a smirk underlining his words. "The goal for this morning is to work through the *Kama Sutra* book. Specifically, the page you marked as interesting."

"Hot damn," Garen breathed, even more interested now. "Great plan. Wait, who's taking which position?"

"As for that—" Nico started, only to break off. His head lifted, a frown tugging at his mouth, and he twisted to look in the general direction of the front door. "Do you hear someone knocking?"

There better not be someone knocking on their door at— Garen lifted his head just enough to check the bedside alarm clock—nine a.m. on a Saturday. Heads would roll.

The doorbell rang, loud and insistent.

Distantly, Wicky's voice called, "My friends, I'm here! Let me in!"

Garen groaned and let his head flop back onto Bel's shoulder. Of course it was Wicky. Of fucking course it was. Ever since Wicky had bought a house down the street from them and moved into it a month ago, he'd been over here near constantly. Normally, Garen didn't mind, but—

Kama Sutra plans. Fun new sex position. Lazy morning sex. He could feel all of that dissipating into thin air.

In a no-nonsense tone, Bel ordered, "Nico, go deal with

him."

"What?! No, that means I have to put on pants!"

Ooh, brilliant. Make Nico go deal with him. Garen backed up this plan one hundred percent. "Nico, he's your problem child. You get to go deal with him."

Nico growled and grumbled but rolled free of the bed, reaching for clothes. "This is highly unfair, and I protest. Vigorously. You two better not start anything without me. I'll get rid of him in five minutes—"

Garen would actually pay good money to watch that happen. Wicky was nothing if not determined.

"—and be right back in bed with you twenty seconds after that. See if I don't."

The doorbell rang again.

"Wakey, wakey, eggs and bakey! I know you guys are awake. Nico couldn't sleep in if his life depended on it!"

Wicky rather had them there.

In a whirl of displaced air, Nico was out of the bedroom and down the stairs, already calling ahead.

"This better be important, you nut job!"

Bel didn't even give Nico five seconds to get down the stairs before swinging a leg over Garen's hip and going back to kissing him. He was not to be deterred, eh? Garen smiled into the kiss.

He'd make it up to Nico later. Right now, he had an amorous blond who required all of his attention.

Thank you for reading *Aussie Terrors*! The next goal for this world is to write Wicky's book which will happen sometime later this year. Be on the lookout for the audiobooks which will come out Fall 2022.

In the mood for magic? Have you tried the series Jocelynn Drake and I created with dragons, mages and fated mates? Dive into an epic urban fantasy complete with castles, hoards, and secret clans!

Origin

Looking for a funny (cracky, let's be honest), slice of life read? Poor Ross is up to his ears in supernatural problems, which is what happens when you're a PA for a supernatural clan. It's a good thing his vampire boss is so sexy. And gives him hazard pay. That helps too.

The Tribulations of Ross Young, Supernat PA

Books by AJ Sherwood

Gay 4 Renovations
Style of Love
Structure of Love*

Jon's Mysteries
Jon's Downright Ridiculous Shooting Case
Jon's Crazy Head-Boppin' Mystery
Jon's Spooky Corpse Conundrum
Jon's Boom-Shaka-Laka Problem
Jon and Mack's Terrifying Tree Troubles*

Mack's Marvelous Manifestations
Brandon's Very Merry Haunted Christmas
Mack's Perfectly Ghastly Homecoming
Mack's Rousing Ghoulish Highland Adventure

R'iyah Family Archives
A Mage's Guide to Human Familiars
A Mage's Guide to Aussie Terrors

Unholy Trifecta
How to Shield an Assassin
How to Steal a Thief
How to Hack a Hacker

The Warden and the General
Fourth Point of Contact
Zone of Action

Short Stories
Marriage Contract
How to Keep an Author (Alive)

AUTHOR

Dear Reader,

Your reviews are more important than words can express. Reviews directly impact sales and book visibility, which means the more reviews I have, the more sales I see. The more books I sell, the more I can write and focus on producing books that you love to read. You see how that math works out? The best possible support you can provide is to give an honest review, even if it's just clicking those stars to rate a book!

Thank you for all of your support. See you in the next book!

AJ's mind is the sort that refuses to let her write one project at a time. Or even just one book a year. She normally writes fantasy under a different pen name, but her aforementioned mind couldn't help but want to write in the LGBTQIA+ genre. Fortunately, her editor is completely on board with this plan.

In her spare time, AJ loves to devour books, eat way too much chocolate, and take regular trips. She's only been outside of the United States once, to Japan, and loved the experience so much that she firmly intends to see more of the world as soon as possible. Until then, she'll just research via Google Earth and write about the worlds in her own head.

If you'd like to join her newsletter to be notified when books are released, and get behind-the-scenes information about upcoming books, you can join her NEWSLETTER here, or email her directly at sherwoodwrites@gmail.com and you'll be added to the mailing list. You'll also receive a free copy of her book *Fourth Point of Contact*! If you'd like to interact with AJ more directly, you can socialize with her on various sites and join her Facebook group: AJ's Gentlemen!

Made in United States
North Haven, CT
29 May 2025